He was Anton of Gifford, the son of the Marquis of Malchester: the man who had saved her on the Field of the Cloth of Gold.

He was as she remembered and yet he was so different. He looked older, stronger—his eyes cold and unsmiling as they moved over the assembled nobles and their ladies. He gave no sign of recognition and she felt a little pang of disappointment as she realized that he did not know her.

She held back the rush of tears that suddenly threatened. How foolish of her to imagine that he might know her! Why should he? Too many years had passed and she had changed. Something in her had known him instantly despite the changes to his appearance, but he felt nothing.

She sat back, struggling to control her disappointment. Even if he had remembered her, it could make no difference. She was married and had borne her husband a child. Nothing had changed, but her insides churned with emotions she could not control. That day had been enshrined in her memory as something magical, helping her through the worst days, helping her to do what she must.

* * *

Fugitive Countess
Harlequin® Historical #279—March 2010

ANNE HERRIES

Award-winning author who lives in Cambridgeshire, England. She is fond of watching wildlife, and spoils the birds and squirrels that are frequent visitors to her garden. Anne loves to write about the beauty of nature, and sometimes puts a little into her books—although they are mostly about love and romance. She writes for her own enjoyment, and to give pleasure to her readers. She invites readers to contact her on her Web site, www.lindasole.co.uk.

Fugitive Countess
Anne Herries

HARLEQUIN®

TORONTO • NEW YORK • LONDON
AMSTERDAM • PARIS • SYDNEY • HAMBURG
STOCKHOLM • ATHENS • TOKYO • MILAN • MADRID
PRAGUE • WARSAW • BUDAPEST • AUCKLAND

Recycling programs
for this product may
not exist in your area.

ISBN-13: 978-0-373-30588-9

FUGITIVE COUNTESS

Copyright © 2010 by Anne Herries

For questions and comments about the quality of this book
please contact us at Customer_eCare@Harlequin.ca.

www.eHarlequin.com

Printed in U.S.A.

a field of gold, the richness of the gowns and jewels worn by the wealthy men of two countries beyond anything anyone had ever seen. It was, Anton thought, as if the two monarchs wished to outshine each other.

At just seventeen, Anton was already a man of some stature: broad-shouldered and long in the leg, his dark hair cut so that it turned under and just brushed the gold lace ruff he wore about his throat. His jerkin of black velvet was slashed through with gold, and he wore tight-fitting hose of cloth of gold with soft leather boots that came halfway up his calf and boasted tassels of pure gold. His flat cap was black, but in honour of the occasion it had a feather fastened with a huge emerald and gold pin. Across his body was a sash of gold sewn with precious jewels; his sword was encased in a scabbard of leather set with semi-precious stones. He looked what he was: the son of an extremely wealthy man, and his position in the King's train showed that His Majesty held him in some esteem.

Anton took his place in the world for granted, sitting astride his horse proudly as he relished the glittering scene. More and more nobles were entering the field, some of them riding carelessly, their horses jostling for position as they tried to get closer to where the two kings had come together to exchange greetings and promises of friendship. Anton was feeling excited, for his father had told him that King Henry had spoken of giving him a more prestigious position at court. Despite his father's wealth, Anton knew that he was expected to make his own way in the world. He would one day inherit a fortune, but it had always been clear to him that he must win honour and fame for himself.

It was so exciting to be a part of this momentous occasion. Anton did not wish to miss anything, his gaze travelling constantly from one face to another, unwilling to miss a moment. Young and strong, he had proven himself on the training ground and now longed for adventure.

He suddenly noticed a fracas going on to his left, and realized that some of the proud nobles were not satisfied with their position. An English noble he recognized and a French lord he had never seen before were trying to edge each other out, their horses jostling and shying. One of the horses close by was snorting, clearly nervous of the crowd. As Anton watched, it reared up and started to kick out at the nearest horse, which made that beast snort and shy sideways, in turn causing some of the others to panic. It was obvious that some of the horses were on the verge of mad flight. One fine chestnut mare reared up and dislodged her rider.

As the rider screamed and went tumbling, Anton leapt from his own horse and rushed towards the lady, scooping her up out of the way of flailing hooves. The nobles were starting to bring their horses under control once more as Anton pushed his way through the crush, carrying his precious burden to a place where pavilions of rich cloth had been set up apart from the crowd. The lady had been frightened, and clung to him as he carried her to safety, but he thought she was not seriously harmed.

'Are you hurt, little mistress?' he asked as he set her down, for he thought her not more than thirteen or so, and little more than a child. Her breasts were mere buds beneath the silk gown that clung to her slender form. Her

hair carried a hint of red in the gold, and her eyes were
more green than blue. He thought that she was fair, and
would be beautiful one day, and he was angry that she
might have been seriously harmed. 'The fool who caused
your horse to rear like that should be flogged for his life.'

'Oh, no…please…' The girl blushed delicately. She
spoke English well, but with an accent that told of her
French birth. 'I would not have a fuss made, sir. My
father would be angry. He wanted me to ride pillion
behind my groom, but I insisted that I could manage my
horse. I did not expect such a crush.'

'I dare say no harm has been done.' Anton smiled at
her, for she was both pretty and sweet, her face that of
an innocent angel. He glanced round. 'Someone has
rescued our horses, it seems…' He saw his squire
leading his mount, and a French vassal was bringing the
spirited chestnut that had thrown her.

She touched his arm to reclaim his attention. 'Will
you tell me your name, sir? I am the lady Marietta
Villiers…'

'I am honoured.' Anton bowed gracefully. 'Anton
of Gifford—son of the Marquis of Malchester and
Earl of Gifford.'

'Thank you for my life, Anton of Gifford.' Marietta
reached up and kissed his cheek. There was a faint flush
in her cheeks, but her eyes were as bright and clear as
the summer sky. 'I shall honour your memory for as
long as I live. I must go, for my groom comes and my
father will be anxious…'

'It was nothing…' Anton said. He hesitated, wanting
to ask more—who her father was, where she came

from—but he knew that he too was looked for. He must return to the King's train, for he might be summoned to do His Majesty some service. The girl had had a fright, but she had borne it well and she was not alone. She was but a child, and they were not likely to meet again. He must forget her and remember his duty to the king.

He relinquished her to the care of her groom and made his way back to where his father waited. The Marquis had noticed his act of gallantry and nodded, a look of approval in his eyes. It was no more than he would expect of his son.

'That was well done of you, Anton. I dare say it did not go unnoticed by others. As you know, we are to accompany His Majesty to the court of Charles of Spain. Charles has recently been appointed the new Holy Roman Emperor and Henry must pay his respects.'

'Yes, Father. I am happy to be a part of His Majesty's train.'

'I think you will find that Henry thinks much of you, Anton. It may be that you will be given a position of more importance than you imagine…'

Anton felt a surge of excitement. He was not sure what his father meant, but the future held a golden promise. He was strong, ambitious, and impatient for the good things life had to offer. All thought of the young French girl was forgotten as he watched the moment when the two kings greeted each other. It was good to be young and on the verge of something wonderful.

Later he would remember the girl he had rescued and

smile, tucking the memory away deep in the back of his mind, but for now history was in the making!

Marietta looked at the man who stood beside her father, to the right of the French King. It was due to the Comte that they had been invited to this glittering affair, and she must be grateful for the privilege. The Comte was not ugly, for his years sat well on him, and though of a heavier build than she found attractive, he seemed strong and noble. Her father, brought to the verge of ruin by foolish investments, had given her to this knight in return for the right to live in peace on his own lands. She was fifteen years of age and it was time for her to be wed. The Comte de Montcrief would make her a good husband, for she knew him to be a kind and generous man.

However, his smile did not make her heart beat faster—the way the young English knight's had when he'd held her close to his chest. He was so bold, so strong and so handsome! She had felt so safe in his arms! More than that, she had felt a warm melting inside her, like liquid honey that curled through her body, arousing sensations she had not known existed.

Anton of Gifford—the son of the Marquis of Malchester!

Marietta knew that she would never forget the man who had rescued her from what might have been painful injury or even death. Something in her had responded to him as he'd looked down at her with those serious grey eyes. In those brief moments she had experienced the strangest feeling—as though she had met her destiny. She had kissed him impulsively, but wished that he had kissed her back—on the mouth. Instinctively she wanted so much more that in her innocence she did not understand.

She was so immodest! It was as well that neither her father nor the Comte could read her mind. Her thoughts were wild and romantic—the foolish dreams of a young girl. She had listened to the storyteller and his fables of courtly knights too often! The reality was that she must marry a man she did not love or see her father dispossessed of all he owned and both of them turned out to beg for their living.

Marietta might instead have chosen life as a nun, but she doubted she would be taken without a dowry, which her father was unable to give her. Perhaps if she had felt a true vocation she might have chosen that life rather than marry the Comte, but her father would still have been faced with poverty. By agreeing to marry the Comte de Montcrief she had ensured that her beloved father would end his days in his own bed.

She must think of the good she had done, Marietta decided. Her future was not what she would have wished, but she must do her duty. She would be a good wife to the Comte and bear his children—and she would try to forget that *once* a young man had made her long for so much more…

Chapter One

France 1525

'Marietta.' Comte de Montcrief greeted his wife with a smile as she entered his chamber, carrying a pewter cup and a small flask containing a dark liquid. She grew more beautiful with every day, her red-gold hair like threads of silken sunbeams and her eyes more brilliant than any jewel. 'You never fail to bring my medicine when I need it. I do not know how I should have managed without you this past winter. I am sure that without your nursing, my dear wife, I should have died.'

'I know this eases the tightness in your chest far better than the mixture the apothecary sent you, my lord. I believe the fluid on your chest is easing, is it not?'

'Yes. I grow stronger every day, thanks to you, my love. I was blessed when your father gave you to me, Marietta.'

'I have been blessed in giving you a son,' Marietta

replied. 'I failed twice, and thought it was God's will that we should not have a child—but our little Charles flourishes. He has passed his first year, and as you know too well 'tis the first few months that are so dangerous for vulnerable babes.'

'You have given me a fine heir, but I hope he will not inherit too soon…' The Comte frowned. 'It worried me when I was ill, for though I know you are both brave and wise, it would be hard for you to hold the castle against the barons who might seek to take it. The nobles are a greedy rabble, Marietta. If I should die before our son reaches his maturity I have left the care of him and my estate to you, to hold for our son until he is old enough to take it—but I would urge you to choose a husband as soon as you may decently marry. I have no doubt that you will have many offers, but choose wisely. You must take a man with fortune enough that he will not covet our son's inheritance—and one who will treat you well.'

'Please, my lord, do not speak of such things to me,' Marietta begged. 'I am not sure that I would wish for another husband. You have been good to me, and to my late father.'

'Your poor father suffered greatly towards the end, and I was pleased that you should nurse him here in our home. I would do anything to please you. I am too old for you, Marietta. I offered for you when your father told me of his need—but I think I have not been fair to you. You should have had a fine young husband to bed you and give you many sons. It lies heavy on my conscience that I took your youth and squandered it when you might have had so much more.'

'Hush, my lord.' Marietta held the cup out to him. 'Drink this and ease yourself. You have been a kind husband, and many are not. I am content with my life, especially since we have our son.'

The Comte smiled indulgently. 'You have been a good wife. I shall buy you a present. What would you like?'

He took her hand and she felt the press of the heavy gold ring he wore on the middle finger of his left hand. It had a huge cabochon ruby and was very fine.

'I ask for nothing but your affection, my lord—but if you will give me something, let it be a lyre. The one I have has cracked and is no longer sweet in tone.'

'You shall have the finest that can be bought,' the Comte said, and kissed her cheek. 'And perhaps a ring for your finger too. Now, go about your business, Marietta. I would sleep.'

Marietta sighed as she made her way to her solar in the south-facing turret of the castle. When she had married her husband he had given her all the rooms in this tower, so that her ladies might be there to serve her. She had a bedchamber, a chamber where she could sit with her ladies and sew, and there was another chamber where her clothes were kept and her ladies slept on pallets that were stowed away during the day.

Montcrief seldom disturbed her these days. He had always been considerate. Marietta believed that if she had given him a son the first time she had conceived he would not have troubled her again. She knew now that he felt he had wronged her by taking her to wife. The difference in their ages had shown more as the years passed; he was too old for her, and his health had deteriorated suddenly after a fall from his horse. They had been fortunate that she had managed to produce a healthy heir. Her son, to the joy of both his parents, thrived.

Marietta had long since ceased to regret her marriage. She enjoyed being the chatelaine of a fine castle and ran her home with ease. Her child had brought her great joy and made her sewing a pleasure, for she liked to see the boy dressed in fine gowns and spent hours at her embroidery.

Yet Montcrief *was* too old, and although Marietta loved him it was more the love she would give to a dear uncle or friend. However, she had never thought of betraying him…except for once or twice at the start, when the picture of a handsome Englishman had popped into her head as she lay beside her husband.

It was nearly five years since the day she had almost been trampled beneath the hooves of that horse. Marietta sometimes wondered where Anton of Gifford was, and what he had done in all those years. She imagined him living on a fine estate in England. She knew that the countryside was beautiful there for her mother had told her. Baron Villiers had married an English lady of great beauty but little fortune. Jane, Lady Villiers, had been a sweet lady, and had taught her daughter much before she died.

Marietta knew that a distant cousin of her father's had married an English gentleman. Claire Melford had sent a letter when she had learned of Marietta's marriage, and Marietta had written to her a few times over the years. Claire had asked if they would visit, but Montcrief was always too busy. He went often to the

French court. At the start he had taken Marietta with him, but when she'd had her first miscarriage she had asked that she be allowed to stay at home. Now that she had her son, she might accompany her husband next time he went.

She entered her chamber, glancing at the child who lay sleeping in his crib. Charles was resting well, his chubby face flushed and glowing with health. He had recently been weaned and no longer needed the wet nurse's milk. Bending down to kiss his brow, Marietta thought that she must count her blessings. She had thought that her life was finished when she came here as a bride, but she had made the best of it and was happy enough. Only now and then did she allow herself to think of the young man who had saved her life. For one moment she had glimpsed how sweet life might be, but that was mere fancy, a romantic notion that she had put away as she became a woman and her girlish dreams faded.

Anton bent to lay a single yellow rose on Isabella's grave. She had been buried with her unborn child these six months gone. Not one day had passed in all these months when Anton had failed to blame himself for his wife's death. It was because of him that she lay beneath the earth, her young life extinguished.

'Forgive me!' he cried. 'Sweet lady, forgive me, I beg you!'

Tears ran down his cheeks for the guilt was strong. If he had not flown at her in a jealous rage that last day would she have gone walking and fallen, striking her head against a stone at the foot of steep steps? She had died instantly, and her unborn child with her, for her body had not been found until it was too late and the physicians could save neither her nor the son she'd carried.

When they married, Anton had believed himself to be passionately in love with his wife. However, something had changed between them after the birth of their first child. From the start Isabella had shown little response to his lovemaking. He had thought it was simply her innocence, but after their daughter was born she had complained of headaches, begging to be left to sleep alone. The realisation that his wife did not love or want him had been hard to accept at first. But gradually he'd discovered that he no longer felt anything for her, and understood that the marriage had been a mistake. Divorce had been impossible, for Isabella had been a Catholic and Anton's strong sense of duty, both to his wife and his daughter, had driven him to make the most of what he had.

For months he had done his best to please Isabella, and then one night she had come to him in his bed and asked him to love her. He had responded with warmth and pleasure, believing and hoping that they could begin to build something worthwhile that would give them both a measure of happiness. When she had told him she was with child once more Anton had been delighted. He loved his daughter, and hoped for a son, but a little over a month before Isabella's death he was told something in an unsigned letter that made him suspect she had betrayed him with another man. He had carried the nagging doubt inside him for weeks, reluctant to believe that the tale was true.

It must be a lie! Surely it could not be true? His mind had twisted and turned, seeking a way out of his torment, remembering and analysing. His wife had suffered so much during her months of childbearing, always complaining of sickness or discomfort, hardly able to bear the touch of his hand on hers.

The uncertainty had tormented him beyond bearing. In the end he had asked Isabella if the child she carried was his. The look on her face had been such that he had felt as if she had struck a knife to his heart.

'You can ask that of me?' she said, in a voice that was so faint he could scarce hear it. 'You think I would betray you—betray my honour?'

Anton seized her wrist so fiercely that she cried out. 'Tell me, is this story true or a lie?'

'Believe what you will,' Isabella said, her face proud. 'Unhand me, sir. You hurt me. Remember the child I bear, for he is yours...'

'Isabella...' Anton cried as she walked away, her gown making a swishing sound on the marble floors of their Spanish palace. 'Forgive me. It was told to me and I could not forget...'

Isabella did not look back. The next time Anton saw her, she was lying at the foot of some stone steps leading to the sunken gardens, her neck broken.

Anton had wept over her dead body, but it was too late. He was the murderer of his wife and child! Yet he could make amends—must make amends for the wrong he had done his wife.

In his agony over Isabella's death he had neglected Madeline, his beautiful daughter, who was now almost eighteen months old. He had loved her from the moment of her birth, but for months he had scarcely seen her, leaving her to the care of her nurse Lily—an Englishwoman who had come to them after the death of her Spanish husband.

Anton's expression was bleak as he straightened from kneeling by the grave. He could not bring Isabella back, but he would devote himself to the care of her daughter.

He was tired of living in this country, though he was well liked at court and he spoke the language fluently. Isabella had helped him, laughing at his clumsy pronunciation at the start. Because of her he had done well in his position as the eyes and ears of England's king, but now he wanted to return home. To stay here with his memories would make his life unbearable. Here in the home he had shared with Isabella he would be for ever haunted, seeing his dead wife's face at every turn, her dark eyes accusing—always accusing.

He would return to England and make a new life for himself. Isabella had brought him a small fortune in jewels and gold when they married. Combined with the fortune he had won for himself, he could buy a large estate and build a house. Perhaps in time he might find a woman willing to share his life and give him an heir. He could never offer a woman love, for his heart had died with Isabella, but his wealth might be sufficient for some. It would not happen yet. His wounds were too raw to think of marriage. Until his home was built and a mother for Madeline was found he would give the child into his mother's care.

All Anton wanted for now was peace. Perhaps in England he would be able to sleep…

'You will come with me to the tourney?' Montcrief looked pleased as Marietta inclined her head. 'You will do me the honour, wife? You are even more beautiful than when we married. I shall be glad to have your company.'

'You know it gives me great joy to ride—and now that you are well again we shall go out together more.'

'We shall go riding tomorrow,' he promised her. His steward approached, bearing a letter on a salver. 'Excuse me…' He broke the wax seal and frowned as he read what it contained. 'In God's name, what does *he* want here?'

'Is something wrong, husband?'

'Rouen asks if he may visit with us.' The Comte looked annoyed. 'I have told you that he is the bastard my mistress bore me when I was young? She was a woman of Rouen, and he takes her name instead of mine.'

'Yes, my lord.' Marietta's gaze was steady as she met his look. 'I have heard it said that had I not given you a son you might have left your estate to the Bastard of Rouen—is that so?'

'It was in my mind. I have told you that it needs a strong man to hold the castle and lands. Rouen is a good soldier—but coarse like his mother, and baseborn. He would not learn from books when he was young and thought only of fighting. Our son will learn to be noble of mind as well as birth. I want you to make sure of it if something should happen to me.'

'You are well again, husband,' Marietta said. 'You will live long enough to teach Charles these things yourself.'

'I intend to live to see him grown if I can,' Montcrief agreed. 'But I wish you to be aware of these things just in case. Life is never certain, my love. A man may die in many ways.'

'That is true, for many die of poverty and sickness. I tend those I can at Montcrief, taking them cures and food—but the poor are everywhere.'

Montcrief nodded, but she could see his mind was elsewhere. 'I suppose I must allow the visit. I do not wish for it, Marietta. He is a surly brute, and I do not quite trust him, but it is sometimes better to keep your enemy close.'

'You think of Rouen as your enemy?' Marietta was startled, for she had imagined that there was some affection between the two. Why else would Montcrief acknowledge him as his bastard?

'Perhaps I chose the wrong word. At one time I was proud of the boy, but as he grew he became surly and wild, fell into bad company. I would have been loath to see him the master here, though had we not been blessed it might have come to that…' Montcrief looked thoughtful. 'He has learned to expect something of me. I dare say I must make him a gift, though not lands—but money. Yes, I may offer him five hundred silver talents. We may see him at the tourney. Perhaps the deal may be struck there.'

'Five hundred silver talents is a great deal of money, my lord.'

'You are right—but 'tis a fraction of my fortune. Our son will inherit much more when I die, Marietta, and you will have your portion. You do not begrudge Rouen the peace offering?'

'No, my lord. I would never seek to influence your judgement in such matters. You must do as you wish.'

'Well, I think it best. I do not wish him to feel resentment against Charles. With his own small fortune he may buy land, if he wishes, or seek out a trade.'

Marietta smiled and left him to his thoughts, for they both had many duties.

'We should stop for a while,' Lily Salacosa told her master. 'Madeline suffers from a fever. I do not think it serious, but constant travelling is making her tired and fractious. Could we not rest at the next inn for a day or two?'

Anton looked at the babe she held in her arms with concern. His daughter's face was flushed, and when he touched her face she felt too warm.

'Yes, we shall rest, mistress,' he told her. 'I sent ahead to take rooms at an inn near Rouen. We shall break our journey there. If Madeline continues to be unwell you must summon a physician to her.'

'I think it merely teething, my lord, but she will recover sooner with a few days of rest.'

Anton smiled and bent to kiss his daughter's forehead. She would be as beautiful as her mother one day—a fair, pale goddess who would set the hearts of her suitors racing. Anton knew that he had not been Isabella's only suitor. She had seemed pleased to wed him, and happy in their marriage at first, but had she hidden her true feelings from him?

Anton squashed the thought. That way lay madness! His wife was gone and he would never know the truth. He must think only of the future and his beloved daughter.

A poster nailed to a tree caught his eye. A group of men were clustered about it excitedly, chattering and laughing. He called out to them in French, asking what was going on.

''Tis the day of the tourney,' one of the men responded. 'The winner of the games may win a silver arrow and all may enter. Only a man skilled in wrestling, throwing and archery can win. Men come from far and wide to enter.'

Anton nodded. As a youth he had often entered such tournaments, and the idea appealed to him. Since he must tarry a few days for the sake of his daughter, why should he not take a little time to amuse himself?

The day of the tourney had arrived. Marietta dressed in a gown of rich dark blue embroidered with silver beads and braiding, her long hair covered by a hood of matching cloth laced through with silver.

She felt proud to be riding by her husband's side as they approached the field outside the city of Rouen, where the great fair was held every year. Nobles and freemen from all corners of the land would journey here, for the contest was a rich one. The young men entered contests of running, throwing a spear, shooting arrows at a barrel and wrestling. For the past weeks posters had been placed about the countryside, inviting all the young men to enter, and they would come from all over France. To win the silver arrow a man must be the winner of all four events. If the arrow was not won small prizes were given to the individual winners.

Marietta took her place in one of the most prominent seats, smiling as she looked about at the happy faces of the populace. The people were of good cheer, and they waved, calling out greetings to the nobles they knew or served as they arrived.

A fanfare of trumpets announced the arrival of the contestants and some twenty men rode into the arena; these were the nobles who had entered the tourney and would give the spectators a magnificent show. The battles were merely to show skill and strength, and there would be no fights to the death, as there had been in years gone by. Behind the nobles came the freemen, sons of noblemen and burghers, who were to enter the contest for the silver arrow.

For the first hour Marietta watched the nobles tilting with their fearsome lances, trying to unseat one another. Some of them went on to fight with heavy broadswords until one or the other asked for quarter. She applauded the winners when they came to take their bows. One knight vanquished all five of his opponents and was given a fine dagger with a jewelled hilt as his prize.

After the show of valour by the nobles there was a display of tumbling and dancing bears. Then the trumpets announced the contest for the silver arrow was about to begin.

The men were announced one by one. The Bastard of Rouen was the tenth man to present himself, and the cheers for him were deafening for he had won this prize twice before and it was obvious the people considered him their champion. He was a tall man, thickset, with a reddish beard and a scar at his temple.

He came to bow before the watching nobles, bowing his head to his father and to Marietta. She had an uneasy feeling, a trickle of ice sliding down her spine as she felt his gaze on her. Lifting her head proudly, she gave him a cool smile and saw a flicker of anger in his eyes.

The next man to present himself gave his name simply as Anton. He too was a tall man, strong with dark hair and grey eyes—and Marietta tingled as she knew him. He was Anton of Gifford, the son of the Marquis of Malchester: the man who had saved her on the Field of the Cloth of Gold. He was as she remembered, and yet he was so different. He looked older, stronger—his eyes cold and unsmiling as they moved over the assembled nobles and their ladies. He gave no sign of recognition, and she felt a little pang of disappointment as she realised that he did not know her.

She held back the rush of tears that suddenly threatened. How foolish of her to imagine that he might know her! Why should he? Too many years had passed, and she had changed. Something in her had known him instantly, despite the changes to his appearance, but he felt nothing.

She sat back, struggling to control her disappointment. Even if he had remembered her it could make no difference. She was married and had borne her husband a child. Nothing had changed, but her insides churned with emotions she could not control. That day had been enshrined in her memory as something magical, helping her through the worst days, helping her to do what she must.

The contest had begun. The men were lined up for the race, which started from a line in front of the dais and continued over the surrounding countryside, ending back at the same spot. Once the men had left the field on the start of their gruelling race, the nobles and their ladies were served with food and wine.

Marietta ate little. It was foolish, but much of her pleasure in the day had disappeared when she had looked into a pair of cold grey eyes and seen no flicker of recognition. In her dreams, which she had treasured, when they met again Anton of Gifford had smiled and told her that she had remained in his heart and mind all these years—but such dreams were foolish!

A cheer went up when the runners returned. She saw that two of them had far outpaced the others: neck and neck, they raced to the dais and arrived at precisely the same moment. Wild cheering for the Bastard of Rouen broke out as the crowd chanted his name.

The master of ceremonies held up his hand and the crowd quietened.

'For the first event we have two winners, for they could not be parted. It is the first time this has happened and each has one talent to take forward.'

Some cheered wildly, others grumbled, for they had wanted the Bastard to win. However, the second contest was announced and the spear-throwing began. Each man had three throws. The first to throw was the Bastard, and his spear reached to the second marker. Another contestant stepped forward, his spear flying through the air to within a fraction of the Bastard's. Three other men threw, but could not reach the second marker. Then Anton stepped forward. His arm went back and the spear flew through the air, almost reaching the third marker.

The Bastard stepped forward to throw again. His spear landed a fraction behind Anton's; the next contestants could not reach even the second marker. Anton threw again, but this time he did not reach his first try.

People were calling out, cheering wildly as the Bastard stepped forward. He drew back his arm, putting all his effort into the final throw, and his spear went past Anton's first marker by no more than a handspan. A huge cheer greeted his efforts, especially when none of the others could come near. Then silence fell as Anton stepped up. He drew back his arm and threw for the final time. The spear flew through the air and finished level with the Bastard's.

There was a buzz of excitement as the crowd waited to hear who would be announced the winner. The master of ceremonies stood up, holding his hand up for silence.

'On the third throw they are equal,' he said. 'But Anton threw further with his first spear. He is therefore the winner.'

Marietta was watching the Bastard's face. He looked furious, for it meant that he could not now win the silver arrow. Only Anton could win this coveted prize, if he gained both the archery contest and the wrestling crown.

The archery came next. People were murmuring with excitement, for though some stayed loyal to their champion, others were willing the stranger on. It was known that archery was the Bastard's weakest skill, and they wondered if Anton could win yet again. He could and did, easily.

Last came the wrestling. No one had ever beaten the Bastard of Rouen at wrestling. A hush fell over the crowd as the master of ceremonies stood up.

'It has been decided that the contest shall be settled by three bouts between the Bastard of Rouen and Anton…'

Marietta gasped as she heard the announcement. Her gaze flew to the Bastard's face. She saw the gleam of satisfaction in his eyes and knew that he was confident of winning this contest. She sat back, feeling that she could not bear to watch, for she did not wish to see Anton humbled. He was such a worthy champion, and she guessed that the Bastard meant to humble Anton if he could.

As the contest began, Marietta closed her eyes. She was sure that the Bastard would do his best to cripple or injure his opponent. Once she had seen a man suffer a broken arm, and she could not bear to see Anton hurt in this way. She was so tense that she thought she might faint.

Hearing the gasp of astonishment and a new buzz of excitement, Marietta opened her eyes to see that Anton had taken the first fall. Her gaze fell on the Bastard. She was shocked by the look of hatred in the man's narrow-set eyes. He looked as if he would like to murder Anton!

Her heart beating wildly, Marietta sat forward to watch. The Bastard had never been beaten in this contest. Surely Anton could not best him again? She turned her nails into her hands as the two men came to grips. The Bastard was so strong, and he seemed to have Anton in his grip. He must win this time!

It happened so quickly that Marietta scarcely realised what had occurred. One moment the Bastard seemed to have Anton in an unbreakable hold, the next he was lying face down in the dirt, his arm twisted behind him and unable to move.

Wild cheers broke from the watching crowd. The nobles were on their feet applauding, the ladies threw scarves and flowers to the champion. A hush fell as the master of ceremonies stood up and announced Anton as the winner of the silver arrow.

Marietta's husband stood up. It was his privilege to present the prize to the winner. She was shocked when he turned to her, presenting the silken cushion with the arrow.

'Take it, Marietta,' he said, and smiled. 'Today my wife will present the winner with his trophy.'

Marietta hesitated, then picked up the arrow and went down the steps to where Anton was standing. She smiled as he made her an elegant bow, and a thrill went through her as she saw the gleam of triumph in his eyes. He might not recall the day he had saved her life, but he had been her champion since that time and she was delighted that he had won this prize.

'You were a worthy winner, sir,' she said. 'I am proud to give you the silver arrow.'

'I thank you, my lady,' Anton said, inclining his head. For a moment his gaze intensified as he looked at her, but no flicker of recognition showed in his eyes. 'I am honoured.' He turned and showed the arrow to the crowd, bowing as they cheered him.

Marietta turned to leave. She put her foot on the first step leading back to the benches where she had sat with her ladies, and then suddenly a dog came rushing towards her from nowhere. It was a huge fierce hound with a brindle coat, and his mouth was drawn back in a snarl. A scream left her lips as the hound sprang at her for no reason, sending her to the ground. Putting up her arms to protect herself, she felt its teeth graze her flesh, and then someone was there, pulling the hound away from her, whipping it with the flat of his sword. The sound of its howling as it fled from the angry avenger was terrible.

'Lady, are you hurt?'

Half fainting, blood trickling from the wound to her arm, Marietta felt herself lifted in strong arms. She was being carried away from the scene. Dimly aware that it was the champion of the day who had saved her from the dog, she tried to thank him.

'I need no thanks, lady,' he said as he strode towards a tent. 'That beast should be destroyed. I believe it was meant to attack me, not you.'

Marietta was feeling too faint to enquire more as she was set down on a pile of soft cloaks and silks in a tent she realised must be the one the knights used to change into their armour. The man she believed to be Anton of Gifford kneeled at her side. He took her arm and examined it, his fingers firm and gentle.

'The beast merely grazed the skin,' he said, and poured water from a flask onto a linen cloth, bathing her arm and wiping away the blood. 'It will hurt for a day or so but there is no real harm done.'

'Thank you. You saved my life.' Marietta was beginning to revive. She wanted to confirm if he were indeed the young man who had saved her life once before, but before she could say anything more the tent flap was lifted and her husband entered together with the Bastard of Rouen.

'Marietta, are you harmed?' the Comte asked anxiously.

'This knight acted promptly and drove off the beast,' Marietta told him. 'I was faint for a while, but I am feeling much better thanks to my brave rescuer. He has bathed the wound and I believe I have taken no harm.'

'The brute should be put to death,' her husband said, and glanced at the Bastard. 'It belongs to Rouen. I have told him he must get rid of it after what it did to you.'

''Tis a hunting dog and knows no better,' the Bastard muttered. Marietta saw him glance resentfully at the knight who had bested him, and felt an icy shiver down her spine. He would not forget this day!

Marietta stood up. She was still trembling, but felt better. 'I am well enough to leave now, husband.'

'If you are sure we shall leave at once.' Comte de Montcrief turned to Anton. 'You have my gratitude, sir. I hope that you will allow me to repay you in some way?'

'I did only what any knight of honour would do, sir. I am glad to have been of service and need no repayment.'

'Then I offer you friendship. If I may be of service to you, you have only to ask.' The Comte offered his hand and they clasped hands. He turned back to Marietta. 'Come, my dearest, take my arm. You must tell me if you feel faint and I shall help you.'

Marietta took his arm. At the door, she turned back and smiled at the knight who had saved her for the second time.

'Thank you, sir. I shall not forget…'

He inclined his head to her but made no answer.

Anton felt a deep satisfaction as he walked away from the field. To become the champion and save a beautiful woman from a savage dog in one day was an achievement that sat well with him.

It was mere chance that he had entered the contest at all. He had told his men to wait for him at the inn, to guard his daughter and her nurse, but it was really because he'd wished to enter the contest incognito. He had been in no mood for the knightly display of skill. Had he wielded a weapon of war, he might in his present mood have struck too hard and killed his opponent.

When he'd seen the notice announcing the contest for the silver arrow he had been intrigued and amused, intending at first to be a spectator. Then he'd seen men lining up to enter the contest and something had driven him to sign his name. As a young man he had loved sport, and he had been the champion of many a fair. He had entered on a whim, unsure that he would excel in all the contests, but the years of training and exercise in the Spanish sunshine had kept him strong.

In the first race he had suddenly felt alive in a way that he had not since Isabella's death. The black shadows had fallen away from him as he'd sped over the course. He had run for himself alone, and he had been surprised to discover that he had been one of the winners. The feeling had exhilarated him, giving him such pleasure that he had thrown himself into the rest of the contest with gusto.

He was laughing inside, because he had never thought to win the prize and was still surprised that he had thrown the great bear of a man who called himself the Bastard of Rouen.

Anton knew that in winning the wrestling so easily he had made himself an enemy. He shrugged. What did it matter? He would be in England within a couple of days and it was unlikely he would see the man again.

A frown creased his brow as he thought about the young woman who had presented him with the silver arrow. What was her name—the Comtesse de Montcrief? He had taken little notice of her until the dog attacked her, but when he had carried her to the tent to tend her wounds he had been tantalised by the scent of her hair, which had wafted towards him. He had felt as if he should know her.

Had they met before? Anton could not think it. It was years since he had been in France and that for but a brief time…

Surely not? A vague picture came into his mind. There had been a child…a young girl he had rescued from beneath the flailing hooves of her horse.

Anton could not be certain that the beautiful woman he had helped today was the young girl he had rescued from the hooves of a terrified horse all those years ago. It was unlikely that fate should bring them together twice in similar circumstances. He struggled to bring the earlier memory to mind but the child's face was unclear; she had been forgotten in all that came after.

Anton was fairly certain that the dog had been ordered to attack. He was the most likely intended victim, because he had humbled Rouen in a sport in which he believed himself invincible. Surely he would have no reason to want to harm the wife of the Comte de Montcrief? He frowned as he wondered if he ought to have told the Comte of his suspicions.

Why did it matter? The woman's husband was responsible for her protection. She was the wife of a powerful man, and could mean nothing to Anton. Besides, he had no wish to marry yet. When he did it would be to a deserving widow, an older lady, someone gentle and kind who would love his motherless daughter. The suspicion that Isabella had betrayed him with another man, and that the child she had carried with her to the grave had not been his, was like a bitter taste in his mouth. She had seemed so innocent and lovely when he wed her; how could he ever trust again?

'I have written to the Bastard,' the Comte told Marietta the next day when he came to her as she sat sewing in her solar. 'He disappeared after the contest and I fear he was displeased that the prize went to another. I believe I must make my offer soon. I would not have him my enemy.'

'I did not like the way he looked at me,' Marietta said. 'I believe he resents me. It is very strange that his dog should attack me.'

'The brute was out of control and has been dealt with. Rouen resents the truth, which is that you have given me a legitimate son.' The Comte sighed. 'I was wrong to let him believe that he would succeed me here. I should never have recognised him—but my first wife could not bear a living child and I thought I might never have an heir.'

'Then you must make your peace with him, husband.'

'Yes, I must.' The Comte smiled at her. 'You were much admired yesterday, my love. I think that we should give a feast for our neighbours soon—perhaps after the Bastard has visited us.'

'Yes, we should…'

Marietta held her sigh inside until her husband left her. It was ridiculous to feel so unhappy. Nothing had changed just because she had seen a man she had never thought to see again.

Anton of Gifford. The years had been kind to him, for he had grown stronger and more handsome. Watching him as he won the silver arrow had made her realise all that she had lost, but had the incident with the dog not happened she would probably have found it easy to forget. The memory of him driving off the brute and tending her arm was something that would live with her for a long time. It seemed that it was her destiny to be rescued by Anton of Gifford, for she was certain in her own mind that it was he.

She shook her head. It was useless to repine. She had never had a chance of being the wife of the man she admired. She knew nothing of him other than that he was bold and strong. He might be a rogue! He had certainly not declared his true title when he entered the contest. Marietta must never think of him again. She must be satisfied with what she had, and, indeed, most of the time she was content.

It was just that she could not help wondering where Anton was now and what he was doing…

'I am glad to be home, Father,' Anton said as his father came down the stairs to greet him in the large hall of their home. 'I have done all His Majesty bade me, but Spain no longer hath anything to hold me. I believe I shall do better in England.'

'I am glad to see you home,' the Marquis said, and his expression was grave. 'I was sorry for your loss, my son. To lose a wife and child so young was a great tragedy.'

'Isabella was not truly well the whole time she was carrying the babe. Her death was an accident. The physician thought that she had turned dizzy and fell down the steps leading to the sunken garden. I have grieved for her and now I have come home to begin a new life here in England. God saw fit to give us a beautiful daughter and I shall make a new life for her.' The new lightness of mood after the contest had stayed with him and he had begun to make plans for the future. It was time to move on—to try and put the bitterness and his doubts behind him. 'I am come to beg my mother if she will care for Madeline until I can provide a home worthy of Isabella's daughter.'

'You have come back to your family.' His father was nodding and smiling. 'I am glad of it, for I thought at one time that you might never return. You need not ask, my son. Both you and the child are welcome here until you are ready to move on.'

'Thank you. I was sure it would be so. How is all my family, Father? Your steward told me that Mother has not been well?'

'Catherine had a nasty chill that settled on her chest. It has pulled her down and I have been anxious for her sake. She is on the mend now and will be pleased to see you.'

'I shall visit her at once.'

'Stay and talk with me for a moment longer. Your sister is with her. Her women usually tend her at about this hour.' The Marquis was thoughtful. 'Your coming is opportune, Anton. Sarah has been with us for the birth of her child. Now that she is well, and the boy thrives, Lord Sheldon has asked that she join him at court. I would prefer not to escort her there, for I do not wish to leave your mother until I am certain she is truly recovered.'

Anton was silent for a moment. He had hoped to have some time with his family before visiting the court. It was possible that the King would have some task for him once he presented himself, and Anton was not sure that he wished to serve at court. He believed that he might prefer life as a country gentleman. However, his father had asked a favour of him and he would be churlish to refuse.

'Of course,' he said. 'I shall be pleased to escort my sister to the court.'

'I would not press you to wed again,' his father said. 'But I hope that in time you will find a lady who can make you happy, Anton. It might be that you'll meet someone at court.'

'I thought a kind, gentle lady—perhaps a country woman who would love and care for my daughter…'

'Such a marriage would bring you comfort, but I am not certain it would bring happiness, my son.'

Anton made no answer. It was too difficult to explain the hurt and anger that lived inside him. He had decided that he would not look for love or passion in his next wife. However, as he left his father and went to find his mother and sister, the picture of a woman's face was in his mind: a beautiful woman who had smiled as she gave him a silver arrow—a woman who had felt so good in his arms as he carried her to his tent.

Chapter Two

Marietta felt the man's hot gaze on her and her skin crawled. She had disliked her husband's bastard the first moment she laid eyes on him, and his behaviour at the tourney had not endeared him to her. There was something menacing in the way he looked at her. She felt as if he stripped her naked with his eyes, exposing her flesh to his lust. For Montcrief's sake she had greeted him politely, but all evening she had longed for the moment she could leave the feasting and return to her chamber. At last the time had come, for the hour was late.

'I shall retire now, my lord,' she said softly, leaning towards her husband to whisper in his ear.

'Yes, do so, Marietta. Some of the men grow lewd and coarse. I do not wish you to be exposed to such behaviour. Go to your chamber now and lock the door. Do not expect a visit this night for I have business that will not keep.' He smiled and touched her hand.

Marietta nodded. She knew that he meant to get Rouen to sign the paper he had had prepared and be done with it that night.

'I wish you goodnight, my lord. May you sleep peacefully.'

'Send some of your mixture to my chamber, my love. My chest feels tight this evening. I do not wish to be ill again.'

'My woman shall bring it to your chamber. It will be there when you retire.'

Montcrief inclined his head, smiled at her and waved his hand. Marietta beckoned to her ladies. The three of them exited the hall together, leaving the men to their drink and their jesting. Beyond the lights of the hall there were shadowed passages and dark corners, the chill of the stone walls striking even the most hardy.

In her bedchamber, Marietta went to her cabinet, unlocked the door and took out a small bottle.

'When you have helped me to disrobe, take this to my lord's chamber and place it on the table by the window. He will see it there and know what it is when he retires.'

'Yes, my lady.'

Jeanne took the bottle and stood it down while she helped Marietta to remove her rich tunic and gown of green cloth.

'I can manage now,' she told her ladies. 'Go to your beds—but do not forget the medicine for my lord, Jeanne.'

When her ladies had gone, Marietta went into the small alcove where the child's cot was placed. Charles was fast asleep. She smiled, resisting the temptation to touch his cheek lest she wake him. Feeling glad to be alone at last, Marietta sought her bed and was soon asleep.

It was barely light when the noise of shouting and lamenting woke her. She sat up as the door of her bedchamber was opened and Jeanne came rushing in, looking strange…almost frightened.

'What is it?' she asked. 'What is all that shouting and wailing?'

'I bring terrible news, my lady,' Jeanne said. 'I do not know how to tell you—your husband is dead. His steward found him lying on the floor of his chamber…'

'My lord is dead?' Marietta gave a cry of alarm and jumped out of bed. She was reaching for her robe as her other women entered the room. 'How did he die? Was it a seizure?' She crossed herself. 'God save his soul.' Tears stung her eyes, for her husband had been good to her despite the differences in their ages.

'He was bleeding from the mouth,' Louise said, and looked awkward. 'Some are saying it must have been poison…'

'Poison? Who would poison my lord?' Marietta looked at Jeanne's face and saw the guilt. 'You do not think that the medicine I sent Montcrief last night would harm him?'

'Of course it would not,' Rosalind said staunchly. 'You use only herbs that do good, my lady. Your cures saved him last winter, for without them he would have died.'

'But some say it…' Jeanne turned red as the other serving women looked at her. 'I do not say it, my lady. You know that I am loyal to you—but Lord Montcrief's steward questioned me. He saw me leaving the master's chamber last night and asked me what I did there. I told him I took the master's medicine to him. The look in his eyes frightened me, my lady: it was a crafty, malicious look. I do not think he likes you.'

'You are right, he does not. Drogbar thinks that I whispered against him to my husband and caused him to lose face. It is true that I suggested we might be served faster at table if the kitchens were brought closer to the great hall, for the food was always cold when I first came here. Montcrief ordered it changed and laughed at Drogbar for not thinking of it sooner. I think the man has not forgiven me.'

'He hates you,' Jeanne said, and shivered. 'He is a powerful man, my lady. He would not dare to speak against you while the master lived, but now...'

'No one will dare speak against her. She is the mother of the new lord of this manor,' Rosalind said. 'Do not forget that she bore the master a fine son.'

'There are those who wonder how it was possible, for the lord was too old to father a child; they hint at the black arts—' Jeanne broke off as all eyes turned on her. 'Forgive me, lady—but it is whispered of you, here at the castle and in the village.'

Marietta's gaze narrowed. 'I have never heard these tales. I have always tried to help people. Why should they say wrong of me?'

'They whisper you are a witch...' Jeanne crossed herself. 'Forgive me! I know that you help people, but there are some who whisper that you could not have saved the master's life had you not bartered with the Devil himself.'

'Be quiet, you foolish woman!' Rosalind said, and her eyes flashed with anger. She had come to Montcrief with Marietta, and known her since they were both children. 'My lady is not a witch. Those who speak so foully abuse her good nature. She has shown you nothing but kindness, Jeanne—nor you Louise.'

'I would not spread such tales,' Louise said indignantly. 'I know my lady is a sweet angel.'

Jeanne looked at Rosalind, and then at her mistress. She fell to her knees before Marietta. 'Forgive me, my lady. I do not believe the tales, but I thought you should know what is being whispered.'

Marietta's face was pale. Inside, she was grieving for her husband, and all this talk of witchcraft was too foolish to be borne.

'Enough of this nonsense!' she said. 'I must go to my husband at once.'

'My lady…is that wise?' Jeanne asked.

Marietta ignored her. She swept out of the chamber and ran down the stairs of her tower. Going through a narrow passageway, she entered the Great Hall and ran across it to the private chambers that belonged to Comte de Montcrief.

As she tried to enter the steward blocked her path, his eyes staring at her with hatred, dark and malicious. 'None may enter here.'

'Stand aside, sirrah,' Marietta commanded. 'How dare you deny me entrance to my husband's chamber?'

'It was the new lord's orders that none should enter.'

'My son is the new lord Montcrief—and I am custodian of his manor until he reaches maturity.'

Marietta's eyes flashed at him. 'Stand aside or I shall have you flogged for your impudence.'

'Do as the lady says,' a voice said from behind her, and Marietta whirled round to look into the face of the Bastard of Rouen. The sneer of triumph on his thick lips sent a chill through her. 'I did not tell you to deny my father's wife the right to pay her last respects. You may go in, lady.'

'By what right do you assume command here? My husband gave me the custodial rights until my son is sixteen. I know his will is lodged at court and once it is read everyone will know that my claim is just.'

'I would not dream of interfering with your ordering of the household and your son, lady.' The Bastard inclined his head to her. He was a handsome man, in a coarse, rough way, his eyes a chilling blue. 'However, I believe you will find that the men follow me. How can you hold this land for your son, lady? It needs a strong man—as you would soon discover if I rode away and deserted you.' He moved closer, towering over her. She could smell an overpowering perfume that hid the smell of dried-on sweat. 'Do not fear, lady. I intend to stay here and protect you and your sweet son, as my father would have wished.'

His mocking smile infuriated her. How dared he take command here? Marietta was tempted to throw the truth in the Bastard's face. She knew that her husband had tried to prevent this very situation, but something had gone wrong. Montcrief had died suddenly and the Bastard had seized his chance. For the moment Marietta was powerless. Instinct told her that it would be foolish to antagonise this man.

'I thank you for your kind thought for me and my

son,' she said proudly. 'For the moment I shall accept your protection.'

'You are gracious, my lady.' His eyes gleamed with anger as he bowed his head to her.

Marietta went into her husband's chamber. One of the men who had served the lord was washing his face, but he bowed his head respectfully and drew back. It was obvious that he intended to leave, but she held out a hand to stay him.

'Tell me, please, how my lord looked before you washed him?'

'There was blood on his mouth. It had run from the side—a mere trickle, my lady.'

'And his expression? Were his eyes open or closed?'

'Open, my lady. I closed them and put the silver coins there to protect him on his journey across the Styx. If he goes prepared he may pay the boatman.'

'You believe in such things, Jolyn?'

'Yes, my lady.' He crossed himself and glanced over his shoulder. 'I know there are many things that we cannot understand. Some speak of the Devil and evil, but these powers may be used for good. I know that my lord spoke often how much better he felt after you gave him medicine, my lady.'

'Thank you,' Marietta said. 'You may leave me with my lord, but return soon to finish what you have begun.'

Jolyn bowed his head and left the room. Marietta bent over her husband and kissed his brow.

'Forgive me that I was not here when you needed me, my lord,' she said, and the tears wet her cheeks. 'I have been fortunate and I shall miss you.'

She bent her head as the tears trickled down her cheeks. Montcrief had treated her kindly and he had protected her. Now she was a woman alone and at the mercy of others. The Bastard of Rouen had taken command here and for the moment there was nothing she could do—except protect her child and wait. If she could get word to the French court perhaps the King would help her, but would she still be alive or would she be the next to die—and her son with her?

'We are pleased to see you at court.' King Henry VIII of England stood up to offer his hand to Anton. He clasped him by the shoulder. 'We were sad to learn of your loss, sir—but welcome you home. You have served us well.'

Anton bowed gracefully. Clad in black from head to toe, with only a fringe of silver to his sash, he was a distinguished man who turned heads as he walked through the court.

'I am honoured to be received privately, Sire. You show me great favour. It is good to be home again.'

Henry studied him in silence for a moment, then, 'You have brought the Lady Sarah to her husband, for which I am sure he expressed his thanks, but what is your intention now, sir?'

'I believe I shall buy land and build my house. In time I may marry again, and I hope to have several sons. My father has but the one son, and if I fail the name dies with me…'

The King looked at him oddly, a glint of displeasure in his eyes. 'It is the hope of all men to have sons, sir.

The Queen hath given me a daughter but as yet I have no living son.' He crossed the room to look down at the courtyard garden below. Through the opened window floated the sound of ladies laughing. The King raised his hand and called out. 'Tell me, my lady Anne—is it warm today?'

Anton did not hear the lady's reply, but when the King turned back to him the look of displeasure had gone from his face.

'The Lady Anne Boleyn is walking with some ladies. I think we should go down and join them, sir. The getting of sons is an ambition I share with you. Choose your wife carefully, my friend. Divorce is no easy thing, especially if you be a king.'

'I imagine it must be difficult, for many in the church would be against it…' Anton knew he must tread carefully, because he had heard the stories and knew of the rumour that the King was seeking a divorce from Queen Katherine so that he might marry Anne Boleyn.

'And you—what is your opinion?'

'I think no man should stand above the King, Sire.'

'You have learned your trade well,' Henry said and smiled. 'I see you are a true diplomat. Tell me, Anton of Gifford—will you do your King a further service?'

Anton bowed his head. It was as he had feared, but he knew he could not refuse. He had become wealthy, and he had learned much from his position at the court of the Holy Roman Emperor—and he had this king to thank.

'Of course, Sire. You have only to ask.'

'It will mean a short journey to France—but we

shall talk of this another day…' Henry smiled. 'It is too pleasant to talk of politics. We must find a way of amusing the ladies—perhaps a game of tennis might please them. Tell me, do you play—are you a good sportsman? Shall we match ourselves for the ladies' pleasure?'

'I have some skill,' Anton replied, smiling inwardly as he recalled the day he had won the coveted silver arrow—and the woman who had presented him with his prize. It was odd, but she had been much in his thoughts of late. He was angry with himself for letting her take root in his mind. Isabella's loss was still a cause of raw grief and he needed to atone for her death! 'Why not, Sire? I may be able to give Your Majesty a little sport…'

'You are sent for, lady,' Jeanne said, her cheeks hot as she avoided looking at her mistress. 'The lord asks that you join him at table this evening.'

'I am in mourning for my husband,' Marietta said. 'Please tell the Bastard of Rouen that I shall not come down this evening.'

'It is forbidden to call him by that name. He is lord of Montcrief now,' Jeanne said, and her eyes were wide with fear. 'He told me that if you did not come he would send men to fetch you.'

'He has threatened you?'

'It was I who took the medicine to the Comte's chamber the night he died. The new lord says that if I do not obey him he will charge me with the Comte's murder.'

'Does he dare to suggest that my husband was murdered?' Marietta's gaze narrowed as the woman hung her head. 'And who is supposed to have put the poison into the medication—you or me?'

'I swear I did nothing wrong!'

'I have accused you of nothing. There was naught to harm my husband in the cure I sent him—but it may have been contaminated later.'

'Will you come, lady? I fear the lord's wrath if you do not. He says I shall be beaten if you do not obey him.'

'Very well. For your sake I shall come.' Marietta waved her away. 'Leave me. I must prepare myself.'

She turned to Rosalind as the door closed behind the other woman. 'Now I am bidden to table because he desires it. Where will it stop?'

'I have seen his eyes on you, my lady. He wants everything that belonged to his father. He wants more than your obedience—and I fear he will take it whether you will it or no.'

'You think he will force himself on me?'

'I think he intends to marry you, my lady. Sandro heard him say as much to Drogbar. It is the only way he can claim your husband's lands legally. At the moment he holds them by force—but if the King sends a force against him he must surrender.'

'You sent my message to the King?'

'It was done at once, my lady, and in secret. The messenger has not yet returned with a reply.'

'The Bastard needs me and my son for the moment, which is why we are still alive,' Marietta said. 'But if my son should have an accident…should die in his sleep…'

'The Bastard of Rouen would be accepted as the

new Comte de Montcrief. He has his father's blood; the master accepted him—would have left the manor to him had you not given him a child.'

'Then if my son were dead he would have all that he craves.' Marietta looked at her, her fear plainly writ on her face. 'I must take the boy to safety, Rosalind.'

'Where will you go, my lady?'

'I do not know…' There was no one in France to help her! For a moment she thought of the man who had once saved her life—the man to whom she had presented the silver arrow. If only he were here! Her instinct told her that he would protect any lady in need. Yet what right had she to ask for his help? Who could she turn to in her need?

Marietta paced the floor, her eye falling on a scarf that had been sent her as a Christmas gift the previous year. 'I shall go to my father's second cousin in England! Lady Claire Melford has asked me to visit so many times. She will help me, and perhaps her husband might intercede with the English King to help me regain my son's birthright.'

'If you run away they may say that you murdered the Comte by witchcraft and were afraid of the consequences.'

'If I stay I may be forced to marry the man I believe truly committed that foul act…'

'My lady…' Rosalind stared at her in horror. 'You think the Bastard murdered his father? If that is true…'

'He will stop at nothing to gain what he wants.' Marietta lifted her head, her face proud. 'I must go down, for he will send an escort to force me if I do not—and I would not have Jeanne beaten, though she thinks me a witch.'

'She cannot!'

'I am certain she believes it. The Bastard has her in the palm of his hand. I do not trust her, Rosalind.'

'You can trust Sandro and me. I swear that we will serve you. We would both give our lives for you and the baby, my lady.'

'Thank you,' Marietta said. 'I believe we must leave as soon as we can arrange it. We shall not be able to take much, but I have some jewels and a little gold that my husband had hidden in his room.'

'If we can get to England you will be safe.'

'I pray that it will be so,' Marietta said. 'Now I must go, before I am taken to the hall by force…'

She walked from the chamber, her head high. Rosalind was not the only one who had seen the look in the Bastard's eyes. His lust was hot and it was the only reason he had not already given her up as a witch. He wanted her. If he could have her as his wife his claim to the manor would be much stronger, and once he had tired of her he would dispose of her as he had her husband. Marietta knew that her life, and that of her son, hung in the balance. She must escape before morning or it might be too late.

Anton reined in as he approached the Castle of Montcrief. King Henry had sent him to the Comte with a message, which he believed was of some importance. A return to France was not something he had wished for, but when he had learned what the King desired he had not felt able to refuse him. And at the castle of Montcrief he was bound to see the lady he had rescued from that brute of a dog.

He was aware of a flicker of something that might have been anticipation. Perhaps during this visit he might learn if the lady who had presented him with the silver arrow was truly the child he had rescued that day on the Field of the Cloth of Gold. She had been much in his mind of late, though he was not certain why. When the King had asked his favour it had seemed as if Destiny had spoken.

He sat his horse, looking at the castle for some minutes before giving the order to move on. His instincts were telling him that all was not as it should be. He could see that the drawbridge was down and the flag was flying at half-mast. Men were on the battlements, but he was not challenged as he and the ten men-at-arms he had brought with him clattered over the bridge into the inner bailey. Anton was clad in armour, his head covered with a helmet. His standard bearer was carrying his own pennant and another that bore the arms of the Tudors, showing that he was an envoy from the English court.

'If anyone questions your mission, tell them merely that I have sent greetings to an old friend,' the King had instructed before Anton left the English court. 'You must deliver my letter into the hands of Comte de Montcrief himself. If for any reason he is not there, you will return it safely to me. The letter is writ in code, but if any other should decipher it, it might cause further trouble between England and her enemies.'

'I shall do as Your Majesty asks.' Anton had bowed his head. 'I shall present my credentials and keep your letter close to my heart until I meet the gentleman himself.'

Now, looking about him, Anton wondered at the lack of order. Where were the men-at-arms training? Where was the steward who should have been told of his coming and been here to meet him? Where were the villagers bringing carts of food and supplies? Instead of order, there was an air of neglect about the place, as if the servants did not care to obey their master. It was not what he would have expected of the powerful lord he had seen at the tourney.

The castle looked almost deserted, apart from a few house-carls in the courtyard. He summoned one to him and the man came hurriedly.

'Forgive us, your honour,' he said, cringing as if he expected a blow. 'The steward is with the lord and everyone else is out searching for *her*…'

'Searching for whom?'

'The witch of Montcrief. She that murdered her gentle husband by foul witchcraft.'

Anton frowned as he remembered the beautiful lady who had given him his prize and a chill ran down his spine. 'Do you speak of the Comte's wife? By what right do you call her a witch?'

'You! To the kitchens, or I'll have you flogged until the skin falls from your back!'

A man had come striding into the courtyard. The Bastard of Rouen! Anton knew him instantly and was immediately suspicious. What had happened here? How came such a brute to be the master of Montcrief's castle? The house-carl had run away as fast as his legs would take him, looking as if the Devil himself were after him. It might be best not to let the Bastard realise that he was speaking to the man who had bested him at the tourney. Anton knew that he looked different in his armour and could only hope he was not recognised.

'Sir, I have come to bring the Comte de Montcrief greetings from Henry Tudor, King of England.'

'Your messenger arrived an hour since,' the Bastard replied, eyes narrowed, calculating. Anton had brought ten of his men into the bailey with him, but more were camped outside, waiting his return. 'You are welcome to stay here with your men, my lord—but I fear your journey has been wasted unless you carry a message you may pass to me? I am the master here now.'

'The message is in my head. It is merely that Henry wishes to congratulate the Comte on having a fine heir—and to assure him of friendship should he visit England.'

'My father died some five days ago. He was killed by witchcraft and poison—and the culprit was his wife. She has stolen her husband's son and fled, taking gold and jewels with her. Most of my men are out, searching the countryside for her and the servants who assisted her flight. They will suffer the same fate as their evil mistress when they are caught.'

'Witchcraft is a wicked crime,' Anton said, resisting the urge to wipe that look of satisfaction from the other's face. 'Has the witch been proved?'

'She escaped before she could be put to the test. I was at first deceived in her, for she pretends to be modest and God-fearing. However, her flight is proof enough. She had heard the rumours that she was to be accused of her husband's murder and fled in the night before she could be apprehended.'

'I see that you have much to occupy you,' Anton said. His instincts told him that this man was not to be trusted. He did not like him, and caution told him that it would be wiser not to take his hospitality. His men would prefer to rest under the stars rather than be murdered as they slept. 'I am sorry for your trouble, and I shall move on rather than cause you more bother.'

He remounted and signalled to his men to follow him from the castle. Anton was aware of a prickling sensation at the nape of his neck. Something was wrong here. He could not tell how much truth there was in the tale of the lady murdering her husband, but he could not believe that she was a witch. Many women were hanged or burned to death as witches, because they had failed the barbaric acts that put them to the test and proved their guilt. The thought of such vile cruelty left a bitter taste in his mouth. He shuddered as he pictured the woman he had seen at the tourney being tortured and then burned in the flames.

He could do nothing to help her. Nor should he if she were truly the murderer of her husband. Yet he could not believe it of the woman he had seen at the tourney. Something was wrong here!

His mission was at an end. Instead of staying here overnight he would turn north towards the home of Lord de Montfort. It would mean one night more upon the road, but his aunt Anne's husband would welcome him and he would deliver a message to their son Sebastien. King Henry had charged him to invite his cousin to visit the English court.

Anton frowned as he gave the order to move north. He

would be glad to put a few leagues between him and the upstart who claimed that he was the new lord of Mont-crief. There had been a look of slyness about the man that made him wonder just what was behind his invitation to stay the night. Anton had no doubt that he and his men would have been killed as they slept, perchance to be robbed for their armour and possessions. He was glad to leave, and could not help but think of the woman who had been forced to flee her home. He remembered how beautiful she had looked that day at the tourney. The wife of a powerful noble, she had had everything she could want—and now she was a fugitive in fear of her life.

Marietta screamed as she saw the small party of men riding towards them fast. She knew the pennant well. These were the Bastard of Rouen's men and they would catch her and take her back with them. She had brought her fate on herself by defying the Bastard, but her son was innocent.

'Take Charles and run that way,' she said to Rosalind. 'I shall go this—perhaps if they come after me, you and Charles may get away…'

'I cannot leave you, my lady.'

'Go! I command it!' Marietta cried. 'I charge you to take care of my son. He must live even if I die…'

She gave her woman a little push, but then she saw it was too late. A larger party of men were coming towards them from the opposite direction. They were caught between them and there was no escape. She screamed despairingly and began to run towards the woods. Perhaps if she could reach them she might escape for long enough to hide her child. Even if she died, Charles must live…

The sound of yelling and screaming made her glance back over her shoulder. She was stunned as she saw that the larger group of men seemed to be attacking the Bastard's soldiers. What was happening? Who were the strangers, and why were they fighting the rogues that would have taken her prisoner?

Instead of fleeing into the woods to hide, as she had planned, she stood, her heart beating frantically as she watched the fight.

After a short skirmish, the men she feared had turned tail and were running for their lives. Marietta stood still as one of the strangers rode up to her; her heart was pounding and she wondered if her last moment had come. She pulled her shawl over her head, trying to hide her face. She was frightened. Did these men know who she was—had they saved her because they wished to sell her to the Bastard for gold?

'You are safe now, mistress,' the knight said, and raised his visor, revealing his face. Marietta's heart stopped as she knew him. For a moment relief flooded through her. It was Anton of Gifford—but would he remember her? Surely he must after that day at the tourney! Would he believe her innocent if she told him her story? She pulled her shawl tighter around her face, hoping that he would not recall that she had given him the silver arrow or the incident with the savage dog. 'Come, I shall take you up with me.'

'No…' Marietta hung back. She hugged the child to her. She was nervous, because she did not know how he would react if he knew who she was and the crimes of which she stood accused. 'Please, allow me to go on my way.'

'If you do not come with us those villains may return. Where are you travelling to, mistress?' her rescuer asked. His eyes were narrowed and intent as he gazed down at her. 'We go north, to the estate of my uncle Lord de Montfort. Then we will travel back to England.'

'I was on my way to England myself,' Marietta told him. 'I need to reach the coast by nightfall.'

'Then we shall take you some part of your way. I am Anton of Gifford, mistress. I shall take you to safety, and then we shall discuss what you should do in the future…'

Had he recognised her? Did he know that she had been forced to flee her home? Marietta trembled inwardly. So far he had been kind, but what would he do if he knew that she had been accused of witchcraft and murder? It would be best if they parted before he discovered the truth.

'You saved our lives, but if you set us down when we have put some distance between us and those rogues we shall do well enough.'

'Will you not tell me your name, mistress?'

Marietta hesitated. 'It is Marie—Marie de Villiers.'

She saw a flicker of something in his eyes. Had he remembered her? Would he denounce her as a wicked murderess?

'Come then, Mistress Villiers,' he said, and offered his hand. 'We waste time and night falls…'

Marietta stood still as he dismounted and lifted her to the saddle, remounting so swiftly that she almost fell as the great horse moved forward. She had slipped the babe inside the shawl she had wrapped around her head and body, leaving her hands free so that she could hold on to the knight's cloak. The knights were regrouping after routing the Bastard's rogues. She saw that one of them, a man with a fearful scar on his face, had taken Rosalind up behind him, and Sandro was riding the pony they had brought with them, their few possessions strapped to his back. It seemed that she had no choice but to go with them.

Sitting behind Anton of Gifford, Marietta was aware of mixed emotions. How long had she dreamed of meeting this man again? Yet now it had happened she had the shadow of murder hanging over her.

Anton called a halt as the gates and wall that bounded the estate of Lord Simon de Montfort came into view. He dismounted and signalled to his men to do the same. He had brought the man and two women this far, and he believed they must now be safe enough to continue their journey. He assisted the woman he had taken pillion to the ground and gazed down at her. He had known her the moment he looked into her face. She was the woman who had given him the silver arrow at the tourney—the wife of the late Comte de Montcrief, the woman whose perfume had haunted his senses since he held her in his arms. So why had she given him a false name? Did she think that he would betray her to the Bastard of Rouen? Did she even remember giving him the silver arrow?

The questions chased each other through his mind

as he considered what he should do now. She had asked to be allowed to go on alone, but if he abandoned her she and her servants would be recaptured within days.

Deciding not to press her for the truth, or reveal that he knew she had lied about her identity, he told her, 'My aunt will give us shelter for the night. You are safe now, lady.'

'I thank you for your kindness, but we travel to the coast for we mean to take ship for England. I should not wish to trouble your aunt…'

'It will be no trouble. You are weary and can go no further this night, Mistress Villiers. Rest here and I shall escort you to the coast in the morning. You will be safer with us.'

'No, no, sir. We should go on…' Marietta hung her head, seeming afraid. Did she think that he would denounce her as a witch? 'I think we should not put you to more trouble, sir. Just allow us to leave and we shall delay you no more.'

Anton looked down at her. She was pale, and she looked exhausted. He felt something stir inside him. This woman could not be guilty of murder! As for the charge of witchcraft—he had no patience with such nonsense.

'You will stay here this night,' he said. 'My aunt will give you a room where you may rest and tomorrow we shall go on board my ship.'

'No. I must go…' Marietta tried to pull away from him, but gave a little cry and stumbled. Anton saw that she was faint from hunger or exhaustion, and caught her in his arms before she fell.

* * *

When Marietta came to herself once more she was in a small chamber that might belong to a servant of some importance. It was clean, and the sweet-smelling sheets on the bed were fresh, though of a coarse cloth that felt hard to someone who had been used to the finest of linen and silk. She moaned slightly and someone came to her, bending over to apply a cool cloth to her head.

'You fainted, mistress,' Rosalind told her. 'It has all been too much for you—and you have not eaten properly for two days. Lady de Montfort has sent you soup and bread. Will you not eat a little?'

Marietta sat up. Her head was aching, but she could smell the beef broth and it was good. She was suddenly aware of a ravenous hunger.

'My son, Charles—where is he?'

'Lady de Montfort took him. She says that she will feed and care for him until you are better. She likes children, and she has but one son who is full grown.'

'Has she asked questions?'

Rosalind brought the soup and bread on a board, placing it over Marietta's knees. 'I think the lord told her something. She has been nothing but kind, my lady.'

'You must not call me that,' Marietta warned. 'Marie or Mistress Villiers will do.'

'I do not like to address you so,' Rosalind objected. 'But if you wish it I shall try.' She hesitated, then, 'The lord seems fair-minded—could you not tell him your story?'

'No! We do not know him,' Marietta said. 'How can I trust a stranger? He might believe that I am a witch and that I murdered my husband.'

'Surely he would listen if you told him the truth?'

'I dare not risk it. We must leave here tonight and make for the coast ourselves.'

'Is that wise, mistress? Even if we reach the coast safely, we may not be able to find a ship to take us to England. If word hath reached the coast they may be looking for us…'

Marietta sipped the soup and found it good. She ate a mouthful of bread and then some more soup, looking at her serving woman thoughtfully. Perhaps Rosalind was right. Perhaps it would be better if they stayed with the men who had rescued them until they could find safe passage to England.

Anton of Gifford was brave and honourable. He had saved her twice before. Surely he would do nothing to harm her? Yet if he thought her a murderess he might feel it his duty to give her up. She had no choice but to accept his help, but she would not reveal herself to him just yet.

'You speak wisely. I thought to flee, but that would merely arouse suspicion. We shall accept the lord's escort until we are safely able to get to England.' She crossed herself. 'I pray that neither he nor his men guess who I am…'

Anton opened the door of the guest chamber with caution. He did not wish to wake either the woman who called herself Marie de Villiers or the maid who slept by her side, yet he had been unable to rest without seeing for himself that she was well and safe.

He approached the bed softly, his bare feet making no noise on the stone flags. Gazing down at her face as

she slept, he felt his heart contract with an odd pain.
How beautiful she was! She looked innocent as she
slept, murmuring something that was indistinguishable,
one hand beneath her cheek. How could a woman like
this be guilty of murder?

He felt a wave of anger sweep through him as he
thought of how cruelly she had been treated by the
Bastard of Rouen. The man was a rogue, and Anton suspected that he had begun this tale to rid himself of his
father's wife and gain all Montcrief's wealth for
himself.

If that were true the woman had been cheated of her
rights. Yet how could he be certain that his instincts
were true? He had believed Isabella as innocent as she
was lovely, but she had turned from him to another. Was
it wise to trust any woman?

Even if she were innocent, it would be better to
deliver her safely to her chosen destination and forget
her. Isabella had taught Anton a hard lesson. He had
thought he loved her, but her coldness, her petulance
and her betrayal had made him realise their marriage
was a mistake. He still felt the guilt of her death heavy
on his conscience, for even if she had taken another man
as her lover she had not deserved to die. He hoped that
he would have been man enough to release her and let
her find happiness if she had confessed the truth to him.
Yes, he had raged at her, but in the end he believed that
he would have done what was right.

When the time was right he would marry again, but
he would take great care in his choice of a wife. A
woman such as the Widow Montcrief was beautiful, but

if he were foolish enough to let himself be caught she would wind her fingers about his heart and eventually destroy him.

Turning away, Anton closed the door softly behind him. He did not know why this woman had touched something inside him, but he would not allow her to take root in his heart.

Chapter Three

'Who are they?' Anne de Montfort asked of her sister's son later that night. 'I think that the mother of this delightful child is a lady, despite her clothes. I saw her face as we put her to bed and her features are too delicate to be those of a peasant.'

'She says that her name is Marie de Villiers.' Anton thought carefully. He considered that it would be best to tell no one that he knew the lady to be the widow of Comte de Montcrief. 'In truth I do not know who she is, Aunt. I rescued her from rogues upon the road and that is all I can tell you. I dare say she would have gone on her way had she not been overcome by faintness. She says that she wishes to travel to England—and since I have a ship waiting…'

'You intend to take her there.' Anne smiled. 'I think my sister is blessed in her son, Anton. I love Sebastien dearly, but he tends to be wild and reckless. Mayhap he has been spoiled because he was our only child. You have such fine manners and it is a pleasure to have your company.'

Anton murmured something about her son being young as yet. He was vaguely troubled in his mind concerning the lady he had brought to her house. If the lady were indeed the Comte's widow, as he firmly believed, she might be guilty of her husband's murder, though he had instantly acquitted her of witchcraft. He knew that some of his men would certainly look at her askance if they suspected anything of the kind. Fortunately, he believed that none of them had been present at the tourney where he had taken the silver arrow from her hand and then rescued her from a savage brute of a dog.

He frowned, because the idea that she might actually have killed her husband left a bad taste in his mouth. He knew that women could be faithless. Had he not been given ample proof? Isabella had been lovely and seemed innocent but she had destroyed his faith in women. This French woman was beautiful, but was she also a wicked murderess? No, surely not!

He decided that he would deliver her safely to England, but after that he would leave her to make her own way.

'It has been good to see you,' Anne told him, and kissed his cheek. 'One day you must bring your daughter to visit me.'

'Yes, I shall—one day.'

Anne wondered at the odd look in his eyes. She supposed that the sad, sometimes desperate look she had seen there at times must come from the grief he felt at the loss of his wife—but what else had made Anton so serious?

* * *

Marietta glanced back at the château as they rode away. Lady Anne had spoken kindly to Rosalind before they left, giving her food for the journey. Rosalind had been taken up behind the knight with the scar on his face. She knew that his name was Miguel Sanchez, and he had told Rosalind that he was a friend of Anton of Gifford's. As yet she had not spoken to him herself, but she had noticed him staring at her and something in his look had made her nervous. Did he know who she was? Would he betray her?

Marietta was riding just ahead of Anton of Gifford. Dressed in his black armour, with a visor over his face, he seemed a fearsome warrior, and his grip on her wrist when he had refused to let her go on her way alone had been strong. She had been well treated at the home of Lord and Lady de Montfort, and she was feeling better for the rest and good food, though she had seen nothing more of her rescuer until this morning.

She had been surprised when the horse had been brought out for her to ride, because it was a fine specimen and the kind of mount only a lady would ride. She feared that the man who had rescued her was aware that she was not who she pretended to be—but did he know her real name? Had he remembered her from the tourney at last?

'Why am I to ride a horse like this?' she had asked as he had offered to help her mount.

'It is fitting that you should, lady,' he said softly. 'Come, there is nothing to fear. Believe me, I mean you no harm.'

'I believe you, sir,' she said, and took his hand,

allowing him to help her up into the saddle. She gazed down at him, wishing that his visor were up so that she might see his face. 'You are generous and I thank you for everything you have done for us.'

'It was little enough.' The knight's eyes gleamed behind the visor that masked his face. 'We shall soon be on board my ship, and within a few hours you will be in England.'

'Thank you…'

Marietta's stomach tightened with nerves. This knight had such a strange effect on her. His touch made her tingle, and she was apprehensive of what he would say if he ever discovered that she had been accused of witchcraft, and yet instinctively she wanted to trust him. If only she dared tell him the truth and throw herself on his mercy!

Anton chose to ride just behind Marie de Villiers, as she called herself. He could watch her and stop her if she tried to ride off alone—or protect her if another attempt were made to snatch her. He had seen the puzzled look in her eyes earlier, and knew that she was wondering about him. Was she afraid that he would betray her to her enemy? Was she worried that he'd heard the rumours about the death of her husband?

Anton had dismissed the idea of witchcraft instantly. He was aware that many believed in the power of evil, and feared it, but he was inclined to think that evil lived in the minds of men who practised it. He would sooner believe the Bastard of Rouen capable of murder than this gentle lady.

Some would no doubt say that she had cast her spell over him. Even his friend Miguel might turn against her if he knew that she was accused of witchcraft. If he were to deliver her safely to her destination Anton would need to be careful. It would be better to plead ignorance than admit that he knew her. Once they were in England she should be safe from the man who wanted her dead.

Anton had no doubt that the Bastard of Rouen had seen his chance to take what rightfully belonged to the Comte's legitimate son. It would not be the first time it had happened and would not be the last. The Comte's widow might be able to prove her innocence and try to take back her husband's estate once she reached England—but could she hold it? The Bastard of Rouen was not the only man who might try to take it by force. A woman alone was not safe in turbulent times, and the barons of France were fiercely independent and jealous of their privilege—hungry for power and wealth, they would see his widow as a prize to be taken.

The Comte had neglected his duty. He ought to have set men in place who would protect their mistress to the death—but perhaps he had. They might already be dead or imprisoned…

Anton frowned. It was not his place to enquire. He had a duty to return the King's letter and tell him what had happened at the Castle of Montcrief. Once the lady was safe in England he should forget her. A wry smile touched his mouth, for it was easy to make the decision but not as easy to carry it through.

* * *

Marietta stood on board the ship and watched the shores of France slip away into the mist. She felt strange, as if she had said farewell to everything dear and familiar to her. It was doubtful that she would return to France—unless she could find someone who would intercede with the King for her?

'You should go below, lady.'

Marietta turned as Anton of Gifford came up to her. 'I wanted to watch until the land was gone, sir. I am not sure that I shall ever return to France.'

'You do not know that, lady. Things may change in the future.'

'They cannot change for me. I do not mind for myself, but I would have justice for my son.'

'Indeed? In what way?'

'It does not matter.' Marietta turned away. She did not dare to trust him, for even in England a witch could be hunted and condemned to death. 'You said that I should go below. I shall do as you ask, for I would not wish to be in the way…'

'It was for your own sake that I advised it,' Anton said. 'The captain tells me that there may be a storm.'

'I see…' Marietta inclined her head. 'Excuse me, I must make sure that Rosalind and my son are safe. I speak a little English, but my…friends have none.'

'How is it that you understand the English language so well, mistress?'

'My mother was an Englishwoman. I learned to speak the language at her knee. Excuse me, I must go below.'

She did not look back as she walked away and started

to descend the ladder leading to the cabins on the next deck, but she was aware that he was watching her.

Anton had discarded his heavy armour as soon as the swell became too great. If the storm should become too fierce and the ship sink, neither he nor his men would stand a chance wearing their armour. Accordingly, they had all removed it, and were wearing only their short jerkins and tight-fitting hose, with shoes that could be kicked off in an instant.

Anton was an experienced sailor. During his time as an ambassador at the court of the Holy Roman Emperor he had often travelled between Spain, France and Italy. He had gone back on deck when the storm struck, to see if he could be of help, and also because he knew it was easier to ride the heavy swell on deck rather than lying on a bunk in his cabin.

He was watching a particularly large wave coming towards them when someone touched his arm, and he turned to look into the face of the groom Sandro.

'How may I help you?'

'Forgive me, my lord, but my lady is very ill. We have nothing to give her, and we wondered if you had a little wine to settle her stomach?'

'I have something better than wine, though 'tis best given *in* wine. I shall go to my cabin now and fetch it for her.'

'Thank you, my lord…' Sandro looked a bit green in the face, and suddenly dashed to the side of the ship, retching over the side. Anton smiled grimly. At least the man had the sense not to vomit into the wind!

He left the man staggering back to safety and went down to his cabin. It took him only a moment or so to find the powder given him by a Spanish doctor who was part Arab, and another to mix it into a cup of wine. He hung onto a wooden beam as the ship lurched, protecting the cup and managing to keep it upright.

The ship righted itself as Anton made his way to the cabin next door and knocked. Rosalind, who looked little better than Sandro had a few moments earlier, opened it.

'I have brought this for your lady,' Anton said. 'You look ill yourself, mistress. Go up on deck for a moment and get some air. It may ease you.'

'I cannot leave my…' Rosalind gasped and rushed for the chamber pot, vomiting into it. 'Forgive me, my lady…'

Anton went towards the bed. He saw the woman lying on the bed, her hair in disarray about her on the pillow. She had her eyes closed and she was moaning, clearly in great distress.

'Come, lady, you must drink this,' Anton said. He perched on the edge of her cot, slipping an arm beneath her shoulders to lift her. Marietta's eyes flickered open. A little sigh escaped her, but she parted her lips, swallowing obediently. 'Drink it all. In a little time you will feel much better. I never travel without this cure. I am seldom ill these days, though I have suffered in the past.'

'Thank you…' Marietta lay back, a tear slipping from the corner of her right eye. 'You are so kind…'

Anton stroked back the damp hair on her forehead. How did she manage to look so lovely even while she was ill? Seeing her like this moved him, arousing strong emotions; he felt protective, wanting to ease her.

'Do not try to talk. I shall go to prepare a cup for your serving woman and return in a moment or so…'

Marietta made no answer. Anton returned to his cabin and made up more of the mixture. He took the mixture back to Rosalind, who gulped it down gratefully.

'Go on deck for a while,' Anton advised. 'The mixture will work in a short time and the air will refresh you.'

'My lady…' Rosalind glanced at the bed where Marietta lay.

'Is safe with me. I give you my word of honour as a knight and nobleman of England.'

'God bless you, sir!' Rosalind said, and stumbled through the door, clearly still feeling groggy.

Anton went to stand at the foot of the bed and gazed down at the woman who lay there. Her red-gold hair was spread on the pillows and she looked beautiful, desirable, despite her distress. The colour was returning to her cheeks. He smiled, because he saw that her hands had unfurled and she was no longer moaning. The mixture had begun to work its magic—though it was no magic but just a simple cure that the physician had learned from his brethren. The Arabs had many cures that would be thought witchcraft by some.

This lovely woman could not be a murderess! Anton swallowed hard as he gazed down at her face, feeling something move about his heart, as if a shadow that had lain there had shifted and eased. How could anyone accuse her of such evil? She had the look of an innocent angel. He thought her one of the most beautiful women he had ever seen—and he felt the first stirring of forgotten desires deep in his loins. He moved towards her, driven by the need to touch her. The strength of the feelings she aroused shocked him. Even when he had courted Isabella he had never experienced such an over-whelming desire to touch and hold as he felt now. Bending over the Frenchwoman, he smoothed her damp hair back from her forehead. Her eyelids flickered and she looked up at him.

'Are you feeling better, Mistress Villiers?'

'A little…yes. I am better than I was. Thank you…Anton of Gifford. Why are you so kind to me?'

'I am at your service, lady. Do not fear me. I shall not betray you. Your secret is safe with me. I know you are not a witch, for I do not believe in such tales, and I cannot think you guilty of murder.'

'You knew me from the first?'

'You are the late Comte's wife. Of course I remem-bered you from the day of the contest, when you gave me the silver arrow and that dog attacked you.'

'You must believe that I didn't murder my husband. I cared for him deeply, despite the difference in our age. I am innocent of the charge against me…' Marietta said, and sighed. Her eyelids flickered. 'I am so very tired.'

'Sleep in peace, lady,' Anton said softly. He knew that she was hardly aware of what she had told him, for her mind was confused by sickness. Bending his head, he placed a gentle kiss on her brow. 'No one shall hear your secret from me. You are safe now.'

'Thank you, Anton,' Marietta said, gave a faint sigh and fell asleep.

Anton stood for a while, watching as she slept. She had sworn that she was innocent of any crime and he wanted to believe her. He did believe her! He might be a fool to accept her word, and yet his instincts had told him from the first that she could not be guilty of murder.

Would she tell him everything once she was well again?

Her plight touched his heart—a woman and child alone save for her servants. What would become of the young Comte now? He was but a child, and had lost both his father and his birthright. At least his daughter, Madeline, had her father and a loving family, but who did the young Comte have to protect him?

The thought occurred to him that he could stand as both the young Comte's and his mother's protector. If he championed her cause something could be done to put right the wrong that had been done mother and son.

Anton shook his head. To become too involved in this woman's story might be foolish. Perhaps it was best if they parted without speaking of the truth. He had brought her to safety, but when they reached England he would let her go on alone.

'Where are you headed?' Anton asked as the horses were brought. Foolish as it might be, he had discovered that he was reluctant to abandon her to her fate. A slight detour on his part would be no trouble. 'I must go to London soon, but if it is on my way I could escort you to your destination.'

'I go to stay with a distant cousin.' Marietta fumbled with the strings of her purse. 'I have her letter here. Lady Claire Melford. She is the wife of…'

'Sir Harry Melford. He is my uncle, and has lately been made the Earl of Rundle for services to the King.' Anton frowned. 'How come you to know the lady Claire?'

'Her father was cousin to my father,' Marietta said. 'She has written many times, inviting me to stay, but…my husband was too busy to accompany me and I would not desert him.' Her eyes were on his face. 'How strange that we should have family ties and not know it.'

'Fate, perhaps?'

'Yes, perhaps.'

'What makes you think Lady Claire will receive you?' Anton's eyes narrowed. 'Will you tell her the truth? Will you tell her that you were accused of murdering your husband by witchcraft?'

'My husband did not die by my wish nor at my hand,' Marietta said. Her cheeks were pale and she would not look at him. 'I was falsely accused because Rouen wanted me to take him as my husband and I would not. He threatened me, tried to force me to wed him, so I ran away…and then he accused me of murder and witchcraft.'

'I suspected as much. The Bastard of Rouen is a rogue—but had you no one to protect you?'

'My husband was trying to protect both his son and me,' Marietta said. 'He required his bastard to sign a paper renouncing all rights to his fortune in return for money.'

'But he died before it was accomplished. Does that not seem suspicious to you?'

'I believe he may have killed my husband, but I could

not prove it. People believe the tales that I am a witch, perhaps because I have some skill in healing.'

'Yes, I know that women healers are sometimes suspected of using the black arts—but you do not dabble in such things?'

'Never!'

'I thought not. I do not believe in such powers but many do—and it can be dangerous for women.'

'I know…' Marietta looked uncertain. 'I mean to tell Lady Claire—but perhaps she will not wish to see me…'

Anton hesitated, then, 'May I see Lady Claire's letter inviting you to stay?'

Marietta felt inside her purse and took out a sheet of vellum, handing it to him. Anton read the letter and saw that it was addressed and written in fond terms that would indicate a liking on the part of his uncle's wife. It was clear that Lady Claire liked and approved of the Comtesse.

'I believe you should give Lady Claire a chance to hear your story,' Anton said. 'It will not trouble me to see you safely there, lady—if you should wish for my escort?'

She seemed to hesitate, then lifted her clear eyes to meet his. 'You have done so much for me already, sir. I cannot repay you, but if you would be so good as to see me to my kinswoman's house I should be grateful.'

'Then we shall accompany you, lady.' Anton inclined his head.

It was foolish to feel pleased that she had accepted his help. Their lives must soon turn in different directions, for he was certain the King would have more work for him and she was not for him—yet there was something that drew his eyes to her again and again as they rode. She was beautiful, but he had met others as lovely. There was pride in her, but something more... something that tugged at the secret core inside him.

His lips settled into a thin line. It would be wrong for him to think of love and marriage with a woman like this, because his stupid jealousy had caused his first wife's death. Even if Isabella had betrayed him, she had not earned her cruel fate. He did not deserve to find love again and he would not look for it.

He would deliver Mistress Villiers to her kinswoman and then forget her. It would be better for both of them so.

Marietta was aware that Anton looked at her often. What was he thinking? Did he suspect her of murdering her husband?

He had been so gentle when he gave her the medicine that had eased her sickness. For a moment as he had stroked her forehead and comforted her it had been almost as she had seen it in her dreams—when he held her and kissed her and vowed to love her. Her dreams of romantic love had sustained her as she cared for and nursed a husband who was more suited to be her father, but they were all foolishness. She had known marriage, and a kind of love, but the feelings she longed to experience were merely the imagination of a lonely girl.

Marietta fought down the wave of longing and regret. If only she hadn't been obliged to marry the Comte. She had accepted her fate, and been a good wife to him, but now she was alone, with only a few jewels to help her make her way in the world. Having always been loved and indulged, she was not sure how she could make a living—unless perhaps she could take on some sewing? Her embroidery had often been praised, but would it be good enough to earn enough food to keep her child and her servants alive?

Her thoughts were heavy, sometimes dark and fearful as they rode through countryside that seemed very different from that she had known all her life. England was beautiful in its own way, but it was not France—it was not her home. Her knowledge of the language was not as strong as it ought to be if she were to live here, and not everyone would speak French as well as Anton of Gifford. Her servants would find it even more difficult to adapt, for they knew hardly a word of English.

'You have looked pensive all morning, lady,' Anton said when they stopped for refreshment. She was sitting on a fallen tree, her child in her arms, a picture so enchanting that his heart caught. 'Does something trouble you? The boy is not ill?'

'No, Charles seems to thrive. I believe he is enjoying the adventure.'

Anton knelt down, looking at the boy's face. His eyes were wide and enquiring, and, as he saw that he was the centre of attention, he chortled with glee and leaned forward to touch Anton's hand. Caught by this unexpected gesture, Anton reached out and lifted him, then swung him high above his head, holding him safely so that Charles shouted and laughed, clearly enjoying the encounter.

'You are good with children,' Marietta said, and smiled as Anton returned the child to her arms. 'His father played with him that way sometimes.'

'He will miss his father, I think.'

'Yes. We shall both miss the Comte…'

'Is that why you are sad? Because your husband is dead?'

'I grieved for his death because it was cruel and wrong, but I am not sad because of it…'

'Then why?' Anton's eyes quizzed her.

'It is just that everything is new and strange here,' Marietta said. 'I dare say the countryside will seem more familiar as time passes.' She did not say that she feared for what her future must be without a husband to care for her and her son.

'Yes, it must seem different,' Anton agreed, and looked thoughtful. 'But we shall soon be with Lady Claire, and then you may feel more comfortable. You will be able to care properly for your son there.'

'He is very precious to me.'

Anton nodded. 'I can see that, *madame*. I have a daughter, perhaps a few months older. I think much of providing a good home for her future, for she is all I have left now.'

'Your wife died?'

'Yes. It seems that we have something in common— a shared loss. You must cleave to your son and find happiness in him, lady.'

'Yes, I shall.' A delicate blush touched her cheeks. He had been married and widowed! How foolish all her dreams had been! He had never thought of her after that day on the Field of the Cloth of Gold. 'If I can stay with Lady Claire for a few weeks I may find some way to earn my living.'

'I am sure the Countess has room for one more lady in her household.'

'I am good with my needle.'

'Then I am sure she will be happy to have you as one of her ladies.'

'Yes, perhaps…'

Marietta was thoughtful as they remounted and started on their way once more. Seeing Anton with her son had shown her another side to him. He had a daughter he loved and he had once had a wife. Perhaps the reason he sometimes looked so stern was that he was grieving hard for his wife.

She tried not to think of what might have been. Her future was in the balance, for she could not know how she would be received when they reached the home of her kinswoman.

Marietta was sitting in the inn parlour nursing her son when Anton entered. Charles had been crying and his face was flushed. She thought that he might have a tooth coming through, and she ran her finger over his gums, rubbing on a little of the mixture she used when he suffered this way.

'What ails the boy?' Anton asked, frowning.

'I believe he has a tooth coming,' Marietta replied without looking up. 'He cried when I gave him his milk this morning, and he is not usually fretful.'

Anton picked up the little pot she had been using and

held it so that he could smell the substance inside. 'This smells like honey?'

'It is a mixture of many things, but I sweeten it with honey so that he does not refuse it.'

Anton nodded, his eyes going to her face as she nursed the boy.

'You look tired. Where is Rosalind?'

'She is rinsing some cloths for the boy. I cannot expect her to care for him all the time. He kept us both awake last night.'

'Give him to me,' Anton said, and took the child into his arms. As if by magic Charles's cries stopped, and he lay looking up at Anton, eyes wide with wonder.

'He feels safe with you,' Marietta said, and smiled.

She could see that he was accustomed to handling a child and wondered at it, for it was unusual in a knight of his standing.

'My husband loved the boy but he seldom had time for him. Though when he did make the time Charles loved it.'

'A father should always have time for his son.' Anton handed the boy back to her. 'We could rest here for today if you wish? If the travelling is too much for you or the child it would add but one day to our journey.'

'I thank you, but I am sure you have more important business, sir. Charles will come to no harm if we continue our journey.'

'Yes, perhaps it is best, for once we are at your kinswoman's house you will be able to rest and see your child properly cared for.'

'Thank you…' Marietta felt a pang of regret. It might have been nice to take the journey more slowly, because it would have given her time to get to know Anton of Gifford—yet perhaps it was for the best after all. 'You have been kind, sir.'

'I did what any honourable knight would do when finding a lady in distress,' he said, and then turned on his heel and walked away.

He was a man of many moods! Marietta held the sigh inside. It would only bring her heartache if she began to like Anton of Gifford too much...

'Marietta, dearest!'

Claire embraced her, the delight in her face evidence that she was thrilled that her kinswoman had come at last. 'I am so happy that you have come to visit me. When I wrote I thought you might be too busy to leave your home, for I dare say there are many duties to keep you there?'

'Once I had many duties, but no longer...' Marietta saw the questions in her cousin's eyes. Her heart ached, for she could not tell if she would be welcome once she had confessed the truth. 'I would tell you privately.'

'Of course. I have many questions, but they can wait. You have travelled a long way and must be tired. When Anton's messenger told us you were coming I prepared a chamber for you. I shall take you up, my love, and you may rest and take a little food and wine before you join us.'

'You are very kind, Countess.'

'No, my dear. You must call me Claire. I insist on it.'

Marietta smiled, allowing the Countess to lead the way up the wide staircase to the gallery above. A servant sprang to open a door and they went into a room of fair proportions. At once Marietta saw that this was to serve her as a bedchamber, but also as somewhere she could sit alone with her embroidery if she wished to be quiet. She knew instantly that it was one of the best chambers and her guilt was heavy.

'I shall leave you to rest, my love. We shall talk later.'

'It is best that I tell you now,' Marietta said. 'I would not wish to deceive you.'

'You look so serious. Tell me, then, since it concerns you.'

'Sir Anton saved my life. I was being pursued by men who meant to force me to stand trial as a witch. I should have been condemned on the word of a man who has stolen my husband's estate from my son—and I believe may have murdered the Comte. He accuses me of killing my husband by witchcraft or poison, but I swear to you that I am innocent. I did not kill my husband and I am not a witch.'

'Of course you are not! I know well that you nursed your husband through his illness last winter. What a wicked man, to steal what belongs to you and your son. If he killed his father he is evil beyond words.'

'I believe that my husband died of poison. I sent medicine for his chest that night, but he had taken it many times before. I can only believe that something was added to the mixture—something that caused his death.'

'Oh, the wickedness of it! And then to accuse you of the crime to cover his own! He should be punished for what he has done, Marietta.'

'I wish I thought it could be done. I was forced to leave under cover of darkness, which must make me appear guilty in the eyes of many. I swear I have never used what skill I have for anything but good—but there are many who condemn me.'

'It was unfortunate that you were forced to flee, but had you not left you might be dead—and your son.'

'I have no doubt that Rouen would kill Charles if he had the chance. I did not know what to do for the best. All I could think of was to escape and bring my son here…' Marietta faltered. 'I do not know if you wish me to remain now that you know…'

'Of course you must stay, for as long as it suits you,' Claire said. 'My husband would say the same if he were here. He has been called to court, as he frequently is. His Majesty often has some small service that Harry must perform for him, but we have been well rewarded for it so I do not complain.'

'I am good with my needle. If I may serve you as a seamstress…'

'Nonsense! You are my dear cousin, and shall be treated as my equal—as you are. We must see what can be done to restore your son's birthright.'

'Would your husband speak to King Henry for me?'

'The best person would be Anton, for he is much in favour at court.' Claire saw her expression. 'Have you not told him—asked for his help?'

'He knows the truth, but I did not think to ask him to intercede with the King for I did not know it was possible for him to do so.'

'I do not know Anton well,' Claire said, 'for he has

been away some years, but as a boy he seemed honourable and kind. He may still be in the hall downstairs. Why do you not go down and speak to him before he leaves?'

Marietta had moved to the narrow window to glance out at the view. She watched the party of horsemen riding away, Anton at their head. He did not turn back to look for her.

'It is already too late,' she said, feeling a wave of loss and regret. He had gone without saying goodbye to her. She had been foolish to imagine that he might care what became of her. 'He has been kind to me. I suppose he might have helped me had I asked him.'

'Well, all is not lost,' Claire told her. 'I shall send a letter to my husband asking him to visit us, though it may be some weeks before he is able to come home. I know it is distressing for you, but you are safe with me, my dearest. You and your son will have a home with me, and all that is possible will be done to restore at least a part of what you have lost.'

'For myself, I do not mind. I never wished to be a comtesse, or the wife of a rich man, but my son has been cheated of his rights and that hurts me for his sake.'

'I should feel the same,' Claire said, and kissed her cheek. 'My daughter Annabel has been betrothed to a young man some months, and we are to see her married within the year. Once Harry is home the arrangements will be made. I shall leave you to rest for a while, my love. Come down when you are ready and meet her…'

Marietta thanked her. She sat down on the edge of the large bed, which sank beneath her. It had a goose feather mattress, and would be more comfortable than the beds she had slept in as they journeyed here, for the guesthouses at the various monasteries and inns were not given to such luxury.

She felt like weeping. Whether because Claire had been so kind, or whether because she had the odd feeling of having lost something, she did not know. It was unlikely that she would see Anton of Gifford for a long time, if ever. Why should he bother about a woman he hardly knew?

Perhaps she ought to have enlisted his help with the English King—but it was too late now.

Anton had watched as his uncle's wife greeted her visitor with pleasure. It was obvious that she was welcome here, which meant that he could leave with an easy heart. Had the Comtesse de Montcrief been turned away, he would have felt it incumbent upon him to extend his protection. Now he could simply ride away and forget her.

Anton had done his duty. He must think now of the future. The King might ask further favours of him, but for the moment his daughter was safe with Anton's mother. When he had time to return for her, he would look for that sensible woman who would be a good mother for his child and ask nothing more than his name and wealth. It would be wrong to think of finding love again.

He hoped that the King would release him so that he could return to the child he loved and begin to make a new life for them both. He would think no more of the beautiful woman he had left with Claire Melford.

Yet the memory of her scent, and her laughter when he had watched her playing with her son, remained in his mind, like a haunting melody that he could not forget. Was he a fool to cut her from his life? He needed a wife—why should that wife not be Marietta?

No! He crushed the thought ruthlessly. He had learned that beautiful women were faithless. He would be a fool to give his heart to a woman like the Comtesse de Montcrief.

'You say Montcrief was murdered?' King Henry frowned. He took the letter, broke the seal, glanced at it and tossed it into the fire, watching as the parchment curled, turned brown and then crumbled into ash. 'You did well to bring this back to me, Gifford. This man who has taken command at the castle—what is his name again?'

'They call him the Bastard of Rouen, Sire. He has men to follow him, and I believe he is popular with the rabble.'

'What makes you think that?'

Anton explained about the tourney and the way the crowd had reacted, cheering the Bastard until the last, when they transferred their support to him.

'Did he not recognise you as the winner of the contest?'

'Not immediately,' Anton said. 'I was not wearing armour that day—but he may have on reflection, for we were later attacked by rogues I suspect to be his men. I believe he must hate me, for he felt humiliated that day.'

Henry nodded, his gaze narrowed. 'The widow—what do you know of her?'

'Very little, Sire.' It was not quite the truth, but Anton

was wary of telling the King too much at this stage. He still felt protective towards Marietta, though he had determined to put her out of his mind.

Henry looked thoughtful. 'If she has been unlawfully dispossessed of her husband's estate something should be done. My brother of France might take a dim view, but I think some show of power should be made. When a bastard can take what rightfully belongs to Montcrief's son the law is slighted. As for the widow, it depends whether she be guilty of murder or innocent.'

'Your Majesty speaks truly.'

'My father curbed the power of the barons here. It would do my brother of France no harm to copy his example.' Henry glanced out of the window and smiled. 'I must go down and walk with Mistress Boleyn. I shall think on this, Anton. When I have decided I shall speak to you again.'

'Yes, Sire.'

'We must set up a contest. I love to wrestle, and you sound a worthy competitor. I would like to see your silver arrow…'

'I do not have it with me, Sire. Perhaps another time?'

King Hal nodded, a gleam of anticipation in his eyes. 'Come—we must not keep the ladies waiting…'

Anton could only acquiesce. He was impatient to return to his mother and enquire after Madeline, but for the moment he had no choice but to obey the King.

Marietta walked in the gardens near the house. She had been a guest here for three weeks now, and was becoming familiar with her surroundings. At first she had felt uncomfortable, but Claire and her daughter Annabel had been so kind that she had almost lost her fear of intruding in their family circle. It was not and never could be like her own home, but she would do her best to repay the kindness she was receiving and hope that one day she might have her own house again.

A sigh left her lips, because she could not see how that would ever happen. With a cloud of suspicion and disgrace hanging over her, it was unlikely that she would have many suitors. As the widow of Comte de Montcrief with her reputation intact she would have had barons queuing up to offer for her, but as a woman alone with little fortune she had small chance of finding happiness.

Perhaps she ought to have asked Anton for help. Had she done so, he might have interceded for her with the English King.

Marietta glanced round as she heard a twig snap somewhere in the shrubbery. She had been sitting on a wooden bench lost in thought for nearly an hour. Claire would be wondering where she was.

Getting to her feet, she saw one of the bushes move slightly and a chill ran down her spine. Was someone there? Was that person watching her?

'Is someone there? What do you want?'

Silence. Marietta debated whether to investigate, but then she heard a voice call to her and saw Claire at the window, beckoning her to come inside.

Marietta walked towards the house. She told herself that she had been jumping at shadows. Why should anyone be watching her? She knew hardly anyone in England. It was foolish to worry. The Bastard of Rouen had all that he needed. Why should he come looking for her here?

She was safe in her kinswoman's house. And if sometimes she wished for more to occupy her time, she must accept that she was a guest here. In time she would find a way of repaying her hostess's generosity. Thinking on it would surely distract her, too, from her thoughts and feelings for Anton of Gifford.

Chapter Four

'We have made our decision concerning Montcrief's widow,' King Henry said. 'Bring her here to us, Anton. We would hear the lady's story, and if we believe her innocent we shall use our influence with our brother of France. Her lands and all that has been lost shall be recovered if it be possible.'

'I believe her innocent, though she was hunted for a witch, and would almost certainly have been burned had she been taken…'

'I have no doubt the Bastard will kill her if he can. All the more reason for you to bring her to court. If she be innocent she needs our help.' He held out his hand. A fine ring of heavy gold set with a deep red cabochon ruby adorned his little finger. 'Find also the twin to this, if you can, and bring it to me. Montcrief had it and wore it always. If his widow took his jewels she may have it—if not it may be at Montcrief. I would have it if 'tis found.'

'Yes, Sire. I will ask if she has such a ring.'

'Go, then. Bring the lady to court.'

'As you wish.'

Anton bowed deeply and left the presence chamber. His mind was in turmoil. What was he to do now? Should he return to the home of his uncle and warn Marietta? King Henry was a fair man—but supposing he did not believe her story? The punishment in England for witchcraft was hanging; her body would be taken down after she was dead and burned so that she could not return to it—a cruel fate for one so fair.

Superstitious nonsense! Anton instantly dismissed the charge of witchcraft, but that of murder was not so easy to dismiss. Anton believed her innocent, but others might find against her and she could be hanged or beheaded…. No! It would be a crime to see her head parted from her body.

There must be some way of proving her innocence! Anton was frowning as he went out to the courtyard. He mounted his horse, signalling to his men to follow.

When Anton had left Marietta at his uncle's house he had meant to forget her. She was beautiful, and she inflamed his senses, but to fall in love with a woman like the Countess of Montcrief might bring heartache and regret. Yet the sense of duty was ingrained in him: he could not disobey the King. He could take Marietta away, where she was not known, but would she ever be safe unless her innocence was proven? To run away again would seem to prove her guilt. There was nothing Anton could do but take her to the King and plead her cause.

* * *

Marietta stared out of the window. The sun was warm that day, and she was tempted to go out for a walk, but of late she had had an uneasy feeling that she was being watched. She had said nothing to Claire or Annabel, because she did not wish to worry them. Had the Earl been at home she would have told him that she was afraid the Bastard of Rouen's men had found her, but he was away on some business for his estate.

Yet perhaps she was imagining things. She only knew that she was reluctant to walk alone.

Hearing a knock at her door, she called out that whoever it was might enter, and smiled as Claire's daughter came in.

'Annabel,' she said. 'I was just about to ask if you would care to walk in the gardens with me?'

'I should enjoy that,' Annabel said, and blushed delicately. 'My betrothed is here, Marietta. John would be happy to meet you—and to stroll with us.'

'Oh, I have looked forward to meeting him,' Marietta said. 'Will the wedding be soon now?'

'My father has sent word that he will be home in a few days. We shall make the arrangements then.'

'I am sure you are impatient for the day,' Marietta said, and picked up her cloak. 'Shall we go down?'

'We have been followed since we left the court,' Anton told his men. 'I do not know whether they merely mean to pursue us—or to attack once the light fades.'

'We should plan a little surprise for them rather than wait,' Miguel suggested. 'I noticed them an hour since, and I think some of us should gradually split off and wait for them to pass. When you give the signal we shall come on them from behind.'

'I agree,' Anton said. 'We shall come to the forest in a few minutes. Take your chance to slip away one at a time, and then meet up after they have passed. When we reach the clearing we saw as we came this way a month ago I shall turn and face them, and you will lead the charge from the back. We shall see then what they intend…'

There was a murmur of agreement, the men looking at one another, pairing up as they decided to slip away. It was dangerous to travel at any time, for there were bands of beggars and rogues that would attack the unwary, but this was different. They had been followed for hours, and they knew it might mean a fight to the death.

Marietta was at the top of the stairs when she heard a commotion in the hall below. Several people had entered and the voices were all male.

'We were attacked on our way here.' Anton's voice carried to her, and his voice sent shivers down to her toes. 'We drove them off, but it was a bloody fight and one of my men was killed—two more are injured.'

'You were attacked?' The voice belonged to the Earl, who had arrived home the previous day. 'Damn the rogues! Have you any idea who they were—not simply beggars or itinerants if they managed to kill one of your men, Anton?'

'Neither vagrants nor thieves, I think,' Anton said in a cold, angry tone. 'I think I know who sent them, for during the fight I was warned that I should die if I continued to protect her.'

'Protect whom?' Harry sounded puzzled. 'Surely not the lady you brought to us? Who could wish to harm such a lovely creature? Claire adores her.'

'Has Claire told you why she left her home? Perhaps you should know that she was accused of…'

Listening, Marietta felt ice spread all over her. She would have gone down to see if she could help with the injured men, but there were servants enough. The anger in Anton's voice had shocked her. Why had he returned here? Had he come here to take her to court—was she to be tried for witchcraft and murder?

Filled with dread, she fled up to her chamber, locking the door behind her. She was trembling all over, her face hot, her eyes stinging with tears. Anton had sounded as if he hated her. She sensed that he was blaming her because of the attack that had left one of his men dead and others injured.

Marietta felt an overwhelming desire to weep. She brought bad luck to anyone she cared for. Her husband was dead, and now Anton had been attacked and threatened. If she stayed here she might cause trouble for her kind hostess—but where else could she go?

Claire would not hear of her leaving. They had grown fond of one another, and Marietta felt miserable at the thought that she might be forced to leave. Hot tears built behind her eyes but she would not let them spill. She raised her head. Whatever the future held, she must bear it.

Her first rush of emotion conquered, she knew that

she must go downstairs and see if she could be of help. She had some skill in the stillroom and with healing. Anton might hate her, but she must remain calm and hide the pain his anger caused her.

Anton was in the hall speaking with Claire when Marietta went down to enquire if she might do anything to help. She was wearing a gown of pale blue cloth, her hair dressed back from her face and secured with combs, and amethyst earrings suspended from her lobes. His eyes dwelled on her for a moment, narrowing, it seemed to her, in deep suspicion.

'You look well, lady,' he said, inclining his head, a flicker of approval in his eyes. 'Better than when I saw you last.'

'Marietta, my love,' Claire said, smiling at her. 'We are tending the wounded and there is nothing for you to do—but you may talk to Anton. I believe you have something to say to him…'

As Claire walked away, the train of her dress brushing over the marble floor, Marietta found Anton's eyes on her once more.

'You wished to speak to me?'

Her stomach clenched with fear. When he looked at her so sternly she was afraid of his hatred and his anger, and the hurt struck deep into her heart. Dreams died hard, and she had cherished hers for so long, but the man of her dreams was a gallant youth and this stony-eyed man was someone different.

'Claire thought that I should have asked you to intercede for me with His Majesty.' She swallowed back the foolish tears. 'I ask nothing for myself—but for my son…'

'You ask me to plead for you?'

'Yes…' Marietta's breath was expelled nervously as his gaze narrowed, becoming harsher. He looked at her so coldly that she trembled inside. 'I know it is a great deal to ask of you, but Claire thought you the best person because of your position with the King.'

'You have told me you are innocent, and I believe you, but I cannot promise that the King will find in your favour. He has commanded me to bring you to him and I must obey. What would you have me say to him on your behalf?'

'I am guilty of neither witchcraft nor murder. It is true that I sent medicine to my husband that night, but it was the same that had eased him many times. He asked me for it in front of everyone. One of my ladies took it to his chamber, but Jeanne would not have dared to tamper with it. Yet I believe someone did, for I am sure that he was poisoned.'

'Who added the poison—the Bastard?' His eyes seemed to burn into her. 'Did he have opportunity or reason?'

'Perhaps. My husband intended that he should sign a paper relinquishing all right to the name and estate. Montcrief thought it the best way to protect our son, because his own health was uncertain and he feared for the future. Perhaps it made Rouen angry and he killed my husband rather than sign away what he believed his. I do not know.'

Anton looked at her thoughtfully. 'Rouen accused you and you accuse him. Where is the proof?'

'I have none.' Marietta raised her clear eyes to meet his. 'If you or others think me guilty I cannot prove otherwise—but I would never murder anyone. I sought to be a good wife and mother. I have made cures to help people but I do not use witchcraft. If these things are crimes, I am guilty.'

Anton met her unflinching stare. 'The rogues that attacked me said I would die if I harboured the Witch of Montcrief. I believe you innocent, lady—but His Majesty has commanded me to take you to him.'

Marietta looked at him apprehensively. 'Supposing the King does not believe me?' An icy shiver ran through her. 'What will happen to me?'

'I shall plead your case. I think it likely the Bastard killed your husband for his wealth—but the King is the law. If he finds against you there is little I can do.' Anton reached out to touch her hand. 'I would take you away to safety, but unless your innocence is proven you could be accused wherever you go. You would never truly be safe.'

Marietta inclined her head. Tears burned behind her eyes but she refused to weep or beg for mercy. 'I do not mind so much what happens to me, but I fear for my son.'

'Your son shall remain here. If you are cleared of blame I shall bring you back to him—if not I swear on all I hold sacred that he shall be cared for. I know that Lady Claire would care for him, but if you wish it I will take him into my household and he may grow up with my own children.' His words were generous, but to Marietta his manner seemed remote, as if he were deliberately keeping her at a distance.

'Thank you…' Marietta's throat felt tight. She gave

no sign of the fear or the hurt his coldness aroused in her. 'I know that Claire would care for my son, but he should be the Comte de Montcrief. You might be able to help him regain what has been stolen from him. If I die will you do what you can to restore him to his rightful inheritance?'

Anton hesitated, then, 'You have my word. We shall leave for court tomorrow.'

'As you wish, sir.' Marietta turned away. She needed to be alone so that she could weep. Pride would not let her show weakness before this man, but the need was great.

'Stay one moment. Your husband had a special ring he wore often—a large ruby set in heavy gold?'

Marietta was puzzled, but answered truthfully. 'Yes, he never took it from his finger. He said a good friend gave it to him some years before. Why do you ask?'

'Do you have the ring?'

'No.' Marietta frowned. 'I took some gold and my jewels when I fled, but his ring…it was not on his finger or in his chamber. Someone else must have taken it before I saw him.'

'You are telling me the truth?' Anton's gaze narrowed.

'I swear it on my life—and my son's.'

'Then I know you do not lie. Very well, lady. You must rise early, for I wish to set out soon after first light. My uncle will send some of his men with us as an extra guard, though I think we shall not be attacked again for we routed the rogues who planned to murder us in the night.'

'I am sorry for what happened to your man, sir.'

'So am I,' Anton said. 'He died for your sake, lady.

If I ever discover that you have deceived me—I shall kill you with my bare hands.'

Marietta looked into his hard eyes, gave a sob and fled up the stairs to her own chamber. How could he say such things to her? How could he think it? He was cruel, and she should hate him, but he was breaking her heart!

She locked the door behind her, flinging herself on the bed to weep.

Would she never know happiness again? Her husband had been so much older, but at least he had loved and trusted her. There were times when Anton of Gifford looked at her as if he hated her.

Marietta could not rest. Her mind was in torment. She wished that Claire had given her some task—something she could do that would keep her mind from the morning. She had felt safe here, but now she was to be taken to London, as Anton of Gifford's prisoner. Her dreams had been shattered. The hero she had loved from afar was merely the product of a young girl's imagination. She knew nothing of the true man, except that he was determined to do his duty. He would take her to London, where she would face the King and be judged, though there was no proof of her guilt or otherwise.

How could she prove her innocence? She had held herself proudly, telling Anton that she cared only for her child's safety—and that was true. Yet she did not wish to die as a witch. It would be a cruel death and she would face it alone, for she had no one who truly loved her.

It was so unfair! Why should the jealousy of an evil man be believed? She knew that many would take the Bastard of Rouen's word above hers. It was her medicine that had killed her husband—everyone believed it.

Marietta washed her face in cold water from the pewter ewer on her night stand. She had not changed for the evening, and she did not think she could face the others at dinner. Anton would have told them that he had been sent to fetch her—perhaps even Claire would think her guilty now.

She crept downstairs. She could hear voices and laughter in the hall. Turning away, she slipped out of the house by a little door at the rear. The light was fading from the sky but she was too restless to stay indoors. She hardly knew what she wanted. Crying would not help her. She could take Charles and run away, but how far would she get? Anton would find her wherever she went. He would come after her, force her to go to London with him—and then he would be certain of her guilt.

She had his promise that her son would be cared for. Perhaps that was enough. The thoughts churned endlessly in her mind. Perhaps the King might believe her…or be lenient.

Marietta knew that she must stay and face her punishment, whatever that might be. At least her child would be safe, because despite his stern looks and the way he made her want to weep she trusted Anton of Gifford. He might be cold and harsh to her, but he would protect an innocent child. He might even try to regain a part of what had been stolen from Charles, for even if she were condemned as a witch her son was innocent.

Realising that she had wandered farther than usual from the house, Marietta turned back towards it. She shivered because the air had turned cold. It was time to return and prepare for the journey. Farewells must be made, thanks given for all the kindness she had received in this house. Perhaps if God were merciful she might be allowed to return. It was all she could hope for.

She was walking towards the house when she heard the slight noise behind her. Pausing, she looked back just as the shadow loomed up at her. Something struck a blow to the side of her head and she fell, dropping her kerchief on a rose bush at the side of the path.

Blackness had descended. Marietta felt nothing as she was lifted over a man's shoulder, carried some distance and then thrown carelessly into a cart. She did not hear the coarse laughter and the cruel remarks made as she was driven away into the night.

'Have you seen her, Annabel?' Claire asked her daughter. 'It is not like Marietta to stay in her chamber all day. When I enquired, her maid told me that she dismissed her earlier. She thought she was in her chamber, but when we looked she was not there.'

'I believe I saw her go into the gardens an hour or so ago,' Annabel said. 'I would have called to her, but she seemed distressed and I thought—' She broke off. 'She must be frightened. It is a terrifying thing to be summoned by the King.'

'Yes, it is—but she is innocent. How could anyone think her guilty of murder? To look into her eyes is to know that she is innocent.'

Claire glanced up as her husband and Anton came into the hall. They had been searching the house and grounds, but from their looks it was obvious that Marietta had not been found.

'Annabel thinks she may have gone for a walk in the garden.'

'Until this hour?' Anton's brows rose. 'Has she taken anything with her?'

'You think she has run away?' Claire was startled. 'Surely she would not go alone? Her child is here; also her maid. I know she ran away from her home in France, but her life was at risk. Besides, she must know that we care for her. You promised to plead her case and surely the King will listen? No, do not look so sceptical! I am convinced the King would see that she is innocent.'

'I shall search for her outside the grounds,' Anton said, and frowned. 'She may have strayed into the woods, but she cannot have got far on foot…'

'I'll have my people join in the search. If those rogues managed to follow you here she might be in danger.' Harry Melford, newly made Earl of Rundle, looked at his wife with compassion. 'Try not to worry, my love. I know you are fond of her, and I shall send a letter to His Majesty pleading for your cousin.'

Anton stared at him, his gaze narrowed, thoughtful. 'If she has not run away someone may have snatched her. She may even now be dead.' His voice grated harshly. 'God forgive me. I was harsh to her and I shall blame myself if she is harmed.' His skin looked grey as the colour washed from it.

'No! Do not say it,' Claire said. 'Why should

anyone want her dead? She is surely less important than her son to her enemies. While he lives that evil man can never be certain that Charles will not one day take back all that is his…'

'Yes, that is true,' Harry said, looking at his wife with approval. 'If they have snatched her, the Bastard needs her for some purpose.'

Anton was already striding from the hall. If Marietta were dead or taken it was his fault. He had been harsh to her—unnecessarily so. It was not her fault that his wife had betrayed him. The more he thought about his behaviour towards Marietta, the more he blamed himself. He had tried to keep a distance from her because he was afraid of giving his heart, afraid that he might lose her. It had been cruel and heartless of him to treat her so coolly when she needed his help. She must be terrified of what might happen to her! He must find her—or punish the man who had taken her! Anton might never forgive himself for the part he had played in his wife's death, but he did not think he could bear the added burden if Marietta died because he had not offered the comfort she needed.

Because of his harshness she had gone into the garden to seek solitude and she had disappeared. He was reminded of his jealous rage, which had caused Isabella's death. What a fool he was! Because he feared to be hurt he had been cold to Marietta, when all his instincts had been to take her in his arms and kiss her.

Marietta's head hurt so terribly. She did not know for how long she had lost consciousness, but it must have been some hours. Her body felt bruised, as if she had been beaten. Her captors had treated her roughly and she had lain too long in a cramped position. She tried to move but discovered that her legs had been tied, as had her hands. She opened her eyes, but discovered that it was too dark to see anything.

Where was she? She strained to hear, and gradually became aware of movement and the lap of waves against the side of the ship. Her abductors were taking her back to France! Fear coursed through her, because she knew that she would be given no mercy. The Bastard hated her. He would see her dead—and her son! No, Charles was safe inside the Earl of Rundle's house, where she ought to have stayed.

Anton would think she had run away. Would he honour his promise to care for her son, or would he decide that she had broken her word and set him free? What would happen to her poor child? Claire would care for him, but he would never regain his inheritance for her kinswoman had no influence at court. Anton had given his word that he would do what he could, but could she trust a man she hardly knew? She had thought him honourable and generous, but he was no longer the sweet youth she had dreamed of. What had changed him to the cold, stern man he had become? Was it because he suspected she was guilty of murder and witchcraft, despite his declaration that he believed her innocent?

Tears stung her eyes as she lay in the darkness. How could she have been so foolish as to walk alone when darkness was falling? She should have known that the Bastard might try to get her back. Her safe arrival in

England had lulled her into a false sense of security these past weeks and she had no one but herself to blame.

She could hope for nothing. Claire and her family had been kind, but why should they bother to search for a woman who was to be tried for murder and witchcraft? Why should anyone bother to save her when King Henry's justice might condemn her to death? The only person that might have saved her had looked at her so coldly when they last met.

Bitter tears ran into her mouth as she wept. She was alone, and the future held only terror and pain.

'I found this on a bush,' Anton said, holding a kerchief for Claire to see. 'Is it hers?'

'Let me see… Yes, I gave Marietta this myself.' Claire looked fearful. 'It proves she was in the garden. I do not think she has run away.'

'She would not go without the child,' Anton agreed. 'There were signs of a struggle, footprints in the earth near where we found the kerchief. I think she has been abducted.'

Claire gave a cry of distress. 'Those wicked devils! What will they do to her?'

'If they meant to kill her we should have found her body,' Anton said, his mouth pulled into a grim line. 'She has been kidnapped and taken to her husband's bastard, which means that she will be kept alive at least until they reach the Castle of Montcrief. I shall leave at once, and we must pray that I am in time to save her.'

'You will go after her?' Claire looked at him in relief. 'You will try to save her?'

Anton inclined his head. 'She went walking alone because I distressed her. My honour compels me to find her and bring her back if possible.'

He turned and left the hall. Outside, he summoned his men.

'They have taken the lady Marietta, Comtesse Montcrief. She was accused of witchcraft and murder, but I believe her innocent and I intend to bring her back to England if I find her alive. Some of you may not wish to follow me on this mission. If you wish, you may wait here for my return or leave my service. The choice is yours. I am leaving for France now.'

Anton swung himself into the saddle. He did not glance back as he rode off. If they all chose to leave him, he would go alone. Honour demanded it. He could not bear the death of another young woman on his soul!

'We are with you,' Miguel said, his horse coming alongside. 'For pity's sake go a little slower, for the sake of those who cannot keep pace with you. The lady is in God's hands. If she be the innocent you think her, He will protect her.'

Anton's mouth was tight, his eyes bleak as he glanced at his friend. 'I thank you for your company, Miguel. Pray God you are right. For I cannot bear the stain of another sweet lady's death on my soul…'

Marietta opened her eyes as the cabin door swung forward and two men entered. They stood over her, grinning evilly as they saw that she was awake. She knew them as men who had once served her husband, but had transferred their allegiance to the Bastard.

'Untie me,' she demanded. 'How dare you do this to me—your master's wife? You will be punished for this!'

'We serve the Bastard of Rouen, not you, lady,' one of them growled. 'He commanded that you be returned to him.'

'He has no right to command you. My son is the rightful heir—and I am the chatelaine of Montcrief until he comes of age. When the King hears of this, you will all be punished.'

'Shut your mouth, woman. You are a witch and a murderer and will die in the flames.'

'Be quiet, Pierre,' the second man said. 'She is not yet proven. Show some respect.' His dark eyes went over her. 'Forgive us, lady. We but do our duty. I shall untie the bonds if you give me your word that you will not run away. If we do not take you back, the Bastard will kill our children and us.'

Marietta closed her eyes for a moment, then inclined her head. 'I thank you for your courtesy, Boris. You have my word.'

'Do not trust her,' Pierre warned, but Boris bent and sliced through the ropes with his knife. 'Fool! If she escapes you shall bear the blame.'

'Thank you.' Marietta rubbed her wrists. They felt sore and numbed. When she tried to stand she almost fell. Boris steadied her, then lifted her in his arms. 'Forgive me, the ropes have taken the feeling from my legs.'

'You will ride with me,' he told her gruffly. 'Remember that my son's life is forfeit if you run from us.'

'I shall not forget. It was for my son's life that I ran. I do not care what becomes of me…'

Marietta closed her eyes as she was taken on deck and then on shore. She was numbly aware of the horses, and being lifted to a saddle. Putting her arms around Boris's waist, she entwined her fingers in his leather belt so that she would not fall. Her head ached, but the fresh air was rapidly clearing the feeling of faintness, though her sense of despair grew stronger with each league they covered.

She dreaded the moment when she came face to face with the Bastard once more. He would make sure that she suffered for defying him. She imagined that he would enjoy inflicting pain on her.

She must bear it as best she could, for she knew that she could expect no help. She could only pray that death came quickly. If her son was safe she could leave this life without regret. She had nothing more to live for…

Anton stared out into the darkness. It was one of the longest nights of his life, almost as terrible as the night he had sat by his wife's dead body and wept for her. Then he had been helpless, for death was final, but now he burned with the fires of impatience, his sword-hand itching for work. Marietta's abduction was his fault. He should have watched over her more closely. His instincts should have warned him that she was in danger. Why had he not placed guards in the grounds? Why had he been so harsh to her that she had sought solace by walking alone in the gardens?

The truth hit him like a sword-thrust in his stomach, sending a shaft of pain curling through him. His anger had been because he was afraid that she might be condemned as a murderess—and he cared for her! He had wanted her on the ship, but he had fought his feelings of desire. Romantic love was a trap, a source of bitter pain. To let himself be caught by it a second time would be stupid. Isabella had sworn her child was his but he could never have been sure, and the maggot of jealousy had eaten deep into his soul.

Anton did not want to care for another woman. He did not want to feel the agony of loss again—but he was already feeling it. Marietta was in grave danger of losing her life.

If she died at the hands of that evil Bastard, Anton would not be able to bear the guilt.

Marietta allowed Boris to help her down from the back of his horse. She glanced up and thought she saw sympathy in his eyes, but it was quickly hidden. Even if he felt sorry for her plight, his son's life meant more to him. She could not blame him, for in his place she would have felt the same. The Bastard of Rouen was ruthless. He ruled by fear and example, and would not hesitate to kill or maim any of his servants if they displeased him.

Fear was making her tremble inside, but she managed to hide it as she turned and saw him. The Bastard was a handsome man in a coarse, harsh way. Tall and strong, he had eyes the hue of blue ice, his hair worn long, hanging in greasy strands. His clothes looked as if they needed washing, and his beard was in need of trimming, stale food caught in the thick hair. Revulsion coursed through her as she saw the way he stared at her; the heat in his eyes burned her. He seemed to strip away her clothes so that she felt naked, vulnerable.

'So, the witch returns…' He grinned, vastly pleased with himself. 'Where is the brat?'

'We snatched her as she walked alone,' Boris said. 'The child was nowhere to be seen.'

'Fool! I need them *both*.' The Bastard struck him across the face, making him stumble. 'I do not suffer fools, nor failure.'

'We brought you the woman…' Pierre said, and fell to his knees as the Bastard swung round, glaring at him. 'Forgive me…'

'Take these blundering idiots away and whip them,' the Bastard ordered. 'Think yourselves lucky that I don't have you and your families killed.'

'You will never get my son,' Marietta cried, pride making her forget her fear. 'He is cared for and protected and…' Her voice trailed away as the Bastard towered over her. He raised his hand, striking her across the face. She stumbled but did not fall. 'Yes—hit me, kill me—as you killed my husband. I know the truth. You were his murderer, not I. You are a coward and—' Her words failed as he struck her once more and sent her to her knees.

'Take her to her chamber and lock her in,' the Bastard roared. 'If she escapes again I'll hang every last man in the castle.' His eyes glittered with fury. 'I'll speak to you later, witch. You will be sorry you dared to defy me.'

Someone grabbed hold of Marietta's arms and dragged her away.

'You are a bully, a murderer and a thief!' Marietta screamed as they forced her into the castle. 'One day I shall be avenged. My son will be the master here and he will not spare you…'

'Be quiet, lady,' the man who had her arm whispered. 'He is a devil when roused. You would be wise to do as he wants, and then he may let you live.'

'I would rather die than live as his whore,' Marietta said.

On the voyage she had been close to despair, ready to die if she must, but now she was angry. Her feeling of apathy had gone. She would fight him to the last! The Bastard had no right to rule here. Surely God would strike him down!

'If there is any justice he will die first…'

Locked in her chamber, Marietta paced the floor restlessly. Her faithful servants were in England. She had no hope of escape this time, unless she could find a way out of here…

She swung round as a key turned in the stout lock that guarded her door and a woman entered. She was a beautiful woman, with long pale hair and narrow cat-like eyes. Her mouth was thin and hard as she looked at Marietta with dislike.

'So you are the woman he would wed,' she said. 'What have you done to him, witch? Have you put your spell on him? He was mine, but he never spoke of marriage. He thinks of nothing else but you. You must have bewitched him.'

'I swear to you that I have put no spell on him. He wants me only so that he can be sure of my husband's lands and fortune.'

The woman's gaze intensified. 'If he marries you he

will forget me—and he owes me much. I bear his child and I should be his wife.'

'If I could change places with you I would,' Marietta said. 'I mean that I would wish for you to be his wife, not me. Believe me, if I could leave this place again I would not wait to be forced to wed him.'

'You say that, but how can I believe you?'

'I swear it on my life, lady…I do not know your name?'

'It is Claudette. I was but fifteen when he took me from my parents and made me his whore. At first I hated him, but then—' She broke off, eyes glittering. 'If I could think of a way to set you free—would you go?'

'Yes, I swear it.' Marietta moved towards her eagerly. 'Please help me. I have nothing to give you, but…'

'I want nothing from you,' Claudette said, stepping back. 'Speak of this to my lord and you are dead.'

'I swear I shall not…' Marietta's heart sank as the woman went out and locked the door again. 'Please help me…'

She had thought the Bastard would kill her, but it seemed that he still planned to wed her—why?

Had he discovered that he needed her? She was sure that he had expected to rule here, whether she lived or died, but something must have happened to make him realise that he couldn't do it without her.

Marietta clenched her hands, her nails cutting into her palms. She would prefer to die than live as the Bastard's wife, but she might not be given the choice. He could force a priest to do his bidding—and he could force himself on her once she was his wife, for she was not strong enough to prevent him.

She had seen anger in his eyes as he looked at her, but also the gleam of lust. He wanted her. And he needed her. The will her husband had lodged at court must have upheld her husband's wish that she should be in charge of his fortune until his son was of age. Rouen had taken the castle by force, but he could not touch the vast fortune in gold that her husband had lodged with the King's goldsmiths for safety. It seemed that the Comte de Montcrief had outwitted his bastard after all. Much of her son's birthright was safe—but to keep it that way Marietta would have to pay a terrible price.

She fell to her knees beside the bed, head bent as she prayed for help.

If only Anton of Gifford had believed her innocent! She was certain that he would have come to her aid.

'Please, please help me,' she whispered, and it was no longer to God that she prayed.

Now she was remembering the face of the charming youth who had rescued her from certain death, and despite the way he had looked at her the last time they met she was comforted.

Chapter Five

Anton's men were close enough behind the abductors to discover that a party of men and one woman had taken a ship for France the previous morning, but the tide was against them. It would not turn again until the evening.

'Damn them! If he harms her I swear I shall kill him!' Anton's frustration at being held in port was tearing him apart. He stood looking out across the sea, his face like thunder. 'I cannot bear the thought of her at his mercy.'

'Courage, my friend,' Miguel said, clapping a hand to his shoulder. 'We shall bring her back if she lives. If she is dead, by his hand or theirs, they shall all pay for it.'

'There are but ten of us, and he must have a hundred fighting men,' Anton replied in clipped tones. 'I shall not let you all die trying to storm the walls of such a fortress. We should give our lives for nothing.'

'The man Sandro says he knows a secret way into the castle.'

'Is he with us? I had not noticed.' Anton glanced round at the men who had dismounted and were waiting for his orders.

'You have been too preoccupied. The lady's maid stayed behind, to care for the child, but Sandro followed you from the start. We would all of us give our lives to serve you,' Miguel said.

'But I shall not waste lives in vain. If there is a secret way into the castle some of us will go in when the enemy sleeps…' His face twisted in an agony of remorse. 'I must find her alive. I must. If she died because of my neglect I could not forgive myself…'

Marietta lay fully clothed on her bed. She had not undressed, even though one of her own nightgowns had been brought to her and the serving woman had offered to help her. The woman's name was Veronique, but she was new to the castle and Marietta did not know her.

'Thank you, but I can manage alone.'

She dismissed the woman and drank the cup of wine she had been given. A piece of coarse bread and some cold bacon had been sent with the wine. Her hunger drove her to eat what she could, even though it sat uneasily on her stomach.

The walls of her chamber were still hung with the tapestries she had worked herself. All the possessions she had abandoned when she fled were as she had left them, though her lyre had been smashed. She had thought the Bastard might have rent her belongings to pieces, but he had left them undisturbed—all but the lyre, which he must have known was her prized possession.

She touched the silken surface of the wood, which had been smashed apart, then shook her head. What did such things matter? She had left the lyre behind when she fled because her thoughts had been only for her child. His safety and well-being were still of paramount importance.

She paced her chamber, torn between hope and despair. Where was Charles? Did Claire still have charge of her baby? Had he been taken from her— perhaps to become the King's ward, as often happened when there were lands and money involved? The King of England would know that Charles was the rightful heir to a fortune and he might do something for her son—speak to the King of France on his behalf. She herself was beyond help, but it did not matter if her son was safe.

Marietta's lips moved in prayer. She could bear anything if her son were safe!

She stiffened as she heard a key in the lock, and then the door of her chamber opened. She saw a large shadow enter and froze, because she knew instinctively that it was the Bastard. He came towards the bed, the sound of his steps heavy and uncertain. The smell of strong wine hung over him and she guessed that he had drunk deeply at table.

Marietta kept her eyes closed as she sensed and smelled him near. He was looking down at her. Would he throw himself on her? Ravish her? Her stomach churned as the fear curled inside her. She would fight him, but she knew that he would take her for he was too strong for her.

'Thought to escape me…' The Bastard's words were slurred with drink. 'Mine now…always wanted…beautiful but a bitch…'

Marietta tried not to move as she felt his breath on her face. Her only chance was surprise. If he thought she was sleeping he might be careless, giving her an opportunity to escape. She felt the touch of his hand on her hair. He lifted strands of it, sniffing it as if to inhale the perfume.

'Witch…' he muttered. 'I'll make you pay. Not tonight…must be wed…only way to get the gold. Need your signature…won't give me the gold without it…'

He was moving away, unsteady on his feet. She heard him knock into a stool and curse, then the door opened, closed again, and a key turned. Marietta had her answer. It was as she'd suspected. The Bastard needed her to get his hands on the Comte's fortune. He believed that once she was his wife he could force her to do anything, but she would rather die than marry him! She was locked in for the moment, but somehow she had to escape…

'The lord says you must come down—and you are to wear your best gown,' the serving woman said the next morning. 'He is waiting for you in the hall, lady.'

'Tell your master that I cannot come,' Marietta replied, giving a little moan. 'I am sick and must rest. My head aches so much that I can scarce stand.'

'If I tell him that he will beat me.'

'Then tell him I will not come.'

'Are you truly sick, lady?' The woman looked at her uncertainly.

'Look in the pot. You will see that I have been sick.'

The woman fetched it out, recoiling at the sour smell. 'You are sick, lady. I will show him this—but if he comes you must lie on your bed and groan, or he will blame me and I shall be punished.'

'I am too ill to get up today.'

Marietta lay back as the woman took the pewter pot with her. It was true that the coarse food she had been given had turned her stomach, but she had made herself sick by mixing some powders from her medicine chest with water and swallowing them. She was surprised that her herbs had not been taken as proof of her witchcraft, but perhaps the Bastard feared her powers? She had used the mixture before. In the case of poisoning, sometimes the only remedy was to make the patient sick. Sometimes the remedy worked, at others it did not—healing was not a precise form but a matter of trial and error, at least for her.

The mixture had made her feel unwell, and her stomach heaved as she felt bitter bile in her throat. If the ruse worked it would be worthwhile—but would the Bastard accept her excuses?

After some minutes had passed she heard a commotion outside her door, and then it was thrust open and the Bastard entered. She saw that he had shaved and was wearing his best clothes. For their wedding, she suspected.

'What ails you?' he demanded.

'I am sick. Your men hit me too hard and I have been feeling ill.'

'You were sleeping well enough last night.' He looked at her and bent over her, but caught the rancid smell of vomit that she had taken care to spill on her covers. Recoiling in disgust, he glared at her. 'Very well, you may rest today—but tomorrow I shall wed you. You are mine. If you please me I may let you live for a while…'

Marietta gave a little moan and made a retching sound, pressing a cloth to her mouth. She lay with her face buried as she heard the sound of the door slamming.

He was angry, but he could not force her to rise and go down to be married if she was ill. However, the reprieve might not last more than one day. She glanced up as the serving woman approached her.

'Will you ask the lady Claudette to come to me, please?'

'That one is a haughty bitch and will do only as she pleases.' The woman sniffed. 'I shall ask, but I do not know if she will come.'

'Please ask…'

Marietta lay back and sighed as the woman left her. Her head ached, though she could have risen and gone down to the hall had she wished. If Claudette truly wanted to be the Bastard's wife she must realise that she needed to act quickly to prevent his marriage to Marietta, for he was determined to have his way. Marietta had managed to delay the ceremony but he would not be thwarted. Next time he would drag her from the bed and take her with him!

'Please come for me…please…'

Her only hope of salvation lay in the faint hope that Anton would feel it his duty to bring her back to face King Henry's justice—unless she could persuade Claudette to help her…

'Our scouts have spoken to local people. There are still some that remain loyal to their true lord's wife, and they say she is a prisoner in the tower. She has her own rooms and has been given clothes and food. It is rumoured that she would have been wed today had she not been ill.'

'Marietta is ill?' Anton seized on the statement fiercely. 'Damn him to hell for this! He deserves to be hanged for the way he has treated her.'

'It is as well she was ill, for at least it has saved her from worse,' Miguel said. 'If Sandro delivers a way into the castle we may be able to get her out tonight.'

'I pray that we are in time to save her…' Anton's expression darkened. There were worse fates than death, and he could imagine what the Bastard planned for the woman who had humiliated him. 'It is a chance we must take. If she is too ill to walk I shall carry her.'

Miguel nodded, looking thoughtful. 'It is said that the Bastard drinks heavily. We must pray that he will indulge at the table this night, and his men with him.'

'I noticed that there were few guards the last time we visited. His men are ill-disciplined, and it may well be that they are in the habit of drinking too heavily at night…'

Anton's eyes glittered. He had come after Marietta because it was his duty to rescue her and deliver her safely to the King of England—and he would do all in his power to outwit the Bastard of Rouen.

* * *

'You asked me to come?' Claudette looked sulky as she entered the chamber. 'I am not yours to command, even if my lord weds you. My obedience is given only where I choose.'

Marietta met her challenging look. 'I asked if you would come. I know I cannot command you, lady. If you would see me gone from here, I beg you to help me.'

'My lord will kill me if he learns you have fled.'

'He need not know you helped me. Come tonight, when the castle sleeps, and unlock the door. I ask nothing more of you.'

'If he knew I was having his child he might wed me—if you were gone…' Claudette looked thoughtful. 'But he will send for you in the morning, and if you do not come he will order men to look for you. They would find you and bring you back. Nothing would be gained and I might be blamed.'

'If I have enough time I might be far away by the time he realises I am gone.'

'I do not see how that could be…unless…' Claudette's eyes gleamed suddenly. 'I could change places with you—wear your gown and a veil to cover my face.' She looked excited. 'I shall wed him in your place. When he discovers the truth it will be too late. I shall be his wife and you will be far away.'

'Are you certain you wish to do this?' Marietta looked doubtful. The Bastard would undoubtedly be furious when he discovered that he had been duped. 'What will he do to you when he discovers that you have taken my place?'

'He may hit me and shout, but it has happened before. I do not fear him. He knows it, and that is why he loves me. Even if he wed you he would sleep in my bed, for you could not hold him.'

Marietta made no reply. She did not wish to have the Bastard in her bed even on her wedding night, but she would not tell this woman for it would anger her.

'How can you make sure that he does not discover what we have done too soon?'

'I shall put a sleeping draught in his cup when he grows careless. He will sleep late, and when he wakes he will hardly know what he is doing for hours. By the time he realises what has happened you should have a good start.'

'Thank you. I believe you are a brave woman, Claudette.'

'I do this for me, because I love him. He took me when I was but a child. I should be his wife.' Claudette looked her in the eyes, her expression one of pride. 'If he catches you again he will kill you. You are no good to him unless he is your lawful husband. He wants your husband's gold, and you are the key that will unlock the goldsmiths' coffers.'

'I expected him to kill me this time,' Marietta replied. Claudette had confirmed what she had suspected. 'I must think of a way to disappear so that he can never find me again...'

After Claudette had left, Marietta paced the room. She was restless, impatient to be gone, but common sense told her that she must wait for night to fall. The Bastard was eager to make her his wife, and once he had her he would not spare her. He would not kill her immediately. She was useful to him for the moment. But once he had the gold he craved he would find a way to humiliate and destroy her. It would be a slow death and she would prefer to die quickly. If his men recaptured her she would die rather than be brought back alive.

'Anton…' She mouthed the word softly, not realising she spoke aloud. 'Please help me…'

Tears trickled down her cheeks. She was foolish to think of Anton. He had rescued her before, but he now believed she was a murderess. Why would he bother to look for her?

He would not think it worth the trouble. Why should he? She must forget him and think of what she could do once she had left the castle. This time she would have no money, and no one to help her, but somehow she must make her way back to England.

'Bring the witch down to me!' the Bastard demanded. 'I would have her sit by my side this night. I want her to join the celebrations for her wedding…' He laughed and drank deeply from his cup, then wiped his mouth on the sleeve of his robe and belched. 'More wine, dolt! What are you staring at me for?'

'The lady says she is too ill, my lord…' the luckless servant began, and received a blow that sent him staggering sideways.

'Damn her! Damn her black soul to hell…' The Bastard grabbed the wineskin from the serf who presented it and drank straight from the neck. 'Bring her, I say!'

As the frightened servant ran off, Claudette ran her

fingers over his cheek, smiling at him. 'Why do you send for that puling creature when you have me, my lord?' She pouted her red lips at him. 'Let us go to your chamber, and I shall please you so much that you will not want her.'

'My sweet whore,' the Bastard said, grinning at her. 'Your turn will come soon enough, but you must learn to share me with my wife. She brings a fortune in gold. Besides, a man grows tired of too much complaisance. She will fight me, and the thought pleases me…'

'I can fight if you wish for it. I will whip you and scratch you…'

The Bastard caught her wrist as her nails scored his skin, his look suddenly threatening. 'Be quiet, whore! When I want you, I'll tell you.'

Claudette drew back, smarting from his insults. If she was a whore he had made her so. He wanted the gold the late Comte's wife could bring him, but she would do her best to see that his plans came to nothing.

Keeping her smile in place, she took the wineskin he had laid down and filled his cup, slipping the potent liquid that would make him sleep into it while his head was turned. She placed the cup by his hand, and in a moment he reached for it and drank deeply, but he did not finish the contents.

Claudette turned her head to look as she heard shouting, and a scream of anger. The servants had brought the Comtesse to the hall, but she was struggling and protesting, trying to break free of them. All eyes were on her as she was dragged to the high table, and no one but Claudette noticed when the Bastard drained his cup.

'Witch…' he muttered thickly. 'You cannot defy me. I shall teach you a lesson…'

He got to his feet and walked unsteadily along the back of the table where his chief men were seated, then negotiated the steps to the dais unsteadily, finally reaching Marietta. Towering over her, he thrust his hand out and grabbed her by the throat. Bending his head, he forced his mouth over hers. Marietta struggled wildly, and he gave a cry as her sharp teeth sank into his bottom lip. He roared with pain and anger and slapped her, making her stagger back.

Marietta faced him defiantly. His fist curled, as if he would strike her again, then he muttered something and rubbed his hand over his face. A strange strangled sound came from him, his eyes rolling upwards. Sagging to his knees, he stared at her stupidly, and then fell flat on his face.

For a moment there was a stunned silence. Claudette broke it by laughing.

'My lord hath drunk too much,' she announced. 'Take him to his chamber and see that he sleeps well. He will need his strength for the morrow if he is to tame this one!'

Laughter and some coarse remarks greeted her words. Several of the men moved to gather him up and carry him off; they grinned and winked at each other, clearly amused by what had happened.

Claudette came quickly to Marietta. 'You must return to your chamber, lady. I shall lock you in myself.' She hurried Marietta away from the hall before anyone could deny them, her voice soft as she whispered, 'I gave him a strong dose. He will sleep well into the morning. You must lock me into your chamber, so that if he is angry I can blame you. I shall say that you overpowered me and escaped.'

'He will be very angry.' Marietta looked at her in concern. 'He may vent his anger on you.'

'If I am his wife I shall tell him that I bear his son—and that it was for my child's sake that I took your place after you locked me in your room.' Claudette smiled confidently. 'Once you are gone he will forget you. But remember that if you return you will certainly die...'

'I know it,' Marietta said. 'Thank you. We must hurry, for the sooner I am on my way the better...'

Claudette went into the antechamber ahead of Marietta. The next moment she was seized from behind, a hand over her mouth.

'We have come for your lady,' a voice said in her ear. 'Scream and it will be the worse for you.'

'What is this?' Marietta cried as she too was grabbed and held. 'Who are you? What are you doing?'

'Marietta?' A shadow moved towards her out of the gloom. 'We thought you were locked in the bedchamber. Are you at liberty to leave your room?'

'Anton?' Marietta's heart leapt. 'Is that you? I cannot see you...'

'We snuffed the tapers, for we did not wish to alert the castle. We came to take you away from this place—if you wish to go?'

'Oh, yes! Of course I wish to leave. I was about to make my own escape. Claudette was to take my place here. Let her go, for we must lock her in my bedchamber...'

Anton had struck a tinder. Lighting one small candle, he held it high so that he could look at Marietta's face. 'Where is the Bastard?'

'In his chamber. Claudette drugged him, and he will sleep for long enough.'

'Why do you ask?' Claudette was on her guard. 'If you mean him harm I shall scream and bring the guards down on you. You may take her and go in safety, but you will not harm my lord.'

'He may have something I need—a ring.' Anton's hard gaze went over the girl. 'He took it from the Comte de Montcrief as he lay dying. It is fashioned of heavy gold with a large cabochon ruby. Have you seen such a ring?'

'He wears it on a chain about his neck,' Claudette said. 'If you give me your word that he will not be harmed I shall take you to him.'

'He deserves to die for what he has done.'

'She loves him,' Marietta said, and touched his arm. 'Claudette bears his child—for her sake let him live.'

Anton's mouth was a hard line as he looked at her, then he inclined his head. 'Very well.' He turned to Miguel. 'Take the Comtesse and ride for the coast at once. I shall join you as soon as my business is done here.'

'You are not coming with us?'

'I must have that ring.' Anton did not smile as he glanced at Marietta. 'You will be safe with my men. If I should not follow Miguel will take you back to Lady Claire.'

Marietta looked for some sign of warmth in his face but found none. He had come for her, but it must have been at Lady Claire's bidding or because the King had ordered it. For a moment she had thought he had sought her out because he loved her.

She moved towards him urgently, laying a hand on his sleeve. 'I beg you to take care, sir. I would not have you die in my cause.'

'I am commanded to find that ring. You are merely delaying me. Please go with Miguel as I bid you.'

She turned away, fighting her tears as she allowed Miguel to hurry her back down the stone steps of the tower. Near the bottom they heard the sound of voices, and Miguel pulled her back into the shadows until the men had passed.

'There is a secret way beneath the outer walls,' Miguel whispered. 'Your servant is waiting in the stables to guide us through the passage. It is dark, and there are rats and cobwebs, but you must not scream lest someone hears. Remember, Anton is still in the castle.'

'I shall not scream.'

Marietta glanced at his face and saw a strange expression in his eyes. She sensed that he was hiding something, but could not tell what was in his mind. He had come with his friend to help rescue her, but he did not like her. He was hiding it, but she felt strong resentment, even hatred. Perhaps he thought her the witch she had been named?

They slipped out of a side door and ran swiftly across the inner bailey. Reaching the solid stone block that was the stable, Marietta went inside, closely followed by Miguel.

'Sandro?' she called softly. 'Are you there?'

'God be praised, you are alive, my lady.' The groom came towards her, looking beyond her to Miguel. 'Where are the others?'

'Anton and Fitch follow,' Miguel said. 'We are to ride for the coast at once. Anton will do as he thinks best.'

'Then I shall wait for him,' Sandro said. 'He may not be able to find the secret way without me. Take my lady to safety, and may God go with you, sir.'

'If you wait for him then so do I,' Marietta said in a determined tone.

Miguel glared at her. 'You must come with us. Anton ordered it, lady, and he will be angry if you disobey him.'

'I shall not leave without him.' Marietta set her face stubbornly. 'Go on ahead and prepare the ship. I shall wait here with Sandro.'

Miguel's eyes narrowed. He looked furious but, seeing that her mind was set, he turned on his heel and left her with Sandro.

Anton looked down at the Bastard as he lay snoring on his couch. He stank of stale sweat and wine, his hair was lank with grease. Had he been awake, it would have been a joy to kill him, but there was no honour in killing a helpless enemy. There would be a reckoning for the evil that this man had done, but not this night.

'Here is the ring.' Claudette took it from the chain the Bastard wore about his neck and brought it to him. 'Take it and go quickly, but you must lock me in the tower room. I shall tell my lord that you overpowered

me. It will be so much better than the story we planned,
for he might not have believed that she could do it.'

'Why should I believe you? You will raise the alarm
as soon as we leave.'

'You may tie me and gag me if you choose.'

'It might be safer,' Fitch said. 'I will make her secure
without hurting her.'

Anton nodded his assent. 'Come then, lady. We have
no time to waste, for I would be on board my ship by
the time the Bastard wakes…'

Anton pocketed the ring. It was the twin to the one
he had seen on the King's finger.

Wondering at the significance of the matching rings,
Anton was thoughtful as he left the Bastard's chamber.
What was so important about a ring that the King of
England needed it returned?

Anton might never know, for he was bound to serve
the King but not entitled to an answer. He must concen-
trate his thoughts on getting out of here alive!

They had been lucky so far, but could be discovered
at any moment. If the alarm were raised it would be
almost impossible for two men to fight their way out of
this castle. The Bastard of Rouen allowed his men to
drink and neglect their duty, but if roused their numbers
would be overwhelming.

As they made their way back to the tower where
Marietta had been imprisoned Anton heard the sound of
raucous laughter coming from the hall. Twice he
stopped, motioning to the others to keep back as he heard
voices and someone approaching, but each time the men
passed without noticing the figures in the shadows.

They gained the tower room safely. Claudette was bound. Before the gag was placed about her mouth, Anton asked if there was anything she needed.

'For your help this day, I would offer my protection in the future if it is asked.'

'I need nothing from you, sir. Go on your way.'

Bowing his head, Anton signalled that she should be gagged. When it was done they locked her in the room and threw the key into a corner. Let it be searched for!

Running down the steps, they were soon outside in the night air. It was as they approached the stables that Anton heard raised voices. One was Sandro's, the other unknown. As he hesitated, he heard a woman scream.

Marietta! Why was she still here? Had they been caught? As Anton prepared for the worst, he heard a man speaking.

'What are you doing here? Answer me or by God I'll have your tongue—but not before my lord has his fun with you.'

'Do your worst, scum,' Sandro said defiantly. 'Your master will burn in hell for his sins.'

There was the sound of a struggle and a shout of pain. As Anton entered the stable he saw that one man held Sandro's arms behind his back while another struck him about the face. Marietta was being held by a third man; there was no sign of Miguel or his other men. Anton nodded to Fitch and they moved as one. Fitch drove his dagger into the side of the man holding Sandro, just as Anton sprang at the man who had been hitting him, grabbing him by the throat and jerking his arm back until he gave a cry and fell senseless to the ground. Turning to look at Marietta, Anton saw the third man had a dagger at her throat.

'Come any nearer and I will slit her throat,' he warned.

'If you spill one drop of her blood you are a dead man. Let her go and I shall spare you.'

Anton advanced, sword at the ready. The man tightened his arm about Marietta's waist, but she suddenly jerked back, then kicked his shin, and at the same moment shoved her elbow hard into his stomach. He gave a grunt and released his hold sufficiently for her to break free of his grasp. Anton grabbed her, thrusting her behind him. The man dropped to his knees, face pale as he begged for his life.

'Spare me. I was simply obeying orders.'

'Tie him up!'

Fitch moved to obey instantly. The man made no attempt to resist as he was bound and gagged.

Sandro was still on his knees, gasping. His nose was bleeding, and more blood ran from the side of his mouth.

'Why are you both still here?' Anton's gaze went from Marietta to Sandro. 'Where are Miguel and the others?'

'Sandro stayed to make sure you found your way through the secret passages,' Marietta answered him. 'I stayed with him. I could not leave while—'

'You foolish woman! When I give an order I expect to be obeyed! If I miss the tide I can look after myself until I find another ship. You will only hamper me!'

'I beg you, do not be angry with my lady,' Sandro said. 'It was my fault. If I had not waited she would have gone with the others.'

'Are you able to walk?' Anton's attention returned to him. 'You should have persuaded your lady to go with the others—but I know well she is wilful and heedless. I shall not blame you. We must leave at once, for I do not want to miss the tide.'

Anton took hold of Marietta's arm. His strong fingers bit into her flesh, his grip uncomfortable as he thrust her ahead of him into the tunnel. Her throat felt tight, and tears were very close, but she would not shed them. He was so angry with her! She was a burden to him that he would rather not have had, and his harsh words were like the lash of a whip, wounding her deeply.

The journey through the tunnel was a nightmare for Marietta. There was an unpleasant smell, and cobwebs hung from the low ceiling brushing over her face and into her hair. She could hear rustling sounds, and sometimes the squeak of a bat, which made her want to scream, but she held her nerve, the nearness of Anton giving her courage to bear her ordeal.

At last they were out into the open. She gulped the night air, breathing it in thankfully. One of Anton's men had stayed behind to guard the horses. But there were only enough for the men, which meant that she was expected to ride with one of them.

'Come, lady!'

Anton held out his hand imperiously. She took it and he swung her up into the saddle, mounting behind her. Marietta shivered as his arms went about her and she felt his body at her back.

'There is no need to be frightened now.' Anton's

voice was softer. 'We shall be safe once we reach the ship.'

She could not answer him. Being so close to him made her feel safe, and yet she was aware that he was still angry with her despite his words of comfort. She had prayed that he would come to help her, and her prayers had been answered, but she knew that he had not come to Montcrief for her sake. Anton had come for the ring. Claire had asked him to bring her back and he had rescued her—but it was obvious that the ring was more important. She would be foolish to imagine that she meant more to him than duty.

The wind stung her face, getting into her eyes. She wasn't crying. It was just the wind. Anton would take her to his king and abandon her to her fate, whatever that might be. She had escaped the Bastard, but she would not escape the King's justice.

Marietta held herself proudly. It would be foolish to cry for a man who did not love her but she could not help herself. Despite his coldness, he had stirred something deep inside her.

Dawn was breaking when Marietta first smelled the tang of the sea. They had begun the descent of a steep cliff to the secluded cove below. She could barely make out the shape of a ship anchored just off shore, waiting to take her to England. She felt no sense of joy. Anton had saved her from the Bastard's spite but she still had to face the King of England's justice.

He cared nothing for her. Even if the King were merciful the years ahead held nothing for her above the pleasure of motherhood. Yet if she were spared to care for her beloved son she would count herself blessed.

Looking back over her shoulder, she could see nothing but dark shapes and shadows, but knew that people would soon be stirring in the cottages they had passed as they rode. In another hour or so servants would be stirring in the castle. They would take Marietta food, believing her to be locked in the tower. When they discovered she had fled once more they would be frightened. Someone would have to wake the Bastard and tell him. No one would want to be the messenger, and that might give her more time.

Marietta regretted that a servant might be made to pay for her escape. Claudette was sure she could placate him…and she planned to take Marietta's place and wed him.

God protect her! Marietta prayed that the Bastard would not make her suffer too much.

Anton had dismounted. He offered his hand to help her down.

'Praise God, we are in time. The ship has sent a boat for us. We must go aboard at once, for we leave with the tide.'

'Yes…'

His tone was so cold, his manner distant. He was still angry with her. She raised her head, holding the tears inside.

The wind from the sea was cool. It whipped about Marietta, blowing her cloak and her hair. She shivered, but it was not so much the wind but her thoughts that had turned her blood to ice water.

Marietta's stomach turned as she felt his fingers grip her arm. He pushed her towards the water and she stumbled, almost falling. Sailors had got out of the rowing boat and were waiting to take their passengers on board.

'You are tired,' Anton said, and bent to sweep her up into his arms. He waded through the shallow water to where the boat waited.

Marietta's tears were very close. The softer note in his voice had almost broken her, and it was taking all her strength to keep from weeping.

A sailor helped her into the boat. She murmured her thanks, staring back at the beach. The light was strengthening with every stroke of the oars but still there was no sign of pursuit. Claudette's potion had worked well.

Marietta climbed the rope ladder to the deck of the ship, Anton's presence behind her giving her the strength to pull herself up. For a moment she stood facing the shore, the wind whipping her hair into her eyes, her cloak hugging her body. She felt so cold, so lonely and afraid.

'You must go below,' Anton told her. 'You are exhausted. Rest, and we shall talk later.'

Marietta inclined her head. As she moved away from him she saw Miguel watching her. For a moment his eyes held some smouldering emotion, and she knew that she had made him angry by insisting on waiting for Anton. She shivered, feeling cold, lonely and lost.

Left alone in her cabin, Marietta lay on the hard cot, listening to the sound of the water lapping about the ship. The light from the small porthole was dim, and it seemed cold and dark, almost like a prison cell. Her skin was prickling with goosebumps. She might soon find herself incarcerated in the King of England's prison.

Marietta closed her eyes, forcing herself to rest. She was exhausted after the long ride, for she had hardly dared to sleep at the castle lest she was attacked. Her eyes flickered and closed as she drifted into a restless slumber, tossing and turning and crying out in her dream.

Though she did not know it, her cheeks were wet with tears.

'I thought you might miss the tide,' Miguel said as the ship weighed anchor.

'It was as well you waited until the last moment, for had we missed the tide I should have been hard pressed to protect the Comtesse until I could find another ship.'

'She would insist on waiting with Sandro! I tried to force her to come with me but she is proud and wilful.' Miguel's gaze narrowed. 'You should be careful of her, Anton. A woman like that is dangerous.'

'Surely you do not believe these stories of witchcraft and murder? Proud and wilful she may be, but the rest is false.'

'There is no smoke without fire…'

'They are but foolish tales. Believe me, Marietta is no more a murderer than she is a witch. The murderer remains at Montcrief.'

'You did not kill him?'

'He lay in a drugged sleep. Had he been awake I should have found satisfaction in making him confess his guilt—but I had a more important mission.'

'You found what you wanted?'

'Yes.' Anton was thoughtful. 'Excuse me. I have something to do below. We shall talk more of this later.'

He walked away, descending the iron ladder to the cabins below. Apart from the incident in the stables, and Marietta's foolish decision to wait for him, everything had gone almost too well. Anton would have preferred a reckoning with the Bastard of Rouen, for he suspected that the man's rage would know no bounds when he woke and discovered what had happened.

He hesitated outside Marietta's cabin. She had suffered badly on her last voyage to England, but there had been a terrible storm that night. This day there were good winds, but no huge waves to toss the ship from side to side. Almost reluctantly, he opened the door and went into the cabin. He hesitated as he saw that she was sleeping.

Her arm was thrown out, her hair spread on the pillows, but she was not peaceful. She was dreaming and it seemed her dream disturbed her.

'Forgive me… I love you…' Marietta cried, and moved restlessly. 'Please do not hate me… I love you…'

Anton frowned. Who was it that she called to in her dreams? Did she have a lover? Was she dreaming like this because she was guilty of some crime? His heart rejected the idea, though his mind told him that women could be faithless. He had believed that he loved Isabella but she had not returned his love. If the letter he had received were true, his wife had betrayed him with another man: the child she had carried when she died would not have had his blood. She had come to his bed that night so that he would not guess the truth. If Isabella could be so false, how could he trust any woman again?

Anton approached the bed. Marietta looked so beautiful. Something inside him reached out to her, despite his resolve not to let her into his heart. He wanted to take her into his arms, to hold her close and kiss away her fears. The temptation to touch her was strong, but he resisted. He should let her sleep, because once they reached England he must take her to London. Anton wished that he could save her the ordeal of facing the King's justice, but he had no choice in the matter. He had been ordered to bring her before the King and must obey. Only if she were cleared of this crime would she be free of the shadow that would otherwise follow her wherever she went.

As he stood staring down at Marietta, her eyes opened.

'What is it? Have we been followed?' She pushed herself up against the hard pillows, her eyes wide with fear.

'We are at sea. You are quite safe now.'

'Are you still angry because I disobeyed you?' Marietta's voice caught with emotion. 'I know you must think me foolish, but I could not leave while you were in danger for my sake.'

'It was foolish, but I am no longer angry. If I spoke harshly it was for your sake, Marietta. Alone, I should have had little trouble finding a ship, but with you…some captains might have refused to take you. I am certain the first thing the Bastard will do would be to send out messengers offering a reward for your capture.'

'I did not mean to cause you so much trouble. If I had stayed inside Lady Claire's home in the first place I should not have been captured. It was foolish to walk alone, but I thought I must be safe at the house.'

'And so you should have been. That was my fault. I should have guarded you better. It was perhaps a little foolish of you to go out alone in the circumstances, but I am not angry.'

Marietta swung her legs to the side of the bed and stood up. She gazed into his face uncertainly. 'Are you not? I did not expect that you would come for me…'

'You should have known I would. His Majesty ordered me to bring you to court. I was merely following orders.'

'Oh… I see…' Her voice trailed away. 'I thought when you came…but that was foolish. You came for the ring, of course.'

'Do not look like that!' Anton said hoarsely. His need at that moment was so great that he hardly knew what he did as he reached out to take her in his arms. 'I would have searched for you if it took me the rest of my life…' He groaned as he held her pressed to his chest, burying his face in her hair. Why did she always smell so sweet? 'I swore that I would never let another woman near, but you have bewitched me…'

'No!' Marietta pushed away from him. 'Do not say such things. I have used no spells to bind you to me, Anton.'

'I did not mean with witchcraft.' Anton bent his head and kissed her. At first his lips gently brushed hers, and then the kiss intensified, becoming demanding, drawing a response from her. Her body arched into his, her arms about his neck, her fingers moving at the nape. 'Only the magic that binds a man's senses and makes him want a woman so much that it is agony to deny that need.'

'Anton…' Marietta breathed. Her eyes opened wider as she sensed his desire. Her body throbbed with need, but she was afraid to believe. 'Do you truly want me? You want to lie with me?'

'Yes, more than you will ever know.' He drew away from her, his mouth loose and soft with aching desire. 'You are tearing me apart, Marietta. I must take you to the King, but I will do everything in my power to persuade him that you are innocent of all the crimes laid at your door. I would not have you die. You must know I would give my own life to save yours.'

'No, I should not want that…'

'I will do everything I can. I give you my word.'

'You can do no more…' Marietta touched his face with her fingertips. Her body seemed to dissolve with wanting and need, moisture trickling between her thighs. Her lips parted on a soft sigh. 'Do not torture yourself for my sake. If you are with me I shall not flinch. I am innocent. Please believe me. I would never have harmed my husband, though I did not love him.'

'Did you have a lover?'

'No…' Marietta faltered. Her eyes met his stead-fastly. 'There was once someone I loved, but he did not notice me.'

'And now?'

'There is only you. You saved my life. I am grateful.'

'I do not want gratitude…' Anton moved away from her, turning his back. Her words had broken the spell that bound him. 'I have things to do. If you need my cure for seasickness come to me…'

'Anton…'

Marietta watched as he left the cabin. Why had she not told him that he was the only man she had ever loved? He had kissed her, told her he desired her—what more could she ask?

She shook her head, for the answer was foolish. Anton desired her. He might make her his mistress if the King did not have her condemned as a murderess, but love was merely a dream.

Chapter Six

Marietta slept for some hours before going on deck. It was close to nightfall when the shores of England came into view, and a cool wind had blown up. She thought there might soon be a storm and was glad that it had not struck while they were still in mid-sea.

Anton's remedy for seasickness had not been needed this time. He had not returned to the cabin, and she would not allow herself to go in search of him. However, he came up to her now, as the ship anchored a short distance from the English beach.

'You look much better, Comtesse Montcrief.'

'Please…my name is Marietta. You called me by my name last night. I would rather you used it always, at least when we are alone.'

'As you wish. We shall go ashore as soon as the boats are launched. This evening we shall stay at the nearest inn. I know of a decent one where we may safely lodge for the night. In the morning we shall leave for London. We shall be two days on the road and will spend at least one other night at an inn, perhaps more.'

'Thank you for telling me, my lord.'

'If I am to call you Marietta, you must use my name in return.' He smiled at her ruefully. 'Do not fear me, lady. I mean you no harm, believe me.'

'I have always felt safe with you—even though I did not tell you my name at the start. I was afraid you might think me guilty of murder. I think at first you did?'

'I was not sure,' Anton admitted. His gaze was intense, seeming to search her very soul, 'When I found you on the road I took your part, as I would that of any lady who was being attacked. I have tried to keep an open mind, but now I believe it was the Bastard who murdered your husband. He took the ring the Comte always wore, and must have done so as he lay dying. If it was not there when you were called to your husband's bedside only he could have taken it—and so the finger of suspicion points at him.'

'I am certain that you are right. My husband feared that his bastard might try to kill him and steal all that should belong to my son. For that reason he took precautions meant to protect us. The Bastard of Rouen needs my signature to release my husband's gold from its guardians. He thought that once I was his wife he could force me—or perhaps he would not have needed my agreement then, for a husband's will takes precedence.'

'I do not know how French law stands, but in England your fortune would pass to your husband's care. However, if your husband made you trustee for his son, your signature will be needed until Charles is of age. Without it, Rouen will find it difficult to persuade the goldsmiths to give up what is in their charge. They could be called to account by your son when he reaches his maturity; they will not lightly part with gold trusted to their charge.'

Marietta nodded her agreement. 'Then that is the reason I am still alive. I refused to marry him, clung to my bed and pleaded sickness. I know my ruse made him very angry, but it gave me more time. Claudette promised to help me…' She glanced back across the water towards France. 'I pray that he does not take too harsh a vengeance on her.'

'We left her bound and gagged. She need only plead that she was overcome.'

Marietta nodded. She remembered Claudette's mad plan to be married in her dress. Perhaps she had thought better of it. She hoped so, for she would not be in Claudette's shoes when the Bastard of Rouen discovered the trick.

'You scheming witch! I swear I'll beat you to a pulp! How dare you trick me so?'

The Bastard towered over Claudette, his eyes bulging. His neck was red with rage. He struck her a heavy blow across the face, sending her staggering back.

'I am your wife…' Claudette cried defiantly. Her eyes were very bright but she would not weep for mercy. 'Beat me if you wish. It makes no difference. You have married me, and only my death can free you—for the church will not let you put me aside in favour of that witch.'

'Damn you!' The Bastard threatened her with his fist. 'I'll see you in your grave before I'll let you ruin all my plans.'

'Will you kill your own son?' Claudette asked, facing him proudly. She placed her hands on her belly. 'My son will be a legitimate child, and heir to all you have stolen from your fa—' She got no further for the Bastard rushed at her, seizing her about the throat. She struggled, putting up her hands to try and force him back, but he was too strong for her. Her eyes widened in horror as his grip tightened and she knew that he meant to strangle her. Her mouth moved in a plea for forgiveness but no sound came, only a sighing breath. It was her last.

The Bastard let her lifeless body fall to the ground. He stared down at her for a moment and then laughed, lifting her with the toe of his boot and kicking her aside.

'So end any that seek to defy me,' he told the silent, watchful servants. 'Steward, have my things packed and tell fifty of my men to be ready. We leave for England within the hour. They will have taken her back with them. This time I shall go after her myself, and she will follow that whore to hell!'

Marietta looked about the inn bedroom. It was sparsely furnished, but clean, and would serve her well, the bed softer than that on board the ship. She imagined it was more comfortable than the cell that might soon be her resting place—but she would not think of that! If her life was forfeit, so be it.

Kneeling, Marietta closed her eyes and prayed. Anton had promised to help her as much as he could, but the King's word was law. She knew that Anton felt something for her, but was it merely the kind of passion that men often felt for an attractive woman? If he loved her he would surely help her to run away instead of taking her to the King? He had said little on their journey to the inn, seeming lost in his thoughts. Had she done something to anger him again?

Her thoughts went round and round in circles. God must know that she was innocent—but would He spare her? She had just risen to her feet once more when someone knocked at her door. Having asked that she might be served supper in her room, she thought it must be a servant.

'The door is not locked…' She turned as it opened and Anton entered. 'Oh…I thought you were a servant with my supper.'

'Forgive me. I came to ask if you would sup with me instead?'

'I am tired. I shall do better alone.'

'Are you angry with me, Marietta?' His gaze was intent on her face. 'I should not blame you if you were—but I must do my duty.'

'Why should I be angry? I thought I had angered you once more. You said little on the way here.'

'I have much on my mind. Perhaps we could talk at supper?'

'If I asked you, would you let me go back to Claire's house? Would you let me take my son and go away— perhaps to Italy?'

'Do you think it is easy for me to escort you to the King, knowing that he could condemn you to a terrible death?'

'I do not know…' She watched his eyes take fire. 'If it distresses you why will you not help me to run away somewhere I am not known?'

'This is what I wished to talk to you about…' Anton's gaze was intent on her face. 'If Henry clears you of both crimes you will be free of the stain of murder and able to live as a woman of your standing should. Your son will be entitled to make a claim for his inheritance—which means I shall do it with your blessing and in your name, so that you are his guardian.'

'You would do that for us?'

'Yes, of course. If you run away again it will confirm your guilt in the eyes of the world.' Anton's voice was soft, caressing. 'You would never feel safe, Marietta. You would spend your life looking over your shoulder, afraid that someone would recognise you.'

'Yes, that is true,' she said. 'But supposing the King does not find in my favour?'

'This is what we must discuss. Believe me, if judgement goes against you I shall not just stand by and watch you hang. Come down now and we shall make plans…'

'Very well. If you wish it I shall come down.'

'I do wish it. I believe we need to talk in private.'

'We are private here.'

'If I stayed here too long I should think of other things rather than talking.' Anton smiled at her, but the flame in his eyes told her that he wanted her. 'I do not think you are aware that the scent you wear arouses a man's senses.'

'I am not wearing perfume. I washed at the castle.

Perhaps the perfume of my special soap lingers in my hair.'

'It does…' Anton's eyes went over her hungrily. 'Come down to supper, Marietta.' He held out his hand to her, a smile on his lips. 'I would not dishonour you, but being here alone with you tempts me beyond bearing.'

'If you want me…' Marietta's cheeks burned but she forced herself to speak. 'I should not deny you. I have been married. I am not a shy maiden to run away from the truth of men's desires. My husband did not often trouble me, but I do not fear physical union. I do not seek to turn you from your duty. All I ask in return is protection for my son…that if I am dead you will try to recover his inheritance.'

'I have already given you my word on that,' Anton said, his voice hoarse. She was so beautiful, and the scent she claimed not to wear was inflaming his senses. 'You do not need to offer me anything, Marietta.'

'Yet I have—I am offering more…' she said, and moved towards the door, turning the key in the lock. 'This is not just for you, Anton. Tomorrow or the next day may be my last day of freedom. I have just two nights left before I must face the King's justice, and I would not spend them alone.'

'You are certain?' Anton moved towards her, taking her into his arms. 'I do not want gratitude, Marietta.'

'It is not gratitude I offer.' She lifted her face to his, her tongue smoothing over her lips, wetting them. They were moist and soft, tempting. 'I want to spend tonight in your arms, and tomorrow night. I want the pleasure I know you can give me…a pleasure I may never know again.'

If she told the truth she would spend every night of her life in his arms. Perhaps he would never love her, but she would be happier as his mistress than she had ever been as her husband's wife.

'God forgive me, I cannot resist…' Anton bent down, scooping her up behind the knees and carrying her to the bed.

He had the smell of horses on him, and his own masculine musk, and it sent her senses spinning. Her body cried out to him, wanting, needing this gift. Perhaps it was not love, but his desire was strong. She felt his heat and it warmed her to the core.

'You are so beautiful…so lovely…'

'Take me, love me for as long as we have,' Marietta whispered. She felt his lips at her throat and arched towards him, her body begging for his touch. Her mouth opened to the delicate flicking of his tongue. She met him, teasing and duelling in a dance of pure pleasure. Drawing him down to her, she gave herself to him, moaning softly as his hands sought out the most intimate places of her body. Heat pooled low in her and moisture ran as she welcomed his touch.

'You are so hot and wet for me,' Anton murmured as he entered her. 'I have burned for you almost from the first.'

Marietta gave a cry of pleasure as he thrust deep into her. Her body arched to meet his, taking him deeper and deeper. Never once had she felt such pleasure in the act of love. He was young, strong and well made, his manhood filling her, stretching her despite the fact that she had borne a child. White heat licked its way through her body. She sighed and screamed, her fingers digging into him as the climax took her.

Anton looked down at the woman as she lay in his arms. He was not sure at what period they had shed their clothes. Was it after the first time he took her or the second? His need had been great, for it was many months since he had lain with a woman. The first time had been too swift, and his desire nowhere near slaked. Even now that he had loved her thrice he still burned with desire, wanted to feel the moist heat of her silken sheath enfolding him once more. At the moment she slept, her lips parted a little. She looked so beautiful, so soft and sweet, that he could hardly keep from kissing her body.

He had thought that once he'd lain with her the need would go, but it seemed stronger. It was almost as if he were bewitched, for he did not remember a night such as this with his wife. He had believed he loved Isabella at the start, but she had not set him on fire as this woman did. Isabella had been a shy virgin. In the beginning she had flinched from him, and he knew that his loving had hurt her at first, but even after their first child was born she had not welcomed his attentions in bed.

Isabella had rejected him, and the few times they had made love it had been cold and passionless. On the other hand Marietta was a passionate woman, her kisses warm, her body willing and welcoming. She aroused feelings in him that he had never known were there.

Anton rose from the bed. Marietta had no bad dreams to disturb her this night. Instead she smiled as she slept, one hand beneath her face. Was she a wanton? She had given herself to him fearlessly—but was he the first besides her husband to receive her favours? If he let down his reserve and took her into his heart would she break it? Jealousy turned inside him like a handful of maggots, eating at his stomach.

He was a damned fool to care! He should simply take what she offered and then move on. Yet he knew that she had found a way to penetrate his being; she was inside him, whether he willed it or no, and he would not be able to forget her as he had intended.

Anton wanted to wake up and find her by his side every morning! He wanted to lie by her side each night and make love to her until they both slept. He was not in love with her. Desire was not love. He wanted Marietta with a passion that surprised and even frightened him, but he would not let himself love her.

Yet if Marietta died it would tear him apart.

She would not die! Somehow he would persuade the King that she was innocent. He must, because he could not lose her.

He felt for the ring in the inner pocket of his jerkin. The Bastard of Rouen had taken it from Comte de Montcrief and the King wanted it returned. Why? He looked at it carefully, turning it over to examine it from all angles. The back of the stone was not open to the light but encased in gold. Anton had seen rings like this before, and knew that sometimes there was a little compartment behind the stone. The trick was to open it, and that was not always easy. He could see no obvious signs of a catch...

'Anton?'

Hearing Marietta's voice, Anton slipped the ring on his finger and turned to her. She was smiling at him sleepily, and as he hesitated she pushed back the covers, inviting him to return.

'Do not leave me yet, I beg you.'

'I shall not leave you,' he murmured against her ear. In his heart he knew that he would never want to leave her. Love was not necessary when she could give him such pleasure!

He breathed in her perfume, the wonderful scent of her skin, her essence. She needed no other, for her own scent was intoxicating. Already he could feel himself hardening, feel the heat building, pooling deep in his belly. He wanted her again. He would never have enough of her.

'I shall never leave you, little one.'

'Anton...make love to me,' Marietta cried as he began to kiss and suck at her breasts. Her body arched towards him as he slid his hand between her thighs. She was ready for him instantly.

'My precious, wonderful woman,' Anton said, hardly knowing that he spoke. 'So warm and lovely. I want you more than I can tell you.'

He plunged deep into her, feeling her wetness as she took him in. She arched and whimpered beneath him, abandoned and wild with desire as they moved together. He had never known such pleasure in a woman. She was beyond anything he had ever dreamed.

Marietta woke again and saw that Anton was dressing. It was dawn, and the first rays of light were beginning to creep into the room.

'I slept so long,' she said. 'I did not mean to sleep at all.'

'We both slept,' Anton told her, and bent to kiss her once more. 'If I stay longer everyone will know I spent the night with you. I must leave, or you will have no reputation left.'

'Do I have any to lose?' Marietta asked, and sat up. Her long hair tumbled over her breasts and fell across her face. Her skin was flushed, her body pliant and sensuous, a feeling of well-being stealing over her. 'It matters little to me, Anton. If the King spares me I shall be proud to be known as your mistress—for as long as you wish.'

'My mistress…' Anton looked at her. 'You have the right to more, Marietta. You are of gentle birth.'

'I was the wife of a nobleman of France, but it brought me little happiness. Last night you gave me more than all the jewels my husband heaped on me. I shall be content as your mistress—and when you tire of me I shall ask for nothing more than a place to live. For my son I ask much more.'

'You love the child, and would see his fortune and rank restored to him.' Anton nodded. 'You have my word that I shall do all I can for him. As for the rest…we shall speak of this when the King has made his judgement.'

Marietta saw the ring on his finger. 'You wear my husband's ring?'

'I was trying to discover its secret. He did not show you?'

Marietta knelt up in the bed, her body pink and warm from sleep. 'Does it have a secret? He never spoke of that to me, though once he said a good friend gave it to him. I wondered why he chose it above all others.'

'Perhaps it is merely sentiment,' Anton said, and tugged at the ring. 'It went on easily but now it will not come off.'

'You must wet your hand with soapy water. If the water is cold it will make it easier, and the ring will slip over the knuckle.'

'Yes, I shall do so when it must come off. For the moment it is safe enough on my hand.'

'Why is it so important?'

'I do not know,' Anton told her. 'I am leaving now, to order breakfast and prepare the men for our journey. You should dress and come down for we must be on our way soon.'

'Yes, of course.'

Marietta sighed as he closed the door after him. He was still determined to take her to London to the King. Had she hoped that he might change his mind after spending a night in her arms? She had given him pleasure, but his will was still strong. A little chill slid down her spine.

Anton desired her, but his duty to the King still came first.

Anton glanced at the woman riding just ahead of him. She sat her horse well, and pride was in every line of her body. What would he do if the King condemned her to a terrible death?

Wild thoughts of delivering the ring but not the lady had been running through his mind. He could send her to Spain, where he had friends and she would be cared

for until he came for her. Surely he had done all that his
royal master had asked of him?

Yet it would not sit well with his honour to lie. If he
told Henry the truth he could well find himself in the
Tower, his head on the block. Marietta would be alone,
with no one to help her, and she might be sent back to
England to face justice, or worse still to France. Even
if they managed to escape the King's justice, others
might somehow hear of it and condemn her. Only with
the King's pardon could she be free.

No, he would not disobey his King, for that way lay
dishonour and despair for them both.

He would plead Marietta's case, use all his influence.
Perhaps his father and uncle would add their voices to
his if he asked it of them. Henry must listen, for
Marietta was innocent of any crime. Anton would never
believe her guilty of murder. She was too warm and
beautiful to harm anyone.

Had she bewitched him? A smile tugged at the
corners of his mouth as he remembered the night he had
passed in her arms. She was beautiful, warm and desirable. He had felt things that he had thought dead in
him…desire, warmth…love?

Anton's smile dimmed. No, he would not give her
his heart. He had been hurt once, and only a fool offered
himself to the fire twice.

The feeling of despair swept over him, causing his expression to become severe, his mouth to set in a hard line.
Even when Marietta turned her head to look at him Anton
could not smile in response. He had good cause to know
that women were faithless. When he lay with Marietta

he had come close to giving her his heart and soul, but now the doubts were creeping back into his mind.

Why had she invited him to lie with her? Was it because she hoped that he would help her escape the King's justice? Would she have lain with any man to gain her own way?

He tried to rid himself of the unworthy thought, but it worried at him like a wild dog at a dead sheep, tearing at his guts. Somehow Marietta had got beneath his skin. Even though the doubts had returned to torment him, he could not wait for the night, when they would lie together once more.

Marietta had seen the harsh expression on Anton's face. How could he look at her so if he cared for her? Had the night they spent together meant nothing to him?

Holding her head high, she fought off the tears that threatened. She would not let anyone see that she was unhappy. Anton had made love to her so sweetly, yet now he looked through her, as if their night of love had never been.

Pride came to her rescue once more. She had learned to bear so many things. Anton's indifference was just one more. Perhaps he believed that she had bewitched him…that she was a witch. He desired her, but she had not touched his heart.

Turning her head to glance at Miguel, she surprised a look that came close to hatred in his eyes. Why did he look at her so?

On the ship she had sensed that he was angry. What

had she done that he should look at her that way? Miguel became aware of her gaze and smiled. Perhaps she had misjudged his look? Perhaps her fear made her see shadows everywhere?

She turned her head away, her heart aching. The journey seemed long and the day was cold, wind blowing into her face and whipping her hair into tangles. She pulled the hood of her cloak over her head, as much to hide her face as to keep out the cold. It would shame her if Anton realised that she was breaking her heart for him. Let him think her a wanton if he would!

When at last they stopped at an inn to take refreshment, it was Miguel who came to assist her from her horse. His hands were firm about her waist as he lifted her clear, his fingers bruising her flesh beneath the thin gown. She looked into his eyes and saw a spark of something she did not at first understand.

Breaking from his hold, she moved towards the inn, her head held proudly. She had recently seen that look in another man's eyes—the Bastard of Rouen had looked at her with a mixture of desire and resentment.

Surely Miguel did not feel anything of that nature for her?

Could a man want a woman and yet dislike her at the same time?

Marietta shuddered. She had known what her fate would be at the mercy of the Bastard. Was Miguel another such man?

No, surely not! He was Anton's friend and his confidant. He would not lust after her because he must know that Anton had spent the night with her.

Was that the reason she had seen anger in his eyes as they rode? Was he jealous because he wanted her for himself? Or was there another, deeper reason for his hatred? He must believe her a witch!

Perish the thought! A man like Miguel would not hesitate to see her put to the test. She dared not think what might happen to her if Anton abandoned her.

Perhaps it was all imagination? Miguel had treated her with nothing but the respect due to a lady. Her experience at the Bastard's hands had made her too suspicious. He was Anton's friend and he had helped rescue her from the Bastard of Rouen. She must stop seeing enemies at every turn.

Marietta's thoughts were confused and fearful as she forced herself to eat a little of the bread and meat, and drink the ale provided. The future loomed dark and dangerous. Her instincts told her that even if she escaped the King's justice she would not be safe.

Why was she so cursed? Would she never find the happiness she craved?

When they finally stopped for the night, Marietta was bone-weary. Alone in her room, she brushed her long hair and undressed, getting into bed. She had locked her door, because she was not sure that Anton would come to her and she did not wish anyone else to walk in as she slept.

She lay for a long time, listening to the wind in the eaves. Somewhere a shutter was loose, and every now and then it shut with a bang. Her eyelids seemed heavy, closing even though she tried to stay awake, listening for Anton to come. For a long time Marietta struggled against the weariness but in the end she fell asleep.

She did not hear the soft knock at her door, or Anton's voice as he asked if he might enter. The latch was lifted but the door did not open, and after a moment or two he walked away.

Waking with a start as a loud knocking brought her from her strange dreams, Marietta jumped out of bed and went to the door. It was morning. She must have slept all night! A tavern wench had brought her water to wash, and some bread and honey to break her fast.

'The lord said that he wants to leave as soon as you are ready, lady.'

'Thank you. I shall not keep him waiting long.'

Marietta dressed quickly, washing her face and hands. She combed her long hair back from her face, securing it with jewelled clips. Eating some of the bread and honey, she hastily gathered her things.

Had Anton come to her room after she had fallen asleep? She had meant to stay awake for him, but the journey had tired her too much.

She went downstairs to the hall and saw that Anton was standing there, talking to Miguel. Both men turned to look at her, but neither of them smiled. They looked so serious! She feared that they both expected the worst—that she would be hanged as a murderess.

'Forgive me if I have kept you waiting,' she said. It took all her pride and courage not to give way to tears. 'I was tired and slept deeply.'

'No matter,' Anton said, and his tone was harsh, his manner shutting her out as if that night of passion had never existed. Why did he not smile at her? Did he think she had locked her door against him—or was he accepting that she would soon be a prisoner in the Tower? 'We should reach London this evening—unless we are delayed.'

Marietta looked from one to the other. 'Is there some reason why we might suffer delay?'

'Miguel thought he saw men lurking in the woods when he went to the stream to wash. I do not think it can be Rouen's men, for I doubt he could have caught up with us so soon, but it is a reminder to be on our guard. There are always rogues and bands of roaming beggars ready to set upon the unwary traveller.'

'You think he will come after me?' Marietta studied their faces, wondering at their grim expressions. Was it because they were expecting to be attacked that they looked so grim? The hurt inside her eased a little as she realised that Anton was not angry, but anxious. She had misjudged him.

'He needs you if he is to gain control of your husband's fortune. I expect he will come.' Anton's expression softened. 'Do not fear him, Marietta. We are a match for the Bastard's men—but we must keep a strict watch lest he take us by surprise.'

'I see…' Marietta's pulse raced. 'What am I to do?'

'First we must get you to court,' Anton said. 'Come, lady, we must leave. It is possible that Rouen's men might catch up to us if they had a fast ship and rode all night.'

'I am a great deal of trouble to you, sir. You must wish that you had never set eyes on me.'

'You speak foolishly,' Anton replied. 'I deal in what is real. Whether I wish it or not, you are here and my responsibility. I must get you safely to court.'

'And then?'

'I have told you I shall plead your case. You must have faith, lady.' Marietta swallowed hard, because the closer they got to London the more anxious she became. 'I am a man of my word, Comtesse. Whatever happens, I shall do my best for your son.'

'Then I am content…' Marietta hesitated, then, as he came to help her mount, 'Forgive me. I meant to stay awake but you did not come.'

'The hour was late. I had much to do.'

A little pulse flicked in his throat. Marietta was not sure if he was angry or the victim of some strong emotion.

She smiled tremulously as he lifted her effortlessly to the saddle, and for a moment he smiled at her, making her heart lift.

'Do not give up all hope. Henry is a fair man, and he likes beautiful women. He may find in your cause— and then he will bring his influence to bear on your son's behalf.'

'Thank you…' Marietta's voice was no more than a whisper.

She glanced at Miguel. He was standing close enough to hear what had been said, and as he returned her look she saw something in his eyes that worried her.

Why did he look at her that way? She could not decide whether he disliked her or felt some resentment because she preferred Anton. Perhaps it was just imagination. Miguel had given her no reason to believe that he felt either desire or hatred for her.

Anton was striding away, mounting his own horse. His manner to Miguel showed that he trusted and relied on him, thought of him as a friend. Marietta was misjudging him, just as she had mistaken Anton's mood earlier, thinking he was angry when he was merely anxious.

Her fear about what would happen in the King's court had made her too sensitive. She must trust Anton and his friends, for there was nothing else she could do.

London was a sprawling and dirty city. The narrow streets were choked with filth: rotting food, excrement and dead rats lying at the side of the road. No one cleared the rubbish away, and consequently the smell in some parts of the city was foul, disease carried in the air. The houses were mostly of timber, with overhanging top storeys that made them look as if they might topple over and fall down. Some of the larger houses belonged to merchants; they had brightly painted signs that showed which guild they belonged to—the guild of shoemakers, metalworkers, cloth merchants, bakers, tailors, goldsmiths or physicians.

There was so much noise, and the roads were clogged with wagons and horses, the iron rims on the wheels clattering over cobbles. Men drove sheep to market, costers plied their wares, calling out to the people who passed by on foot or on horseback. Dogs barked and fought over the offal they found lying in gutters, and the fashionable ran to avoid the slops tossed out from bedroom windows; many held pomanders to their nostrils to block the foul odours.

When Anton's train finally came to a halt in the courtyard of an impressive house, Marietta looked about her curiously. It was far more modern than her husband's castle or her father's manor in France. There was an undercroft for the horses and servants, but the upper storeys had paned windows of dull grey glass crossed with lead.

'You must be tired,' Anton said, as he came to her. His hands clasped her waist, lifting her from the saddle effortlessly. For a moment her breath caught, for she sensed strong feeling in him, but he suppressed it ruthlessly. 'I shall send word to the King that you are here, but I do not think he will see you until tomorrow at the earliest.'

'Is this your house?' Marietta asked, looking about her.

'It belongs to my grandfather, Lord Melford. You will be safe here and may rest in peace.'

'Thank you. I am tired, but not—' She broke off as she saw Miguel staring at her. 'I must spend the night in prayer. If God has mercy, I shall be exonerated of all the accusations made against me.'

She turned away and went into the house. A woman in a grey gown and white cap came to greet her.

'My master sent word. Your chamber is ready, my lady. I dare say you would like some good hot broth after such a journey.'

Marietta thanked her. The woman seemed kind and uncritical. Perhaps she had not been told that Marietta was to face a trial for her life.

Marietta found the house welcoming and comfortable. The furniture was good solid English oak, as was the panelling on the walls of the bedchamber she was shown to. At once she noticed how much warmer the wooden house was than the damp stone walls of the older inns. Her husband's castle had always been cold, even on a summer day, but this had a comfortable feel.

The crimson velvet hangings about the tester bed matched those at the window, edged with gold braid and draped back with twisted threads of gilded rope. The floor was also of wood, and partially covered with a red and gold carpet. Marietta had always thought carpets too precious to be used on the floor, for they were costly and often used to adorn tables or hang on walls. She thought that the Melford family must be very wealthy.

She had learned something of Robert Melford's history from Claire. He had been with Henry Tudor when he took the throne of England, and his family had served the monarch since that time, rising from humble beginnings to great power and wealth.

'I will send hot water and food, my lady,' the housekeeper said, and bobbed a curtsey.

Marietta explored the room after she had gone. There was a large armoire, carved and polished, coffers and a padded stool, also a lyre and a music stand. She opened the armoire and saw gowns of costly silk lying on the shelves. They must belong to a lady of the house. Marietta touched one with reverent fingers. As the Comtesse she had owned gowns almost as fine as these, but they had been left behind. All she had was the dress she was wearing. It was travel-stained and looked creased after so many days of being constantly worn. She would ask the housekeeper if something could be done to freshen it, so that she might be presentable when she was brought before the King.

What did it matter what she looked like? A wave of despair swept over Marietta. She clutched the silver cross she wore on a chain about her throat and kissed it, then sank to her knees.

'If I have sinned, forgive me,' she whispered. 'I ask only that the truth be believed…'

Hearing a knock at the door, she called out that the servant might enter, but when it opened she turned to see that her visitor was Anton. She rose to her feet, heart pounding. She wished that he would take her in his arms, kiss her and tell her that he could not give her up—but she was dreaming again! He would not risk his King's anger for her sake.

His dark eyes went over her, his expression grave.

'I came to see that you have all you need. I hope your chamber is comfortable?'

'Yes, quite comfortable. Is this Lady Melford's chamber?'

'Once it may have been. She does not come to London these days. My grandparents stayed here often in the past, I believe, but now they allow my parents to use it. My cousins and uncle stay here too, when attending court. Uncle Harry is most often here, I believe, for he is called to attend the King several times a year.'

'Will the lady whose chamber this is mind that I am using it?'

'This is a guest chamber. It is not a family room these days.'

'I thought…the gowns in the armoire…'

'Are for you. I commissioned them before I left London to return to my uncle's house, for I knew that you had none of your own. If the King allows you to return to my cousin's home, you may take them with you.'

'They are very costly. I cannot repay you…'

'I ask for no payment, Marietta.' He moved towards her, his gaze suddenly intense, burning her with its heat. 'Forgive me for bringing you here. I should have fled to Spain and taken you with me…I could do it still…'

'You fear for my life…' Her eyes opened wide and she gasped, because she sensed his urgency. 'I thank you for the thought, sir—but I shall not allow you to put your own life at risk for my sake. If you disobeyed His Majesty he might punish you—he could punish your family too. Besides, you were right when you said that I should never be free if I did not face the King's justice.'

'Henry is just. I believe he will treat you fairly.'

'Then why do you fear for me? Do you still doubt my innocence?'

Anton stared at her, his face working with passion. 'I do not wish to think you capable of any wickedness, Marietta. However, life has taught me not to trust a woman's smile.'

She felt chilled as she saw the look in his eyes. 'I think someone has hurt you, sir. You are at times bitter…angry. All women are not faithless. My father married me to a man many years my senior. I did not love him as I might a young, passionate lover, but I tried to be a good wife. I denied him nothing he asked of me—and I nursed him faithfully when he was ill. If that makes me faithless or a witch, then so be it.'

'Marietta…I have promised I shall speak to the King in your favour, and I shall keep my word.'

'Even though you do not trust me?' Her clear eyes met his. 'Tell me, do you think I lay with you so that you would help me to evade justice?'

He hesitated, then, 'I do not know.'

'If you do not know there can be nothing more to say, my lord. If you will excuse me, I need to wash away the dust of the road—and then I should like to be alone.'

Anton stared at her, then inclined his head. 'You are angry, and justly so. I am little better than the man you ran from in terror, for I took advantage of your vulnerability. Yet I *do* care…'

She shook her head, unable to bear more of this. 'Please go now.'

Marietta was fighting to hold back her tears. How could he not understand that she loved him?

Someone had hurt him so badly that he could not love or accept love. She had fallen in love with a bright-eyed young man, eager for life and its pleasures. This man was not the man she had enshrined in her memory for so many years. He was honourable, and he would help her, but he could not love her.

Someone had robbed him of the power to love.

Chapter Seven

Anton stood staring out of the window at the long garden that ran down to the river Thames. It had begun to rain, the wind howling through the trees that fronded the river's bank. He felt as if he were being torn apart, little by little. His body ached to know the delight he had found in Marietta's arms, but still his mind would not let him accept her for what she seemed. Her beauty beguiled him, and her smile turned his insides to molten fire, but was she honest? If he trusted her, asked her to be his for ever, would she betray him?

Miguel had made it plain in little ways that *he* did not trust her. He had said nothing outright, couching his words in innuendo and suggestion rather than saying outright that he believed her a witch and a murderess.

Was Anton a fool to feel as he did about her? Despite his doubts and his caution, the scent of her haunted him. He longed to snatch her up on his horse and ride away with her, to keep her safe for the rest of her life.

Yet he knew that if he disobeyed the King in this it might mean that his whole family would be slighted and shut out—his own liberty forfeit if he ever returned to England. It was foolish to think of such wild plans. Marietta would never be safe until she had the King's pardon, and with it his protection.

'Your message has been sent.'

Anton turned as Miguel entered the parlour. He knew that his friend hoped they would be rid of the French-woman once she was taken before the King. Miguel was no coward, but he saw no point in spending lives to keep her safe. Indeed, Anton strained the loyalty of his men by asking it of them, for she was no kith or kin to any of them. Only if he offered her the protection of his name could he expect the men to give her their whole-hearted loyalty.

'You sent word to His Majesty in my name?'

'It was the reason you brought her here—or has she bewitched you?'

'Yes, perhaps she has,' Anton replied, his eyes thoughtful as he returned his friend's stern gaze. 'I have almost felt that I could find happiness with her.'

'You were betrayed once. Do not put your trust in women, Anton. If you let her rule your heart she will destroy you—as Isabella did.' Something flickered in Miguel's eyes as he spoke Anton's wife's name.

'I swore I would never love again, but this woman…'

'She uses witchcraft to bind you to her. Do not trust her, or you may rue the day you saved her life.'

'Perhaps you are right. I have been wondering…but you did what I ought to have done as soon as we reached

London.' Anton's expression softened. 'I do not know what I should have done had you not been my friend when Isabella died.'

'I shall always be your friend. You should marry again, Anton—but choose wisely, a good woman you can trust. The Frenchwoman is too beautiful. Her kind take a man's heart and bring him to his knees. You should choose a plainer, gentle lady.'

'You dislike her very much, do you not—the Comtesse?'

'I do not trust such as she. I fear her magic for your sake. After Isabella was killed I thought you might lose your mind for a time.'

'Was killed? What do you mean? She tripped and fell to her death…' Anton's eyes narrowed. 'Do you know something I do not? Have you kept something from me all this time?'

'It was a slip of the tongue, Anton. As you say, Isabella slipped and fell…' He made as if to turn away, but Anton crossed the distance between them swiftly, catching his arm.

'What do you know?' he demanded. 'You must tell me!'

'It will do no good…' Miguel faltered, and then inclined his head. 'The servants whispered that she had been pushed. I kept it from you, because it was nonsense…'

Anton's eyes narrowed. 'What else did they whisper?'

'Nothing.' Miguel's mouth tightened as the pressure on his arm increased. 'If you will have it…they thought that you had killed her in a rage when you discovered her faithlessness. Raised voices were heard by a gardener—a man and your wife's, he said. I questioned him and told him he would be dismissed if he continued to slander your name. He ran away and the whispers stopped.'

'I wish that you had told me. I should have liked to question him myself. I did not follow Isabella into the garden that day. I was too angry, too hurt—but she may have been pushed by someone else...' His eyes became flinty. 'If the gardener heard a quarrel it could have been with someone else—her lover. Perhaps he wanted her to run away with him.'

'There was no one in the garden. The man imagined it all.' Miguel's eyes slid away. 'I should not have told you. You will brood on it and the pain will send you mad.'

'No.' Anton frowned. 'I thought I had driven her to her death because I was cruel to her—but if she argued with someone, if she was pushed, it means that he and not I was responsible for her death.'

'The gardener ran off. You could not have questioned him. At the time you were in such despair. I did what I thought right.'

'I know that you acted out of concern for me, and I thank you for it,' Anton said. 'However, in future I want to know everything. I shall send to Spain when this business is over and see if the man can be found.'

'I had a search made for him. I doubt you will find him, but you must do as you see fit.'

'Yes...' Anton nodded. 'Your advice has served me well in the past, Miguel, but in this you were wrong.'

He turned back to the fireplace, taking a glass of wine from the mantle. 'I shall not rest until I have the truth…'

Anton remained staring into the fire. He did not turn as the door closed when Miguel left the room.

Marietta was ready when the summons came. She had chosen a dark blue gown, very plain, with a squared neckline and a band of gold braid beneath her breasts. It suited her well, making her look what she was—the widow of a wealthy nobleman. She had only the silver cross she had been wearing the night she was abducted, for her other jewels and possessions were still with Lady Claire. Her hair was dressed simply and allowed to fall onto her shoulders, covered only by a black French cap.

She went downstairs to find Anton waiting for her. He was dressed finer than she had ever seen him, in black and silver, a jewelled sword at his side. She made him a curtsey and he smiled.

'You look very well, lady. I am glad that you did not spurn my gift.'

'I did not wish to wear a stained gown to meet the King of England. It was thoughtful of you to provide gowns for me, sir.'

'I have done no more than was owed you. Everyone is entitled to a fair hearing—and you should wear clothes befitting your rank.' Anton's face was expressionless.

Marietta inclined her head. 'You sent for me. I am ready.'

'Then we should leave. Today you will ride pillion with me.'

'Do you think I might try to escape?'

Anton smiled briefly as he saw the flash of pride in her eyes. 'Many might in your position, but it would be useless. I shall deliver you to the court, as I must—but I have promised to speak for you, and I shall see His Majesty first.'

'I thank you for your goodness, sir.'

Anton hesitated. 'I would do more for you…' It was on the tip of his tongue to say that he wished to offer her his hand and fortune, but at the last he drew back. 'Do not fear too much. I have a little influence, and I shall use it on your behalf.'

'Thank you.' She glanced at his hand. 'I see you no longer wear my husband's ring. Did it come off easily?'

'With some effort. It is in my pocket. I shall give it to the King before he speaks to you.'

'I do not know why it is so important.'

'Perhaps that is a secret known only to your husband and the King of England.'

Marietta's eyes widened. 'My husband went often to court in France. Do you think…?'

'I think it is not for us to speculate.' Anton held out his hand. 'Come, we must leave, for if we are late the King's temper will not improve.'

'Anton of Gifford. We are glad to welcome you back to court, sir.' Henry looked at him. 'We are pleased that you have succeeded in both the commissions we gave you.'

Anton bent his head. 'I hope this is the ring you sought, Sire.'

He held it out to Henry, who took it, twisted the

gold-encased cabochon and took something from the cavity inside. He glanced at the small piece of parchment, seemed to read something, and then threw it into the fire with a grunt of satisfaction.

'You did not discover the secret, then?'

'If I had, Sire, I should not have disclosed it to anyone else—but I was unable to solve the mystery.' Anton's tone was bland, his expression unchanging, but there was a hint of something in his eyes.

Henry's gaze narrowed, an expression of anger mixed with appreciation about his mouth. 'We thank you for your loyalty, sir. There are things I would not have my ministers know concerning certain negotiations…if you understand me?'

'How should I understand, Sire? I have heard rumours that you seek an annulment of your marriage to the Queen from the Holy Father, but that is not my affair…'

'Indeed—though others seek to make it theirs. I shall not be thwarted, Gifford. In this I shall have my way— the future of England depends upon it. I need a son!' Henry had dropped the royal *we* to speak plainly.

'Yes, Sire. A King must have a son to follow him.'

'Then you understand that this business must remain within this room?'

'You have my word as a gentleman and nobleman of England.'

'Then this is done…' Henry's gaze narrowed as he slipped the ring inside his jerkin, returning to his royal stance. 'You have served us well, sir. Have you a request of us?'

'Yes, Sire.' Anton met his eyes. 'There is something I would ask of you…'

* * *

Marietta looked around the small chamber where she had been told to wait. The walls were hung with rich silk tapestries, perhaps from France, she thought, for the work was very fine. There was but one small table in the room, and a Bible lay on its surface.

Had it been placed there to comfort or to threaten? The priests threatened the pain of everlasting hell for the crimes of murder and witchcraft. Marietta wished that she might sit down. Her throat was dry, and she would have liked a cup of water or ale, but there was no one to ask. She felt like running away, but she suspected there were guards outside the door. She would not get far, and it would seem to prove her guilt. She must wait and pray.

She walked to the window to look down, and saw several ladies walking together. They were laughing and talking, clustered about one very beautiful lady who seemed to be the centre of attention. The sun had decided to shine and the rain of the previous day had gone.

How much longer was she to be kept waiting? Marietta paced the floor, her nerves as tight as the archer's string. Anton had been with the King for so long. When would it be her turn—and would His Majesty listen?

She turned in sudden fright as she heard footsteps, and her heart raced when she saw the servant. He did not smile as he beckoned to her and she feared the worst.

'Will His Majesty see me now?'

'You are to come this way, lady.'

Marietta followed him down the narrow passage. He stopped in front of a pair of large doors, which were gilded and embossed with symbols of royalty. The man pushed open the doors and indicated that she should go in, closing them behind her with a sharp bang that made her jump.

At first glance she thought that the room was empty. It was richly furnished with hangings and heavy furniture; some pieces were fashioned of walnut and carved, the legs twisted in the Dutch manner, some oak, plainer, and clearly English. Then, as she hesitated, a heavy curtain moved at the far end of the room and a man entered.

She knew at once that this must be the King of England. He was a tall, well-built man, handsome, with red hair and beard, his clothes richly embroidered with jewels. As he came nearer she was aware of his eyes on her. For a moment she met them, then she sank into a deep curtsey, her head bent.

'So you are the Comtesse Montcrief. Your husband was our good friend, *madame*. We are glad to have been of service to you. Sir Anton tells us that he snatched you from the bastard who stole your son's inheritance.'

'Yes, Sire. I owe everything to Sir Anton.'

'He has performed a service for us. In return he asks that we give you a fair hearing—which we are inclined to do. Tell me, *madame*—did you cause your husband's death?'

Marietta's head came up, her face proud. 'No, Sire. I was a good and faithful wife to the Comte, and nursed him through more than one illness. Without my nursing he would have died last winter. Why should I take his life?

He was good to me, and I had no reason to want him dead.'

'We know he appreciated your skills and your worth as a wife,' Henry said. 'There have been charges of witchcraft made against you, *madame*. Some say that you could not have saved your husband's life if you had not used the black arts—what do you say to this charge?'

'If the use of herbs and devoted care is witchcraft, Sire—I am guilty. I used nothing that cannot be readily found in the hedgerows or the woods.'

'And you did not use incantations to aid his recovery?'

'Had I known one that would save his life I would not have hesitated, but I am not a witch and I have no magic—just a little skill with herbs and healing.'

'It is as we imagined. Your husband was no fool, *madame*. He praised you in his letters to us. We thought you innocent, and that was the reason we asked Sir Anton to find you and bring you here. Your husband, the Comte of Montcrief, has done service for us in the past. Tell us how we may serve you. Sir Anton tells us the Bastard of Rouen has seized the castle and will take your son's inheritance if he can.'

'I would have justice for my son, Sire. My husband lodged his gold with the Jews, who are court goldsmiths in France. Rouen seeks to gain control of it, but it belongs to my son.'

'And it shall be secured to him if England's influence weighs with our brother of France. Your home is another matter. We do not approve of fighting amongst the barons, and to instigate a siege at Montcrief would cost many lives. However, we shall see what can be done.'

Henry held out his hand to her. Marietta curtsied once more, and kissed his ring—very like that her husband had worn, she noticed.

'You are gracious, Sire.' She hesitated. 'Am I acquitted of all charges?'

'There were none to face. We had you brought here for your safety. You may remain at court if you wish—unless you have somewhere to live?'

'My father's cousin, Lady Claire Melford, would take me.'

'The choice is yours. You are free to leave, but we would see you again in the future—and the lady you claim as cousin. The Earl of Rundle and his wife are always welcome at court.'

Marietta curtsied deeply. 'I am so grateful, Sire. I shall hope to visit the court with my kinsfolk another time.'

Henry waved a hand at her. 'Go, then. You may attend the banquet with Sir Anton this evening if you choose.'

Marietta thanked him again, curtsied, and left the chamber. Outside the door, she found Anton waiting for her. His eyes searched her face and he nodded.

'Henry has used his good sense. You are acquitted.'

'I am free to stay at court or go.'

'And you choose?'

'I shall go back to your uncle's home. My son is there, and I am anxious for his safety. Before that...' She shook her head. 'His Majesty said there was a banquet at court this evening.'

'I am to take you with me?' Anton inclined his head. 'If you wish to attend?'

'Yes, I should like that,' Marietta said, suddenly shy and unsure. 'If you would wish to take me?'

'We accede to Henry's wishes,' Anton said, his expression giving her nothing. 'He has been gracious, and it would be foolish to ignore his command.'

Marietta looked at him. 'Afterwards, you will take me to the Lady Claire and my son?'

'Of course. Why should I abandon you now?'

'I thought…I have already been a great deal of trouble to you…' Her eyes searched his face, but she could not read what was in his mind. 'You spoke once of your daughter. Do you not wish to go to her?'

'In good time. Madeline is safe with my mother for the moment. In the other matter, I have but done my duty. Henry commanded me to bring you to court. I acted in his name. You have nothing to thank me for, Comtesse.'

'My name is Marietta.'

'It would not be fitting now. His Majesty has seen fit to restore your good name. You are the Comtesse de Montcrief and must be treated as your rank deserves.'

'I see…' Marietta shot a glance at his profile as they left the palace. She sensed a barrier between them. Anton looked stern, a little pulse flicking at his temple. It was quite clear to her that nothing had changed. The King had declared her innocent because of his friendship with her husband—but that did not mean that Anton Gifford believed it. She knew that he desired her, but did he feel anything more?

She sighed inwardly. If he cared for her his reaction would surely have been very different.

* * *

Anton refrained from looking at the woman who rode her horse so proudly. He had wanted to sweep her into his arms and shout with joy when she told him she was acquitted, but his conscience had held him back.

She was innocent of murder, but he was not. His anger had driven Isabella to her death that day—at least that had always been his belief. Miguel's suggestion that she might have been pushed down those steps had set him wondering. If Isabella had been pushed, it meant that he was not directly guilty of her death. Yet there must have been a reason for her murder…

Marietta glanced round the large room. It was filled with richly dressed courtiers, light flashing from the magnificent jewels they wore about their person. She had been seated with some other ladies at a table close to the high board, where the King and his favoured nobles were seated. Anton had been so honoured, as had the striking woman Marietta had noticed in the garden earlier that morning.

She touched the arm of a young woman sitting next to her. Bertha had been friendly when they met, and she felt able to ask a question.

'Who is that lady sitting two places from the King? He seems to look at her often, and she is beautiful—her face is lit up from inside when she smiles.'

Bertha giggled. 'Do you not know that she is Anne Boleyn? She is His Majesty's favourite of the moment. Some say that he will marry her.'

'I thought he had a queen?'

'He does, but...' Bertha shook her head. 'You should not ask such questions.'

Marietta looked at the young woman sitting at the high table. She was beautiful, but also proud. Did she think that the King would put his wife aside to marry her? The church forbade such things. Marietta did not see how it could be done, though it would be easy enough for the lady to become his mistress. Perhaps she was too proud for that. But a divorce might rock the security of the English throne.

It was not for Marietta to judge what the King did. She put the thought aside and glanced round the room once more, becoming aware that she was being watched. Miguel's eyes were on her. His expression was so severe that she wondered if he hated her—yet why should he?

Had he hoped that she would be imprisoned and condemned as a witch? Was he angry because she had been released?

Marietta turned away. Course after course of rich food had been brought to table as the evening wore on. Feeling it wiser not to touch some of the richer dishes, Marietta had supped but lightly. She enjoyed the entertainment, laughing at the antics of the jugglers and the fool. He was a dwarf, and ran about the room hitting people with a pig's bladder that was tied to a stick and filled with air.

Towards the end of the evening musicians began to play, and some people got up to dance. Marietta declined one offer with a young, rather handsome gentleman, preferring to watch. In her heart she hoped that

Anton might ask her, but he was in deep conversation with His Majesty. At one point he left the hall with the King.

Marietta felt uneasy. Had he forgotten her? What ought she to do? She was not sure that she could manage to find her way back to Lord Melford's house alone. She wandered over to a window and glanced out. The view was of a secluded courtyard. In the moonlight it looked mysterious and peaceful. However, her reverie was interrupted as a young page approached her.

'You are the lady Comtesse de Montcrief?'

'Yes. Do you have a message for me?'

'Sir Anton Gifford awaits you in the courtyard, *madame*. I am to take you to him.'

'Thank you…' Marietta smiled her relief. She had been foolish to worry. Anton would not forget her. 'Please lead the way. I shall follow you.'

The page started off, and Marietta followed. She had thought he might mean the courtyard overlooked by the Great Hall, but it seemed he did not for he led her down a long dark passage which seemed to go on endlessly and take several twists and turns. Eventually they reached a door, which the page indicated.

'The courtyard is beyond, *madame*. You will find the gentleman waiting.'

As he turned away, Marietta noticed a smirk on his face. Did he imagine she was meeting a lover in secret?

She opened the door and peered through it. The night air was very cool, but the moon was full. Somehow reassured because of the light, Marietta ventured outside.

'Anton…are you here?' she asked, for although there

was a small fountain, a stone bench and what looked like beds of rose bushes and lavender, as yet not in bloom, she could see no one. The courtyard was bordered with high walls. 'Anton... I have come...' She took a few steps into the open space and then heard the door slam behind her. Suddenly fearful, she rushed to the door and tugged at the latch; it would not budge. Someone had locked it from inside. 'Open this at once!' she cried, and beat on the door with her fists. 'I am locked out here and it is cold...'

No answer came. Marietta felt an icy trickle down her spine. She was trapped, because she could see that there was no other way out of the courtyard. Someone had sent the page in Anton's name to lure her here—but why?

She shivered, feeling the cold of the night air begin to seep into her flesh. Who had trapped her here? Was it the Bastard of Rouen? A moment or two of reflection told her that had it been he she would already have been dead or his captive. Someone else had done this—but who could it be?

Marietta began to walk around the perimeter of the small courtyard, hoping that she might find a gate, or some other way of leaving it. However, there was none. Someone had planned this well, but why shut her out here? Was it merely to frighten her, or were they hoping that she would remain here all night? She shivered, crossing her arms over her breasts, hugging herself to try to keep warm. She must move about or she would not be able to bear the cold. If only she had found a servant to send for her cloak—but she had not given it a thought. Usually Anton did these things for her. He had taken care of her and she ought not to have doubted him.

Tears caught in her throat. Anton was often stern, and sometimes harsh, but he was a man of honour. Surely he would look for her when he realised that she was missing?

She went back to the door and banged on it again and again, calling out for help.

'Please help me. I am locked out…' she cried. 'Please help me…'

'I shall wish Your Majesty goodnight,' Anton said. 'The hour is late, and the Comtesse will wonder where I am.'

'Forgive us, Gifford. We have kept you too long. The lady will begin to think that you have deserted her.'

Anton bowed and left him. He was thoughtful as he returned to the Great Hall to look for Marietta. He had made up his mind that he would ask her to marry him. She needed the protection of an honourable man, and their night of passion had shown him that she would be a wonderful wife. His hesitation had been because he was afraid to trust again, but now he decided that he must take the chance. No other woman would satisfy him. He must have Marietta or no one.

Glancing round the huge hall, he saw that it was almost empty now, for people had begun to drift away after the King's departure. A brief glance told him that she was not here, but he saw Miguel talking to one of the ladies and went up to him.

'Have you seen the Comtesse?'

'Not for some time,' Miguel replied. 'Perhaps she tired of waiting and went home?'

Anton's gaze narrowed for a moment, then he shook his head. 'She would have no idea of how to get there. She would have waited for me to take her.'

'Perhaps she went to meet someone—a lover?'

'She knows no one here. You wrong her, Miguel.' Anton frowned. 'She may have wandered off looking for me and got lost. This place is a rabbit warren if you do not know it well. We must search for her. I shall question the servants. Someone must have seen where she went…'

'I can do that for you if you have more important business.'

'You can search outside the palace with some of my men.' Anton looked round. 'I shall start with that serving woman over there. She looks to be ordering the others and may have some sense…'

He left Miguel and went over to a woman dressed in a grey gown made of good cloth, who seemed to be ordering the servants as they began to clear away the debris and discarded wine cups left lying about by the courtiers.

'Good evening, madam. I need to find a lady. This is her first visit to the palace and I think she may have got lost. Can you help me to search for her?'

'Yes, sir,' the woman said. 'I will summon the pages that have not yet retired. They are always about, and see much that happens. One of them should have seen her. Can you tell me the lady's name?'

'She is Comtesse de Montcrief and she is under my protection.'

'I shall help you all I can, sir.' She beckoned to a young woman and spoke to her, then turned back to Anton. 'Bethany will take you to the room where the pages wait until they are required or given leave to go to bed. I am certain one of them will know something.'

'Thank you.' Anton took a silver coin from his jerkin. 'I am grateful for your help.'

He was frowning as he followed the younger woman. Why had Marietta left the hall? Surely she had known that he would return for her?

How long had she been here? Marietta hugged herself to keep out the chill wind. She had walked round and round the courtyard a hundred times, every now and then going to try the door and call out for help. No one had come, and she thought that perhaps this courtyard was seldom used. She might be here for a long time.

Supposing no one came tonight? Supposing no one came for days?

Fear rippled through her. She was close to tears, but crying would not help her. If the walls had not been quite so high she might have tried to climb them, but there was nothing to help her gain a foothold.

She was trapped! She might die here!

Fighting her fear, Marietta went back to the door and tugged at the latch. It moved, and the door opened. She stared at it in disbelief. Why had it not opened before? For a moment she hardly dared to go inside, fearing that someone might be waiting behind the door to pounce on her.

But she must go in or she would freeze to death! Venturing in, Marietta found that the torches which had lit their way here had guttered in their sconces on the wall and gone out. She had been locked outside for what seemed a very long time. She was shivering as she felt her way along the passage, touching the rough stone of the walls. At the end of the hall were some stairs. Had they come this way? She could not recall stairs, but she could see no other way to go.

At least now there was a window and more light. At the top of the stairs there were passages to the left and the right. She took the left. Inside it was a little warmer than outside in the courtyard, but she was still so cold that it was all she could do to stop her teeth chattering.

At the end of the passage there were more stairs, this time leading down. Marietta stood undecided, and then heard the sound of voices from below. Perhaps she could find someone who would tell her the way back to the Great Hall.

She ran down them and saw that she had come into a chamber that was full of men. They were drinking and laughing, some of them in a state of undress. As she entered they turned to stare at her and fell silent.

'I am lost,' she said. 'Can you please tell me the way to the Great Hall?'

'I can show you more than that, lady,' one of the men said in a ribald manner, and made a gesture that made Marietta recoil in horror. As he moved towards her she gave a scream of dismay and ran back the way she had come. As she fled she could hear the drunken laughter of the men. Did they think she was a whore, come in search of some sport?

She ran back along the passage, feeling close to tears. How was she ever to find her way out of this maze? Hearing voices, she stopped, her heart racing. Lights were coming towards her, but this time she was nervous of calling for help.

She stood poised for flight, though she hardly knew which way to turn. The lights were very near now, and she saw that a man and a pageboy were approaching her.

'Please…' she began, and then faltered as she saw the man's face. 'Anton—thank God. I was lost and…'

'Marietta?' he cried. 'Where on earth have you been? I have had the palace searched for you. Why did you not wait for me?'

'I was told you awaited me in a courtyard and I went to meet you. But you were not there and the door was locked behind me.'

'The door was locked behind you? How could that be?' Anton's disbelief was in his eyes. 'Was someone with you?'

'A page took me there, but left before I went into the courtyard. The door shut with a bang and I could not open it. I was trapped for a long time—and then…it was suddenly no longer locked.'

'You panicked and could not open it at first,' Anton said with a frown. 'You say a pageboy told you I had asked you to meet me—but when I spoke to the pages none knew of this…'

Marietta lifted her head, looking into his eyes. Why did he always doubt her?

'I speak the truth, sir. I was summoned to meet you, but when I got there you were not waiting for me. The courtyard had high walls and I could not leave it…' Her eyes sparked with temper. 'It was bitterly cold. Do you think that I would linger there longer than need be? The door was locked. I paced the courtyard because I was so cold, but I tried the door many times. It was always locked, and then suddenly it was not.'

Anton reached out and touched her arm. Discovering that she was icy cold to the touch, he took off his cloak and wrapped it around her shoulders.

'I sent you no message,' he said, and his eyes were narrowed, thoughtful. 'If you were trapped, as you say, someone played a silly trick on you, my lady.'

'Perhaps—though why would someone play a jest on me? I hardly know anyone at court.'

'I cannot think why anyone would do such a thing. It was a dangerous jest, for if you had remained there much longer on such a night you might have died. We must hope that you do not take harm, Comtesse.' He took her arm, his thoughts of asking her to be his wife pushed to one side in his concern. 'Come. You are shivering with cold. I must call off the search and get you home…'

Safe in her bed, with several quilts to keep her warm, Marietta fell into a deep sleep. She slept despite the disturbing dreams that caused her to cry out once or twice, and she did not wake to see the man who watched over her. She was not aware that he stretched out on a coverlet at the foot of her bed, leaving just as the first light began to creep in through the shutters.

Waking some time later, to find a maid had brought her warmed ale, hot rolls, butter and honey, Marietta was aware that she had a sore throat. She had not escaped completely unscathed from her ordeal of the previous night, and knew that if she had not been released when she had been, she might well have taken a chill that would lead to a fatal illness.

She put two spoons of the honey into her warmed ale and drank it. The drink was soothing and eased her throat, though not completely. When she tried to get out of bed she felt a little dizzy. The unpleasant feeling passed in a moment or two, and she decided that she would ignore her feeling of being unwell. She was not certain that Anton believed her story. He probably thought she had been to meet one of the courtiers in the courtyard and turned cold, for he did not seem to have a high opinion of her.

Perhaps because she had given herself to him on the journey here he thought her a whore?

Tears stung Marietta's eyes but she blinked them away. Short of confessing that she had fallen in love with him the first time they met on the Field of the Cloth of Gold, she could not explain her feelings. He would probably think it the fancy of a foolish girl. Besides, to confess her love for a man who clearly despised her would shame her. She was shamed by the wantonness she had shown as they travelled to London. Had she not genuinely believed that she was to die as the murderess of her husband, she would never have done it.

However, she could not take back what had happened. She must simply retain her dignity and hope that once Anton had returned her to her kinswoman she need never see him again.

Chapter Eight

'The Comtesse de Montcrief says that she was sent a message that was supposed to come from me,' Anton said, his eyes meeting Miguel's across the room. 'She claims that she was trapped in a courtyard with no means of escape for a long time—and then the door was suddenly unlocked.'

'The wind must have blown it,' Miguel said. 'It stuck, as doors will at times. What else could it be?'

'But who sent her the message?'

'Can you be certain anyone did?'

'You think she went to meet someone—a man?'

'I do not think anything about the lady, Anton. She is not my concern.'

'No, she is mine. I brought her here, and until she is safe with my uncle and her cousin I must care for her. Had she died it would have been a stain on my soul. I cannot bear the guilt of yet another death.'

'You blame yourself too much. Isabella fell to her

death that day. You were not there to see it, but she ought not to have been careless in her condition, for she carried your child.'

'If the child was mine…' Anton's eyes darkened. 'You know of the letter that claimed she was faithless…that her child belonged to another?'

Miguel looked at him, seeming almost wary. 'You asked the truth of her—what did she say?'

'She denied it, and ran from me in distress. You know this, Miguel. I have spoken to you of my guilt, for you are my closest friend. If I cannot confide in you, who may I confess my sins to—other than the priest?'

'You know I am always here for you.' Miguel's dark eyes were unfathomable as he looked at Anton. 'Do you believe her innocent or guilty—I speak of Isabella?'

'For a while I thought her guilty, and it tore the heart from me, but when I saw the stricken look in her eyes I thought I had misjudged her. She ran from me in such distress. I was never sure if she had deliberately thrown herself down those steep steps.'

'I am certain it was an accident.'

'Then you do not believe that she quarrelled with someone and was pushed to her death—whether by design or accident?'

'Who would she quarrel with—and why? The servants adored her. You were the only one to think ill of her—and you were not there.'

'Do you believe that, Miguel?' Anton's gaze narrowed. 'Or do you think me guilty of yet another sin?'

'Have I given you cause to think so? I told you that I had the gardener searched for. Had he been found I would have brought him to you. If someone else killed her they should be found and punished.'

'I loved her. Even though I believed she had betrayed me, I loved her. My words were cruel that day, but I could never have harmed her—do you believe me?'

'Yes, of course.' Miguel could not quite meet his eyes. He brushed a speck of dust from his black velvet jerkin. 'When do we leave for the Earl of Rundle's house?'

'Tomorrow, if the Comtesse is well enough. It will be a wonder if she has taken no harm from her ordeal. If I should discover the perpetrator of this evil trick I shall punish him, Miguel.'

'I think you should be careful how much you believe of what that lady says. She has been cleared of murder, but she is not as innocent as she would have you believe.'

'What makes you say that, Miguel?'

Miguel stared at him for a moment and then shook his head. 'I have no proof. I merely sense that she is trouble. Do not ask me why. Men have already died for her sake, and they won't be the last.'

'In that you speak truly,' Anton said. 'I have requested an escort from His Majesty when we leave the city. I expect that Rouen may try to waylay us on our return. He is unlikely to give up without a fight. He wants her, dead or alive. Mayhap I should have killed him as he slept. No matter—I shall guard her well. I do not intend to have her snatched from my care again.'

'And when we reach our destination?'

'I am not certain,' Anton said. 'There is much to consider. My duty ends when she is safe in my uncle's care, but the future is not clear. I mean to settle here in England, but I think that you may wish to return to Spain?'

Miguel looked at him oddly. 'Are you telling me that you no longer have need of my service?'

'You are my friend, Miguel. I merely suggest that it may not suit you to continue in my household if I remain in this country. I mean nothing more.'

Marietta went downstairs when she was dressed and ready. She wandered about the house, feeling restless, and finally settled in the back parlour overlooking the garden. She would have liked to go out, but her throat was still sore and she did not wish to risk making herself worse. They would soon be leaving for her kinswoman's home, and she wanted to be ready when Anton gave the word.

She was sitting lost in thought when the door opened and someone entered. Turning, she saw that it was Anton and rose uncertainly, wondering what he would say to her.

'How are you, *madame*?'

'My throat is a little sore. Otherwise I think I have taken no harm. I was fortunate.'

'Yes…' Anton's dark eyes were on her. 'Have you given much thought to the future?'

'Claire told me that I should be welcome to stay with her. I do not know what more I can expect. His Majesty promised that he would do what he could for me, but I am not sure it would be safe to return to France. Even if Rouen were no longer at the castle there might be others who coveted my son's possessions.' She hesitated, then, 'My husband told me that I should find an honest man to marry, a man who would stand guardian to my son and see that he prospers. Perhaps I shall find such a man, but I am not sure it is possible. Some will think me tarnished by scandal, no matter what the King says…'

'It is possible that you may find some still have doubts,' Anton told her and looked grave. 'That cannot be changed. I am sorry for it, Marietta, but there is little I can do.'

She raised her head proudly. 'Why should you do anything more than what you have promised? I am already too much in your debt.'

'You owe me nothing, lady.'

'I owe you my life. The King may help my son regain his fortune, but had you not come to my rescue I might be dead.'

'I do not ask for gratitude.'

'What *do* you ask of me?' Marietta held her breath, hardly daring to look at him.

'There might be something…' Anton's gaze narrowed. 'I have had it in mind for a while to offer you marriage. As your husband I should be the guardian of your son and his fortune—and I would make it my business to recover his inheritance and to protect it for him until he came of age.'

'You are asking me to marry you?' Marietta stared at him, her heart beating wildly. 'Why do you offer me marriage? You have already promised to protect my son's inheritance. I cannot expect more of you.'

'You ask me why?' Anton frowned. 'I believe we

should deal well together, Marietta. I know you are a good mother, for I have seen you with your child. I believe you might find it in your heart to offer love to my daughter. She has been too long without a mother…'

Marietta looked into his eyes. Was his concern for his daughter the only reason he wished to wed her?

'You are generous, sir…' Her heart raced, because a part of her longed to accept his offer. It was what she wanted more than anything in the world but she was uncertain of his feelings. If he could never love her she might find it too painful to be his wife. 'I am honoured that you should ask me, and grateful for your promise to help my son recover his inheritance, but…I am not worthy of such a marriage. Even though the King has pardoned me the shadow of accusation hangs over me. There will always be those who think that I am a witch and that I murdered my husband.'

'Only fools or bitter minds will think it.' Anton took her hand. 'Let me make you safe, Marietta. As your husband I can protect and care for you so much more easily than if we live apart.'

'Would it help you with your daughter if I agreed?'

'I believe you might bring a smile to her face again. She is too serious these days.'

'You must give me a little time to decide. I had not expected this, Anton.' She lifted her eyes to his face. 'You must know that I feel…kindness towards you…'

'I know that you are warm and beautiful, and it would make me happy to spend my life protecting you and our children.'

'I shall give you my answer when we reach Lady Claire's home—if that is agreeable to you?'

'Yes, of course.'

He looked disappointed, and Marietta wanted to tell him that she had changed her mind and would marry him this instant but something held her silent.

'I am content to wait for your answer.'

'Thank you. When do we leave London, sir?'

'Tomorrow morning, soon after first light—if you are well enough to begin the journey?'

'I shall be well enough. The sooner I am back with my son the better.'

'Yes, I imagine you must miss him?'

'I love him dearly.' Marietta smiled. 'He is all I have in the world.'

'Yes, I dare say he is. I believe you are a good mother, as well as a good wife.' Anton's thoughtful eyes studied her. 'Is there anything you wish to purchase in London before we leave? His Majesty gave me five hundred silver pieces for you—so that you might purchase clothes and replace those possessions you were forced to abandon in your flight.'

She stared at him in shock. 'Five hundred... That is a fortune. I cannot take so much.'

'You would not offend His Majesty by refusing his gift?'

'Oh...no...' Marietta looked anxious. 'Do you think I should accept such a gift? I have jewels I could sell.'

'You must keep them for the future, Marietta. Accept what has been given you. I am sure there must be things you would like to order? We could visit the merchants this afternoon, and anything you purchase can be sent on with goods I have ordered myself.'

Her cheeks were faintly flushed, her look oddly shy, making her, had she known it, more beautiful than ever.

'I do not think I thanked you adequately for the gowns you provided for my use. If I may keep them I need little more for the moment—though I would like a lyre. Mine was destroyed, and it is my pleasure to play and sing when I am alone.'

'Then we shall purchase a fine instrument, and anything else you see that takes your fancy. The few gowns I had prepared for you are a mere trifle.' Anton smiled oddly. 'Please do not refuse my poor gift.'

'They are beautiful. I could not have chosen better myself. If you will wait while I put on my cloak, I shall be ready in a few minutes.'

'Wear a fur muffler to keep your throat warm. I believe you will find one amongst your things. I do not wish you to catch a chill.'

'No, for then we should be forced to stay in town longer.' Marietta smiled at him. 'Excuse me, sir. I shall not keep you long.'

Her heart felt lighter as she ran up the stairs to her bedchamber. It was years since Marietta had been taken to visit the shops of merchants; her husband had always ordered anything she needed and had it delivered to the castle. To be able to choose what she wanted was a rare treat and she felt a little thrill of excitement.

She might buy some silk for embroidery, for then she need not sit idle, and material to make clothes for her son, combs for her hair, silver trinkets that would replace the others she had left behind—and of course a lyre. All of a sudden she could think of so many things she needed.

'You must be weary of shopping,' Marietta said when they returned to the house late that afternoon.

They were both carrying some parcels, though the bulk of what she had ordered would be sent on a wagon with goods Anton had ordered for himself and his family. He had taken her to all the best merchants in Spitalfields and Cheapside, encouraging her to spend recklessly. At first she had been afraid that she might spend more than she had, but Anton had laughed and said he would advise her if she became too reckless. He had said nothing more, merely watching her pleasure with a look of indulgence that made her feel almost shy.

'It was so generous of you to give up your time, for I think you must have more important matters. The Comte always ordered my things and had them sent to the castle.'

'Is it not more amusing to choose what you want?' Anton asked, arching his brows. 'You could not decide between the colours you admired easily, so how could anyone else know which you preferred?'

'I was pleased to have new gowns. I did not mind that my husband chose for me—though my father always let me choose before I was married.'

'Your father was a nobleman?'

'Baron Villiers. He was not a rich man, and lost much of what he had in unlucky investments, I believe. It was fortunate that Comte de Montcrief offered for me, or my father might have lost all.'

'So it was a marriage of convenience?'

'My father thought it a good one.' Marietta dropped her eyes. 'I believe I was fortunate.'

'The Comte treated you well?'

'He was kind to me.'

Anton nodded, looking at her thoughtfully. 'Marietta Villiers… I have sometimes wondered if we met before that day I won the silver arrow?'

'Yes, we did. I remembered you even then, because you saved my life, though you had forgotten me…' Marietta's eyes challenged him. 'It was some years ago. The day two kings met on the…'

'Field of the Cloth of Gold…' Acceptance dawned in his eyes. 'How could I have forgotten? I knew that I had seen you before, but the memory eluded me. I thought once you might be that girl, but so much had happened in the years between, and you have changed, Marietta.'

'I am older, and my waist is a little larger…' she said ruefully. 'You should not remind a lady of her age, sir. It is not gallant.'

'I meant no disrespect. You were a pretty girl then, but you have become a woman—a very beautiful, desirable woman.'

Something in Anton's eyes at that moment made her heart leap. She felt heat pool inside her, and desire trickled through her veins like molten lead. Her lips parted on a sigh. She longed for him to give her some sign that he felt the same way…to take her in his arms and kiss her. If he truly cared for her she would be so happy to be his wife!

'I…thank you,' she said a little shyly. It was on the tip of her tongue to say that she would wed him, but the words would not come.

'Marietta—' Anton began, but broke off as he heard footsteps and Miguel entered the hall. 'You should go up now, lady. We have a long journey, and I do not wish to waste time in the morning. You should see that the servants have packed all you need.'

His words were a curt dismissal that made Marietta turn away. How could he go from gallant lover to the reserved man she hardly knew so suddenly? She met Miguel's cold stare and wondered what was in his mind. He had told her that he was glad the King had pardoned her, but she was not certain he meant it.

'Yes, I would not wish to keep you waiting,' she said to Anton. 'Excuse me, gentlemen. I shall dine in my room this evening, for I wish an early night. I am tired and I would rest.'

Marietta found that she slept better than she had expected that night. In the morning she woke refreshed and ready for the journey. When she went down to the courtyard she discovered that Anton's men were assembled, also some ten others that she did not know who all wore the King's livery. His Majesty had sent the escort he promised.

Anton was engaged in conversation with the captain of the royal guard, and did not see her as she approached her palfrey. Instead, Miguel came up to her. She was reluctant, but could see nothing for it but to accept his help. He stood for a moment looking at her, his expression telling her that he was angry, and resentful about something.

'You have been fortunate, lady. Do not imagine that Anton's attentions mean more than mere courtesy. He has no love for such as you. His wife was a beautiful angel and his heart lies in her grave—where he put her.'

The words were spoken in hushed tones that only she could hear, but in a way that sent shivers down her spine.

'I do not understand you…'

'He mourns her because he killed her. He may use you as a whore, but he can never love another woman. His sin will haunt him for his whole life, as he deserves. Be warned for your own sake.'

Marietta shuddered as he took her and threw her into the saddle none too gently. For a moment she looked down at him. Miguel's intense look sent shudders through her. She had thought previously that he disliked her, but he had never spoken out like this—did he hate her or was he jealous?

Could he be jealous of Anton? Surely not? She had always thought they were the best of friends, and she was sure that Anton trusted him.

Why had he said such things to her? Marietta did not truly understand what lay beneath the warning. Was he warning her against Anton? He had claimed that Anton had killed his wife…almost accusing him of murder.

There was some mystery here. She sensed that there were things she could not know…things hidden in the past that cast a long shadow and would affect the future.

Anton was mounting himself. He glanced at Marietta

and nodded his head, then turned and smiled at Miguel. The friendship between them was plain to see. For a moment Marietta had thought she should speak to Anton, tell him what Miguel had said to her, but his smile made her change her mind. He would not believe her. He would think she had made it up.

Marietta thought she understood Miguel's outburst. His manner had always puzzled her, but now she thought she had solved the puzzle. He wanted her himself, and because she had shown her preference for Anton he had tried to turn her against him.

She could not tell Anton because he would think she was being spiteful. Besides, she did not wish to cause trouble between them. If she decided to accept Anton's offer of marriage, Miguel would have to accept it or return to Spain.

They had been riding for the best part of the day before Anton finally called a halt. He had chosen to stay at a different inn from the one they had used as they journeyed to London.

'I am trying to stay away from the high roads,' he told her as he came to help her dismount. 'If we were followed to London our enemy may be waiting for us to return the same way. At the moment we are too many for Rouen to risk falling on us in open countryside, but in woods the advantage might lie with him.'

Marietta looked at him anxiously. 'Do you think he will try to snatch me again?'

'I think he might kill you this time.' Anton's expression was grave. 'If you were dead he might try to claim guardianship of your son. He does have a claim, for he is Charles's half-brother.'

'He would kill him!' Marietta's eyes opened wider as she stared at him in horror.

'If the claim was made Henry would take the boy as his ward. He has told me that I would be appointed Charles's guardian until he came of age.'

'So the Bastard must kill us both…'

'I am sure he would wish to be avenged on me for more than one reason,' Anton told her. 'I know that the reckoning must come, but I want it to come on my terms. Once you and the child are safe with my uncle I shall seek him out and settle this thing.'

'You will risk your life again for my sake?' Marietta felt her throat tighten. 'I…do not wish you to die in my stead.'

Anton laughed softly. 'Have you not forgotten I bested him once before, lady? This time I shall kill him.'

'Can it not be settled some other way? I would not be the cause of any man's death—and I do not want you to risk your life.'

'You should not concern yourself, Marietta. These things are best left to men.'

'Yes, perhaps…' She sighed. 'I am tired and my mind sees too many terrors.'

'You need to rest. I sent ahead to secure rooms for us at the inn. Go to yours and lock your door. Open it only to someone you know, or the host's wife. I think it would be best if you supped alone again.'

'Yes, perhaps you are right.'

Marietta felt tired after so much travelling. She wanted to see her son again, to feel safe and relaxed in Lady Claire's home. Perhaps then she would be able to think clearly about the future.

Marietta turned her head as Anton brought his horse alongside hers the next day. She had hardly spoken to him since they had left the inn that morning, but she knew that he had to be alert to all the dangers they might face on the journey, and did not expect to be noticed. He had more important matters on his mind.

'We shall spend one more night on the road,' he told her. 'Tomorrow at dusk we should reach my uncle's house if we continue to make good time.'

'I shall be glad of it. I must confess that I begin to feel weary.'

'It is not to be wondered at,' Anton said, looking at her in concern. 'We have been constantly on the road since we returned to England. But I thought you would wish to be with your son as soon as it could be achieved.' He lifted his brows in enquiry.

'Yes, I long to see him. Thank you…' She met his searching gaze. 'Last evening, if I seemed to question your judgement…please forgive me.'

'It is forgiven. You know little of me, Marietta. I took you to London, where you might have met your death, and I have sometimes been harsh with you. How should you know what kind of man I am?'

'You have saved my life and pledged to help my son. Believe me, I trust you no matter what…'

'You have heard something ill of me?' Anton's eyes

darkened. 'I believe I may guess. Please accept my word that I regret sincerely what happened. If I could bring Isabella back to life—' He broke off as one of his men shouted to him. 'Excuse me. I must see what is going on; there may be a trap up ahead…'

Marietta watched him as he rode on with two of his men to investigate a small commotion. The rest of the party was told to halt, and she saw that the men had their hands on their sword-hilts lest this was a diversion to mask an attack on them. However, a shout that all was clear started the train of men moving again, and as Marietta came up to the little cluster of wagons and horses in the clearing ahead she saw that they were travelling players.

She greeted Anton with a smile as he rode back to her. 'Is all well, sir?'

'They are a band of travelling players, Marietta. I have asked them to join with us. When we stop for the night they will perform one of their miracle plays for us.'

'A play?' Marietta's laughed. 'It is a long time since I saw a play. Sometimes the players and mummers came to my father's house, but at the castle we had our own troubadours who played and sang for us. The Comte did not encourage bands of players for he thought them vagabonds.'

'Some undoubtedly are, but others are honest entertainers. You will enjoy the performance, and so will my men,' Anton said, looking more cheerful than he had when he'd left her. 'We are almost at the inn, Marietta, and then tomorrow we shall reach our journey's end.'

And then she must give him her answer, as she had promised. The only trouble was that she was still not sure he wanted her for herself and not just as a mother for his daughter.

Marietta joined some other ladies who had assembled in the inn yard to watch the players set up their scenery. Torches blazed in every corner of the yard, concentrated around the stage so that everyone could see the actors. A mood of excitement had descended, because it was not often that such a treat was offered.

Anton had set some of his men to patrol the yard so that others might watch in safety, but still the feeling was relaxed. Marietta had begun to hope that perhaps Rouen had stayed in France. Perhaps he had decided to be satisfied with what he had—though she knew that the revenues he could extract from the peasants would not long pay for his extravagances. The Bastard must get his hands on her husband's gold, or he would have to find some way of earning more for himself.

The entertainment opened with a display of tumbling, juggling and fire-eating, which brought some gasps from the watchers. Then the play began. It was the story of the adoration, telling of how the three kings and the shepherds heard the news of Christ's birth and came to worship him in a stable.

'Only one more night and then you will be safely with your cousin.'

Anton's voice made Marietta turn to him. His face was in the shadows and she could not read his expression.

'Shall you be glad, Marietta?'

'I shall be glad to rest for a while,' she said, 'and to hold my son in my arms. I have missed him, and I am anxious that he has fretted for me, even though I know he has been well cared for. I have always nursed him myself. Even when my milk dried I spent hours holding him and singing to him each day.'

'You are a loving mother—and will, I think, make a good wife to some fortunate man.' A wistful expression was in his eyes. 'I think of my daughter often.'

'You must be missing your daughter. You have left her too long for my sake.'

'She is safe with my mother, but I shall send for her as soon as we reach my uncle's. I intend to stay for a while, and I want you to meet Madeline as soon as possible.'

'Yes, I should like to meet her. I should enjoy seeing you together. You are so good with Charles. I think you are a good father.'

'You are a generous and loving woman. My daughter would be fortunate to have you as her mother—and I to have you as my wife.'

'Anton…' Her lips parted on a soft breath of need. 'I have been thinking…'

'You need not answer yet. Wait until you are with Claire and your son. Tell me your answer then…' He smiled. 'Look, the play reaches its end. Come and meet the players and tell them you enjoyed their work.'

'Yes…' Marietta smiled up at him. When he behaved like this she was certain of her answer. Indeed, she felt foolish to have doubted, for he had shown her that he was an honourable man in so many ways.

She turned her head, feeling that she was being watched. A man was standing in the shadows, staring at them. Was it Miguel? Had she been right to think he was jealous? Or was she letting her imagination run away with her?

For a moment she was tempted to tell Anton that she was disturbed by something Miguel had said to her at the start of their journey, and yet she did not want to spoil this evening. She felt happier than she had for years. There would be time to tell him another day. After all, Miguel was unlikely to do anything to harm his friend or her because of a little jealousy…

Marietta lay sleepless for a while after she retired. She could still hear noises from the inn yard, people laughing and talking. Some of them had drunk too well of their host's good ale and were celebrating noisily.

She had almost made up her mind to accept Anton's offer of marriage. Perhaps he did not love her as she loved him, but he felt passion for her. She recalled the tender way Anton had loved her that night, the exquisite feeling that had taken her to the heights of pleasure. The touch of his hand on her cheek in the yard had sent shivers running through her, making her ache with the need to lie in his arms once more.

Snuggling down in her feather bed, Marietta drifted into sleep. Something at the back of her mind was vaguely troubling her, but she could not put her thoughts into words. Perhaps it would come to her in time…

Chapter Nine

'Marietta, my dear! I am so glad to see you home again.' Claire Melford drew her into a warm embrace. 'I was devastated when they snatched you from us, and I feared for your life.' She drew back to look into Marietta's face. 'You have suffered no harm?'

'None save for a few bruises when they bundled me into the wagon and I fought them.' Her eyes were anxious as she looked at Claire. 'My son is well? Has he fretted for me?'

'He was a little miserable at first, but I have spent time with him and he seems content. I am sure that he will be glad to have you home, Marietta. Come, let us go up to the nursery. Ease your mind concerning his welfare and then we shall take some refreshment, for I am sure you are hungry and tired from the journey.'

'A little weary,' Marietta confessed. 'I am much better now that we are here.' She hesitated for a moment and then turned to Anton. 'I must thank you for bringing me here. When shall I see you again?'

'You will see me in the morning. I too have travelled much, and I do not intend to leave again for a few days at least.'

'Oh…I am pleased…' For some unaccountable reason her heart leaped. She smiled at him, then turned and followed Lady Claire from the room.

'So, do you think you've heard the last of Rouen?' Harry asked as the ladies disappeared from view. 'Did you have any trouble on the way here?'

'The King sent an escort of his own men. I think it would have been a bold man who attacked us. We were too strong a force, and to attack men wearing the King's livery would be treason. If the rogues were taken alive the punishment would be harsh for such crimes.'

'Yes, I know it.' Harry looked thoughtful. 'So you think the Bastard is waiting his time?'

'What would you do in his place?'

'Wait my chance to strike. You were expecting him to move against you. He will seek to take you by surprise.'

'I have ordered my men to patrol outside the estate. I do not think they will try to storm the house, for that would bring the King's wrath on them—but they will try to snatch her again if they can.'

'So what do you plan?'

'He will not expect me to go looking for him. I shall send out scouting parties. If we discover they have a camp nearby, we shall make a surprise attack. The Bastard of Rouen is a vindictive man and a bad enemy. This will not be settled until he is dead.'

'Henry does not approve of the Barons fighting amongst themselves. If you seek Rouen out you risk the King's displeasure.'

'I know Henry would have us all live in peace with one another. His father called a halt to the old way of settling quarrels, and he has followed—but there are times when only blood will settle an affair such as this.'

The Earl nodded. 'I know you speak truly, Anton, but I would still advise you to tread carefully.'

'I thank you for your good advice, but I must do what is necessary to keep her and the child safe.'

'Yes, I see you must.' Harry smiled oddly. 'You know you may call on me for anything you need?'

'Yes, indeed,' Anton smiled at him. 'You are my mother's brother, sir, and she has told me that I may always count on you.'

'Catherine and I were close when we were young, as twins often are,' Harry said. 'I think of her and enjoy her letters, though we do not meet as often as I should wish.'

'Perhaps you will do so soon.' Anton lifted his gaze. 'For I hope that you will attend my wedding?'

'You are to marry?' Harry's gaze was thoughtful. 'Ah, yes, I see—have you spoken to the lady?'

'This business with the Bastard must be settled first—and there is something else I need to sort out. I am expecting news from Spain, though it may not arrive in time…'

'If you have a problem you may share it with me, Anton.'

'My problem is that I am not certain. Something hovers at the back of my mind, but I am not sure enough to speak of it…'

Marietta spent an hour sitting by her son's cradle. He was sleeping peacefully, his fist curled against his mouth, his skin pink and warm. Her heart wrenched with love. The worst part of her ordeal had been the fear that something might happen to her beloved child, but here he was, safe and sound, and now she could begin to put the terror behind her.

She could not help wondering if the Bastard of Rouen was still out there, perhaps hiding in the thick woods that bordered the estate on three sides. On the fourth side were open meadows, where sheep grazed and a river wound its way lazily through the lush valley. The Earl of Rundle's home was a stout building, more comfortable and warmer than the castle where she had lived with her husband. She thought that she could live happily in a house like this, but she was not certain where her future lay.

Lady Claire had said that she might make her home with her, but Marietta knew that she ought to marry if she could—a good man who would help her son to grow strong and learn all the things he should know. Charles had scarcely known his father. She had a duty to provide him with another—a man who would care for him as if he were his own. However, she was not sure that she was worthy to accept Anton's offer of marriage. And could she truly be content to be married to a man she loved so desperately, yet who had never shown that sort of love to her?

Sighing, she left the child to the care of a servant and went to her own chamber. Rosalind greeted her with glad cries, embracing her warmly.

'We feared for you, my lady.'

'I think I should have died had Sir Anton not come for me. The Bastard would have forced me to wed him, and I would have cut my wrists rather than lie with him.'

'Sir Anton is a good man. You should think of wedding *him*, my lady.'

Marietta looked at her for a moment, then smiled. 'He has made me an offer, Rosalind, but I am not sure why he wants to marry me. My future is still uncertain, and I fear that he may only have asked because he is a man bound by honour, not by love.'

'I have seen the way he looks at you. Besides, Sandro told me he was like a madman when he first discovered that you had been abducted. I do not believe that he is indifferent. You should give him some encouragement, my lady. He would make you a fine husband.'

'Perhaps…' Marietta felt warmth spreading through her like molten treacle, thick and comforting. To be Anton's wife would be more happiness than she could ever expect. 'You must not speak of this to anyone else, for I would not have him feel obliged to wed me for honour's sake.'

'I would not breathe a word, my lady.' The serving woman grinned at her. 'But he is a fine man, and would not leave you to lie lonely in your bed at night…'

'Nor should I wish him to,' Marietta replied, and gurgled with laughter. 'I admit it would pleasure me to wed him—but not unless he truly wishes it…'

* * *

Anton was in the hall when Marietta came down the stairs. She was wearing a gown of green silk that clung to her slender waist, flaring out at the hem. Around her waist she had a girdle of silver threads, and a plain silver cross hung from a ribbon at her throat.

She wore her simple clothes with such style that she might have been a queen. Her hair had been left loose, and fell upon her shoulders in rich red-gold waves; her eyes were more green than blue. For a moment his breath caught in his throat, and he could scarce breathe for the racing of his heart. She was so beautiful! Magnificent. Beside her, Isabella would have seemed pale and slight.

How had he ever forgotten such a woman? Anton knew that the memory of the child he had pulled from beneath the flailing hooves of a frightened horse had remained at the back of his mind—but he had never dreamed she would grow up to be a woman like this...

Hearing an indrawn gasp behind him, Anton turned, surprising a look on Miguel's face that shocked him. He realised that Miguel was jealous—but why? Was he jealous of Anton because he wanted Marietta, or jealous of Marietta because he thought she would come between them? There had been a special relationship between the two of them since Isabella's death.

Anton waited as his friend came up to him.

'What are your plans now?' Miguel asked. 'I have been thinking that I may return to Spain in a month or two...'

'If it is your wish,' Anton said. 'I shall be sorry to lose you, though I knew you might wish to return to your home in time. We have been good friends, Miguel.'

'It may be for the best if I go. I should only remind you of things you wish to forget.' Miguel's eyes looked through him. 'I will stay until you have settled with the Bastard of Rouen if you wish it.'

'I shall need all my men for that,' Anton replied, feeling puzzled by his manner. 'Please, accept the hospitality of my uncle's home and enjoy yourself this evening. We have all earned a rest.'

Inclining his head to Miguel, he walked to greet Marietta as she stood at the bottom of the stairs, hesitating a moment. Her eyes seemed to question him and he made her an elegant bow.

'You are beautiful, lady. That gown becomes you.'

'It is one that you chose for me. I believe the style is flattering to me.'

'You look like a queen.' Anton offered her his hand. 'Your son does well?'

'He has been cared for with all love and attention. He was sleeping, and I dare say he has hardly missed me at all.'

'I do not believe that for a moment. Any man would miss you, Marietta. I think that most must love you from the moment they see you.'

'I do not wish for the love of just any man.' Her eyes met his steadily.

Anton inclined his head. 'The man you love will be fortunate indeed.'

Marietta waited, hoping for more, but then Sir Harry came up to them and Claire beckoned. She excused herself and went to her kinswoman.

'I have had a letter from Lady Melissa Melford,'

Claire told her. 'She is Anton's grandmother. Melissa has heard about you, my love, and she wishes to meet you. My husband's mother suffered a great deal at the hands of her uncle before she was wed. When she learned your story she wanted to know if there was anything she could do to help you.'

'We stayed at Lord Melford's house in London,' Marietta said. 'I should very much like to meet her.'

'She knows that you are our guest, and I believe she may make the journey. Lord Melford is well enough at the moment, though he does not go far from home these days. He will not accompany her, but she may come and bring Catherine with her, and Anton's daughter at his request. Lady Catherine is Anton's mother, of course, and my husband's twin. I believe you met their younger sister, Anne de Montfort, in France?' Claire laughed softly as Marietta nodded. 'I dare say that most of the family will choose to visit us soon for Annabel's wedding—though perhaps not the de Montforts. I shall enjoy seeing all my family under my roof for once.'

'You will have much work to do. Perhaps you will allow me to help you prepare.'

'I dare say you would like to be busy.' Claire nodded and looked thoughtful. 'Once you have had the running of a large house idleness hath little to recommend it. We shall oversee the preparations together, but you must have time for leisure. You will wish to spend a little time with Anton before he leaves us.'

'Has he spoken of leaving?' Marietta's gaze flew to her.

'I believe he means to stay a few days, or perhaps

longer. I am not certain. I shall prevail on him to tarry, at least until his parents are with us. However, his visits are not usually of long duration. I know that it is his intention to look for land that would provide him with a good estate—and to employ builders to construct him a sound dwelling.'

'You believe he wishes to settle near here?'

'He likes the area well, I think. I understand Harry has been making enquiries concerning a manor that may come for sale after the death of its lord. It would be pleasant if he were to settle within a few hours' distance of Rundle Park, would it not?'

'Yes…' Marietta was watching Anton as he laughed with his uncle Harry and some of the other men. 'Very pleasant. You would often have his company, for you might dine with each other.'

'Yes, and I should also have the company of his wife.'

Marietta glanced at her. Claire was smiling at her in such an odd way. Could she have guessed that Anton had asked her to be his wife?

Marietta retired soon after supper that night. She was tired from the journey, and wished to rest, but she was feeling content and drifted into sleep moments after her head touched the pillow.

In the morning she woke feeling refreshed and ready to face the day. As soon as she was dressed in a sensible gown she paid a visit to the nursery. Her son shouted and cried when he saw her, but once she had played with him and given him some sweetmeats he quieted and sat on her lap, snuggling up to her contentedly.

It was as she was nursing him that she heard someone enter the room, and turned her head to look. Anton was standing just inside the door, looking at her.

'You both look happy,' he said. 'It is clear that your son knows his mother is home.'

'He cried when he saw me, but he has settled now. I have never left him for more than a day before. I believe he thought I had abandoned him.'

'You would never do that in this life.' He smiled at her. 'I shall leave you, for I must speak with my uncle. We shall meet later.'

'Yes, of course.'

Anton went away. Marietta nursed her son for a while longer, then he grew restless and clamoured to be put down.

Marietta left him playing with a wooden horse that the Earl had commissioned for him, and went down to Claire's stillroom. They were to take stock of what stores were available, so that the Earl could send to Shrewsbury for anything they needed.

After an inventory was made, a list of ingredients was written out, and the ladies began a tour of the house, making notes on what needed to be done. Servants were set to cleaning, and the linen was checked so that it could be washed and beds made up with fresh-smelling sheets in the guest chambers.

In a castle only the most honoured guests and ladies were given chambers of their own. Men of the lower ranks slept in the Great Hall, or in little cells that were only big enough to hold a truckle bed that was stored away during the day. It had been the custom in Medieval times, and persisted even now in older houses. Only the more modern houses had separate chambers, and many of those led into each other, which could be inconvenient.

It was not until after they had stopped for refreshment at noon that Lady Claire declared herself satisfied for one day. She went to her chamber to attend to some private business, and Marietta was left to herself.

She was staring out at the gardens when she heard something behind her, and turned to see Anton enter the room.

'Oh…' She smoothed her gown. 'You have found me in all my dirt, sir. We have been working all the morning and I should change…'

As she turned to leave Anton caught her wrist. She glanced back at him and her heart raced.

'We have scarce had a moment alone,' he said. 'You look charming to me, Marietta. Do not leave so soon.'

'If you wish me to stay, I shall.'

'Please sit down. I have something to say to you.'

Marietta sat in a chair with wooden arms and looked at him.

'I have tried to be patient, but now I wish to speak to you. You said you would give me your answer when we reached my uncle's house, but first I must tell you something you should know. Because I believe you may have been told something, but perhaps not quite the truth.'

'Very well. I am listening.'

'You know that I was married to a Spanish lady I cared for?'

'Yes, I know that, sir. You have spoken of your wife.'

'She was lovely…very different from you. Isabella had black hair and pale skin and she was gentle. I thought her an innocent…an innocent angel.'

'You loved her very much?'

'I believed so at the start, and I thought she loved me. I was content with my life. Our daughter was born and all seemed well. Then one day Isabella told me she was to have another child, and I thought my happiness was complete…' Anton's eyes darkened, became hard as black diamonds. 'Isabella did not carry the second child easily. She was ill and troubled, often complaining, and unwilling to be near me. I thought her manner was simply because she felt ill, and then…then a letter came to my hand. It was unsigned, and I tried to dismiss it as lies from the pen of a coward. The writer said that my wife had betrayed me with another man—that the child was his, not mine.'

Marietta started up. 'How shocking and hurtful that must have been. I am so sorry…'

'I was devastated. I felt that my life was shattered, my trust betrayed. I tried hard to ignore it, telling myself that only a coward would send an unsigned letter—that what it contained must be lies.' Anton turned away from her, his back stiff with tension. 'In the end I could not bear it any longer. In a jealous rage I accused her of betraying me. I asked her if the child was mine…'

'What did she say?' Marietta caught her breath as he turned and she saw the agony in his eyes. It was costing him much to tell her this story.

'Isabella denied the accusation. She looked stunned, hurt…afraid…' A nerve flicked in Anton's cheek. 'I was terrible in my anger. She ran from me in tears and fear—and in the sunken gardens she fell down some steep stone steps and hit her head. She died, and the child died with her. I knew I was being punished for my outburst.'

'Anton!' Marietta stood up, looking at him with a mixture of horror and sympathy. 'How terrible! You must have felt so guilty—as if you had killed her and the babe…'

'Yes. I see you understand me.' Anton ran restless fingers through his hair. 'Some months have passed now since her death, but at first I could not forgive myself for what I had done. I hardly knew how to live. I think I might have taken my life if it had not been for a friend. He was my comforter—the only one who understood what I suffered…'

'You are speaking of Miguel?'

'Yes…' Anton sighed. 'We were as brothers—or so I believed.'

'You have doubts now concerning his loyalty?'

Anton's eyes sought hers. 'Do you wish me to speak plainly?'

'I think it best.'

'I have asked you to wed me. You know that there is something between us? You have felt it, as I have?'

'Yes, I feel it.'

'I saw Miguel's face when you came down last night. I believe he is jealous, but I do not know why—whether it is because he wants you, or because he believes you will destroy the friendship we have had these past months.'

'Why should I come between you and your friend?'

'I do not know. I saw jealousy in his face as he looked at you—it may be that he wants you for himself.'

'Yes, perhaps…there is something…'

'You have sensed it yourself?'

'I know there is something, but I do not know if he desires me or hates me.'

'He gasped when he saw you, and the look on his face shocked me.' Anton shook his head. 'I shall not allow Miguel's wishes to distract me. I must ask you for my answer now. Will you be my wife, Marietta? I do most sincerely wish it, if it will please you.'

'Marry you…' Marietta caught her breath, and then she was smiling, her doubts fading as she saw the look in his eyes. 'Yes, I will marry you, Anton. I should be honoured—if it truly pleases *you*?'

'Marriage to you would please me well,' Anton said. He stood up and offered her his hand, bringing her to her feet. 'However, we must be careful. I am not sure how Miguel will react to the news—and we still have to face the possibility that Rouen will come after you again. Miguel speaks of returning to Spain after we have dealt with the Bastard. I think that perhaps we should keep this agreement private for the moment.' He gazed down at her. 'I wanted to settle this between us. You know it is possible that I may be killed…'

'I beg you not to say it! I do not think that I could bear it…' Marietta caught back the words that would betray her heart. He had still not told her that he loved her. Only that he had cared for his wife and been dev-astated by her death. Perhaps he sought a marriage with a woman who had been married before, a woman who was well versed in the needs of a man, both in his bed and his home. She knew he needed a mother for his daughter. 'I would have you live and be my husband, sir.'

'It is my true wish,' Anton told her. 'Now, I must tell you something more. I have had word that there may be soldiers in the west woods, and I suspect they are the Bastard's men. I am taking a party to search them out…'

Marietta's nails curled into her palm, but she did not beg him to stay. It grieved her that he must leave so soon, but she knew that the future depended on what happened now.

'Take care, Anton. I shall pray for you.'

'Think of the future. It is what sustains me…' Anton moved closer. He reached out and drew her into his arms, looking down at her for a moment before he bent his head to claim her lips. His kiss was soft, tender, deepening as he clasped her hard against him. For a moment the hunger and need was in his eyes as he looked at her. 'Forgive me. I do not wish to leave you— but I must…'

'God go with you…'

Marietta released him as he tore himself from her arms and walked away. She blinked as she felt the sting of tears. She loved him, and if they both lived she would wed him, but she was still not certain of her place in his heart.

Marietta spent some time playing with her son. When she went down to join the others for supper in the Great Hall it was almost dusk. She asked Claire if the men had returned from their search but she shook her head.

'We have heard nothing,' she said. 'Harry went with them, because he said that if the rogues were on his land he wanted to deal with them. I thought they would have returned before this, for they cannot search in the dark—' She broke off as there was a commotion in the hall and then Sir Harry came striding in. He had blood on his clothes and Claire gave a scream of fright, running to him, his name on her lips.

'Stop,' Harry commanded. 'The blood is not mine, but Anton's. He has been wounded in the side and has lost much blood. I came on ahead to warn you. The men are carrying him home...'

'Anton is wounded?' Marietta approached hesitantly, her face deathly white. 'How did it happen? He is such a skilled warrior...'

'They came upon us suddenly, about thirty of them out of the trees. We held our own easily and drove them off. The Bastard of Rouen was killed by Anton's own hand, but somehow in the melee he was wounded.' Harry frowned. 'From the angle of the wound I think a sword was thrust into his side from behind. I doubt he knew his enemy was there. When all is confusion these things sometimes happen, but it is a cowardly way to strike a man—from behind, when he is fighting another.'

Marietta hardly heard his last words for they were bringing Anton. He was being carried on a gate taken hurriedly from its hinges, and his garments were soaked in blood.

Holding back the feeling of terror that swept over her, Marietta hurried to her chamber. She had healing herbs that would be needed, and she would use all she knew to save him—because if he died she did not care what became of her.

When she went to Anton's chamber, Claire was already there. Anton was naked, for they had stripped away the bloodied raiment and the servants had brought water to wash the wound.

'Let me help,' Marietta said, and went to Claire's side. She took the cloth and soaked it in the bowl, wringing out the bloody water and bathing the area around the wound. 'The cut is deep, but I do not think it had penetrated a vital organ. See—the flesh does not open far. If we cleanse the wound and apply salves it will heal…'

'Yes, that is what I thought,' Claire agreed. 'But wounds like this can turn bad so quickly, Marietta. Perhaps we should use the iron on him? The danger will come if the pus turns green.'

'Sometimes the iron can do more harm than good with a fresh wound like this. I could sew the flesh together with silk thread. And I have some herbs that may help. I need to make an infusion to pack the wound. Have I permission to use your stillroom—and to apply the poultice?'

'Do you understand what you do?' Claire's eyes were upon her. 'If he should die…'

'I care little what becomes of me if Anton dies. Please let me try, Claire. He will suffer so if you cauterise his wound, and I think my way will work better in this case, for there is no putrefaction to burn away.'

Claire looked at her oddly for a moment, then inclined her head. 'I know your heart is good, Marietta. Fetch all that you need, and I will send the servants out of the room when you are ready.'

Marietta thanked her and hurried away to the still-room. She soaked the herbs in water that had been boiled, for it was often contaminated, then strained them into a vessel. The mulch would be packed around the wound after she had sewn Anton's flesh together, and the infusion drunk a little at a time.

Returning to the chamber where Anton lay, his eyes closed, she found Claire alone.

'I sent the servants to boil more water and heat the cauterising iron,' she said. 'It is best if they do not see what you do, Marietta, for it would be thought strange—and servants talk. I would not have your goodness taken as something different.'

Marietta nodded. Her skill with healing was at times controversial, and had been learned from various sources, but mostly it came from within. Her instincts were strong in this case.

The wound had been bleeding again. She took a clean cloth and wiped the skin dry, then threaded her needle with white silk. She gathered the open wound, pulling it so that the gap closed, and then pushed her needle through the flesh, pulling the thread behind. Claire made a gasping sound but said nothing, holding the candle nearer so that Marietta could see to work. It took several minutes to complete the seam. Satisfied that only a dribble of blood was seeping through, Marietta packed the mulch of herbs over the wound and laid a patch of clean linen on it. Then she and Claire wound the bandage about him, letting him back gently on the pillows when it was done.

He had cried out a few times as Marietta did her work, but now he merely lay still, his eyes closed, beads of sweat on his brow.

Claire went to the door and took the iron from a servant, sending the girl running to fetch more clean linen. She brought the red-hot poker back and laid it in the grate, then stood looking down at Anton.

'He does not suffer as he would had we used the iron.'

'I once spoke to an Arab doctor. He told me that he had seen cases where the iron killed rather than saved life. It was his belief that stitching was the best way if the wound was clean, and he showed me how to infuse the herbs to guard against infection.'

'Was this when you were at the castle?'

'Before—at my father's house. My father believed in herbs and medicines. As a young man he studied to be a physician, but when his father died he had to take over the ordering of the manor. I think he made a better physician than a baron, for he liked nothing better than studying—and he taught me much of what I know.'

'So it is not witchcraft but the study of medicine?'

'I am not a witch, Claire. If I were a man the methods I use would cause no raised eyebrows. 'Tis because I am a woman, and women should not know these things. Apothecaries have always been men, as have doctors. They are jealous of their privileges and will not share them. My father was frowned on because he accepted new ideas and was friendly with men of Arabia, for they are often not trusted—perhaps because they push the limits of known medicine and dismiss old methods as crude and useless.'

Claire's gaze rested on Anton. 'Will he take a fever?'

'It is possible, indeed likely. He must be made to drink the infusion, though it is bitter and he will fight us—at least until he comes through the worst.'

'Supposing the wound turns putrid?'

'If it does we shall pack it with maggots so that they eat the infection.'

'No!' Claire looked at her in horror. 'That is horrible. How could you think of it?'

'I saw my father use the method on a lad whose arm was badly infected, and his wound healed when everyone thought he would die.' Marietta met her questioning look. 'I shall do whatever is necessary. Anton saved my life more than once—do you think that I would let him die from neglect?'

'I know you love him.' Claire said. 'I will help you to nurse him. But please do not ask me to touch maggots!' She pulled a face of disgust and shuddered. 'I cannot abide the creatures.'

'Have you never fished with them?' Marietta smiled. 'That is another thing my father taught me—to fish with a pole, thin string and a bent pin.'

'It is no wonder you are different from other women. Your father was unwise to teach you so much, Marietta. Did your mother not object?'

'She died too soon. My father had no son. I became his friend, son, and chatelaine of his home. We were happy until he lost all his money—and then I had to marry to save him from the debtors' prison. I did not wish to marry a man so much older than myself, but I obeyed my father so that he might live out his days in comfort.'

Claire nodded. 'I shall leave you to sit with Anton for a while. If you need me, call me. I shall take your place while you sleep.'

'I shall not leave him until I know he will live. I may sleep at the foot of his bed until then.'

'It is hardly proper…' Claire began, and then shook her head. 'You know best. Call me if you need me…'

Marietta waited until the door had closed behind her, then brought a chair close to the bed and sat in it, so that she could watch over her patient. There was no point in Claire taking her place, for if she went to bed she would not sleep a wink.

Anton's fever started in the early hours of the morning. Marietta had been half dozing in the chair when the cry woke her.

'Isabella! Forgive me. I beg you to forgive me. Come back to me. Please come back to me…'

Marietta fetched a cool cloth and went to stand over him. She washed his face and his shoulders, then his arms. His hair was damp with sweat. Smoothing it back from his forehead, she bent to kiss him.

'It is all right, my love. I am here. Isabella is with you. She forgives you. I forgive you…' She stroked his head with her hand. 'My death was not your fault. You must forgive me for hurting you. I did not mean to hurt you. Isabella did not mean to hurt you. Do not grieve for her.'

Anton's eyelids fluttered. For a brief moment his eyes opened and he seemed to look at her, then he closed them again, sighing and settling.

Marietta felt the ache about her heart intensify. He had loved his first wife so much. She could not expect that he would ever feel as much for her. He would wed her, and she would make what she could of her life, but she must not expect too much.

Anton's fever lasted two days, but he was a strong man, and though he gagged on the bitter medicine Marietta spooned into his mouth he swallowed it. On the third morning, he opened his eyes and looked at her.

'Have you been here long?'

'Since they brought you home.'

'You should sleep. I shall do well enough now.'

'Your wound is healing fast and should not take harm. The fever lasted but two days. I believe all will be well with you, sir.'

Anton sighed, his eyes closing. 'Thank you…'

Seeing that he had slipped into a peaceful slumber, Marietta sent for Claire and told her that their patient was through the worst.

'His wound appears healthy. It seems he has been fortunate.'

'More fortunate than anyone guesses, I dare say.' Claire smiled at her. 'He owes his life to you, Marietta.'

'It was the will of God,' Marietta said. 'Please do not give me the credit. I but nursed him as any woman would.'

'You should rest now. Lady Melissa Melford will be here this evening, and Lady Gifford, Countess of Malchester, may be here even sooner. I shall tell them that you nursed Anton, but nothing more.'

Marietta smiled, and left her to watch over Anton for a while. Now that she was sure he would not die of a fever she was prepared to leave him in Claire's capable hands. His wound might yet become infected, but she would watch, and pray that he took no harm.

When Marietta returned to Anton's bedchamber she saw that another woman had taken Claire's place. She was of a similar age to Claire, and beautiful, but when she looked at Marietta there was a flicker of hostility in her eyes.

'Who are you to enter my son's bedchamber without so much as a by your leave?'

'Forgive me. I have been nursing Sir Anton. I did not know you were here, my lady.'

'You are the Comtesse Montcrief?' Catherine Gifford's eyes held the glitter of anger. 'He was wounded in a battle to protect you, I think?'

'Yes, I fear that is so. I am sorry for it, but nothing would sway him. He would go to search for Rouen. He said that we should never be at peace until my enemy was dead.'

'Indeed?' Catherine's brows rose. 'What are you to my son, *madame*? I know only what Lady Claire has told me.'

'I am someone who hath reason to be grateful to Anton of Gifford. He has saved my life more than once. I believe that I have in part repaid my debt. Anything more must come from your son, *madame*.'

'Is there more? You are a widow, and stood accused of your husband's murder—is that not so?'

'Yes, it was so. I was unjustly accused, for I did nothing to harm my husband and nursed him through illness many times—but someone hated me and craved what rightly belongs to my son.'

'I thank you for your care of Anton. However, I am here now, and I shall nurse him myself.'

'That is your privilege, my lady,' Marietta said, and smiled. 'I hope you will continue to use the herbs and infusions I have prepared, for they have seen him through the fever but he still needs them.'

'My mother will be here soon. She is skilled in the use of herbs. I shall ask her advice on this matter.'

Marietta inclined her head. Lady Catherine was hostile to her. She might try to influence her son to turn away from the marriage he had proposed. Marietta would not hold him to his promise if he told her that he had changed his mind.

Would the stigma of murder and witchcraft hang over her all her life?

Marietta was close to tears as she went to her bedchamber. She would begin to make clothes for her son with the cloth she had purchased in London.

Perhaps it was just as well that Anton had told no one that they planned to marry.

Marietta had been at her stitching for three hours when someone knocked at the door. She called out that they might enter, looking up in surprise as a woman she had never seen before came in.

This woman was older, but had a gentle beauty, her once flame-red hair lightly streaked with white, though her face had few lines.

'Madame la Comtesse Montcrief?'

Marietta got to her feet and curtsied, for she knew at once who the lady must be. 'Lady Melford, forgive me. I thought when you knocked it must be a servant come to call me. Had you summoned me, I would have come to you.'

'I have come to thank you for your excellent care of my grandson, *madame*—or may I perhaps call you by your name?'

'I am Marietta, my lady. I did only what was necessary, just simple nursing.'

'You do not need to pretend with me,' Melissa, Lady Melford, said, and smiled. 'I saw your work. It was excellent, my dear, and I believe his wound will heal well now. The herbs you used are much the same as I would have chosen—as I told my daughter. Catherine was distressed. If she was a little harsh to you, please forgive her.'

'She had the right to question me, my lady.'

'She loves her son dearly. I am sorry if you felt slighted. You are of course welcome to return to Anton's chamber whenever you wish.'

'Perhaps it would be best if I left him to his mother and you. I am merely a dependant, living on Lady Claire's bounty.'

'I think that is not quite the case. My grandson asked for you twice. You will oblige me if you will visit him, for unless you do I fear he may try to leave his bed too soon.'

'Oh…the foolish man…' Marietta blushed. 'It is always so. Men are the worst patients. They will never be sensible.'

'I have often found it so,' Lady Melissa replied, and laughed. 'As soon as they feel a little better there is no bearing with them. So you will visit him soon?'

'I shall go immediately. I thank you for coming to me.'

'It was my duty and my pleasure. I have not lived this long without knowing the signs of a man in love.'

'Oh…' Marietta blushed. 'I am not sure… He feels a kindness towards me, I know, but—' She broke off as she saw the amusement in Lady Melissa's face. 'Do you truly think?'

'I know my grandson, even though I have not seen him for some years. He has not changed much: impatient, a little arrogant, quick to temper and sometimes he sulks. At those times he looks grim and will not speak for hours on end.'

'You *do* know him!' Marietta gave a little chuckle.

'I should, for I have been married to a man of the same temperament for some years.' She nodded to Marietta. 'You must go to Anton now, but one day, when you have leisure, I shall tell you my story. I think you may understand a little better then.'

Marietta thanked her and hurried away. She was feeling confused and uncertain, for Anton had cried so pitifully for Isabella in his fever. He must have loved her dearly, but perhaps it was possible to love again?

When she entered the bedchamber, Anton was lying with his eyes closed. He opened them as she approached the bed, giving her a look of reproach.

'Why have you abandoned me?'

'You were better, and your mother and grandmother are here. You no longer need me.'

'Perhaps I do not need your nursing, but I shall always need you.'

Marietta looked down at him, her heart racing. 'I have not told anyone of our…arrangement. If your family do not approve…'

'They may go to the devil,' Anton said, and gripped her wrist. 'I want you for my wife. You have promised me and I shall not let you break your word.'

'I do not wish it. I merely offered for your sake.'

'Then rest easy. I am not a man who changes his mind lightly.'

'I did not think it, but I should not wish to cause a breach…' Marietta smiled as his grip tightened about her wrist. 'Very well, it is settled—now, tell me how you came to be wounded like that. It looks as if you were struck from behind.'

'Have you seen Miguel since the day I was wounded?'

'No…' Marietta stared at him. 'Was it he that wounded you? But he is your friend…'

'He was once my friend,' Anton corrected. 'I do not know it all, but I believe he blames me for Isabella's death.'

'Yes, he said something that seemed to indicate you were at fault as we journeyed here.'

'You did not see fit to tell me?'

'He was your friend. Besides, I thought it was merely a little jealousy. I did not want to sound spiteful, because you were so fond of him and I never thought he would harm you. He seemed to dislike me—but you were his friend.'

'Damn him!' Anton's eyes darkened. 'He waited his chance and this was his way of murdering me. Miguel knows that he could never best me in fair fight, so he struck me from behind as I fought the men who sprang on us from the trees. I killed your first enemy—he will trouble you no more—but I fear we both have another.'

'Was he…was Miguel Isabella's lover?' She saw a flash of pain in Anton's eyes. 'Forgive me. I should not have asked.'

'You have the right to ask what you will of me. I had no suspicion of it until very recently, but I believe you may be right. Miguel has deceived me all this time. It was only when I saw the look on his face that I began to suspect him of something, but even then I did not realise how much he hated. He cried out that it was for Isabella as he thrust his sword into me. I may discover the whole truth, perhaps, when my enquiries in Spain are done. I suspect that someone witnessed what happened the day she died. If the gardener can be persuaded to speak we may have the answer at last.'

'I am sorry Miguel did this to you—not just the wound from behind, which was a coward's way, but all the rest.'

'Isabella's death has played on my mind for a long time.' Anton's gaze narrowed. 'In my fever it seemed to me that she was with me—that she forgave me.'

'I am certain she would if she could. Besides, if she had a lover, she should have begged for *your* forgiveness.'

'Perhaps. However, her father wanted our marriage. I may have pushed too hard. If Isabella obeyed her father while her heart was given to another…' Anton sighed. 'Miguel has little fortune, and no hope of a title. I shall be a marquis one day—a long time into the future, I hope, but it is so. My father holds the titles of earl and marquis…'

'You think that Isabella was obliged to obey her father…as I was?' Marietta looked thoughtful. 'She should have refused, or if she chose to obey remained faithful to her husband…but that is not for me to say. I never knew her.'

'She was not like you. I do not think she would have dared to defy her father.'

'Then I am sorry for her. It is not easy to marry where there is no love.'

'There was love on my side—at least at first.' Anton frowned, holding Marietta as she would have turned away. 'No, do not run away. You must hear me out. I loved Isabella in a way, but she was like a child. She never gave herself to me as you did that night, Marietta. I have come to believe that in time I should have found that we did not suit…though I would always have honoured her as my wife. I might, however, have taken a mistress once we had our sons.'

'But you grieved for her so much…' Marietta was not sure what to think.

'I grieved for her and my unborn child, and I shall never cease to regret the way she died—but I believe I am ready to move on. I wish to make a new life with you, my love.'

Marietta bent down to kiss him on the lips. He caught her hair, tangling his fingers in it to hold her as she would have moved away, deepening the kiss, his tongue demanding entrance to her sweetness.

When he let her go at last, she shook her head at him. 'You are not strong enough for such things, Anton. I meant just a sweet kiss to seal our bargain.'

'Tell me you love me,' he demanded. 'Tell me you want to be my wife, as I want you.'

'Do you not know it?' Marietta smiled. 'I have loved you from the very first time we met…when you held me safe in your arms after you rescued me from the horse's hooves and looked down at me. I wish that the years between had never happened. I would have come to you untouched, a virgin bride—but fate decreed that our ways should part.'

Anton's passionate gaze held her fast. 'We shall never be parted again. I vow it on all I hold dear. I have done with waiting. We shall be wed as soon as I can walk down the aisle with you.'

'First you must get well and strong again.' She laughed as she saw the impatience in his face. 'Do not look so, my beloved. I am as impatient to be your wife as you to have me—but if you do not take care your wound may open again. You might take another fever, and sometimes that leads to death.'

'My grandmother says that you used a method of sealing the wound that she had heard of but never dared to use. She was all admiration for your skill.'

'It is best not to speak of such things. My father taught me the skills of a surgeon, and he studied in Italy and the East—but as a woman I should not know these things. I fear that it would be frowned upon, for the guilds of medicine and healing are the province of men and they guard them jealously. It was my husband's apothecary who grew jealous of my skill at the castle and began rumours that I used witchcraft. He and others had grown jealous of my influence with my husband.'

'And the Bastard saw his chance to seize what was yours.' Anton frowned. 'I thank God that we have seen the last of him, though I do not know what has become of Miguel…'

'Hush, my love. The Earl of Rundle has men searching for the rogue. If he has not already fled to Spain he will be found.'

'You will not be safe while he lives.' Anton frowned. 'He tried to kill me and failed. He may try for you next time.'

Chapter Ten

Entering the nursery some time later, Marietta saw a child standing next to her son's cot. As she watched, the little girl reached out and touched Charles's face, patting him with her hand. This was surely Anton's daughter, though she had a rather exotic look which must have come from her mother. This little girl would no doubt be beautiful one day.

'Baby…' she said, and, turning as Marietta came up to her, she smiled. 'Pretty baby. Maddie like…Maddie want nurse baby…'

'You want to hold Charles?' Marietta asked, a little surprised that she should speak English rather than Spanish—though perhaps her father had taught her. The little girl nodded and sucked her thumb, her eyes widening. 'I see no reason why you shouldn't. Come and sit down on the cushions and I shall give him to you.'

Maddie did as she was bid, her chubby legs crossed as she perched amongst the pile of cushions on the floor. Her dark eyes were wide with wonder as Marietta lifted her son and brought him to join her on the floor. He was free of his swaddling clothes and beginning to find his balance. For a moment he was content to perch on Maddie's lap, but then he wriggled off and began to crawl about the floor, with the little girl copying him. Clearly she had fallen for the golden-haired boy, and seemed fascinated by his every move, while Charles, pleased with the attention, lost no time in asserting his place in the nursery hierarchy.

Maddie seemed to understand his needs, for it was enough for Charles to point at something to send her running after it for him. Marietta laughed as she watched them playing; they might have known each other all their lives!

She was so intent that she was not immediately aware of someone watching her. She glanced up and saw Lady Gifford standing on the threshold.

'May I come in, *madame*? I do not wish to disturb you.'

'I was just watching them. They have made friends.' Marietta smiled down at the children. 'Charles has been restless, for he is teething, but he seems happy with his new companion…'

'My granddaughter is a charmer. I think she will break hearts one day—but for the moment she seems to have met her match…' Catherine hesitated as the door opened and a woman entered. 'Ah, Lily—this is the Comtesse Montcrief. As you see, her son has met your charge. We shall leave them to your care.' She caught Marietta's eye. 'Perhaps we could talk?'

'Yes, of course.' Marietta looked at the nurse. 'I shall return later, Lily.'

'Yes, my lady.'

'I wondered why Maddie spoke such good English, but clearly she has an English nurse.'

'I believe Anton thought it best, as he always meant to return to England.'

The two women left the nursery, closing the door softly behind them. Marietta looked at Anton's mother, feeling a little puzzled.

'Is there something I may do for you, my lady?'

'You may begin by calling me Catherine. I fear I did not start well with you. I felt you threatened my son, but he tells me that it was not your enemy that wounded him so sorely, but his. I have wronged you, lady. I am sorry for it.'

'Make me no apology, Catherine. Anton was only in the woods because they were hunting the Bastard of Rouen to protect me. However, I believe Miguel was waiting his time. He would have made his attempt sooner or later—and perhaps it was as well that the Earl was also present.'

'I am sure my brother did all he could to assist Anton. We are a close family and I hope we shall continue so—which is why I would make my peace with you. Am I forgiven?'

'You sought to protect your son. In your place I should have done the same.' Marietta smiled. 'I have no wish to quarrel with Anton's mother. I believe he has told you we are to marry?'

Catherine nodded. 'My son tells me that he wishes

for the wedding very soon. Can you not persuade him of the need to recover his strength?'

'I have tried, but he is impatient.'

'Anton is much like his grandfather. You will meet Lord Melford when you go to my father's home. Unfortunately he does not travel often these days, but he is more than three score years and that is a great age—especially for a man who fought so valiantly in the Wars of the Roses.'

Marietta smiled. 'Your mother also wears her years lightly.'

'Yes, my mother is as young in spirit as ever, and she will not admit to her years, even though she was unwell in the winter.' Catherine smiled. 'We are a fortunate family, Marietta.'

'Indeed, and powerful. The Earl told me that he has doubled the men searching the woods and countryside. I think it cannot be long before Miguel is found.'

'I pray it may be so,' Catherine said. 'Now, my dear—what do you plan for your wedding gown? My mother has some lengths of ivory and gold-embroidered silk that might look well on you, and if we all help with the sewing your dress can be ready within two weeks.'

'If Anton will wait so long then I should be glad to wear such a gown, but I may have to be wed in a gown I have, for he grows stronger with every hour. I do not think he will be put off for such an excuse.'

'Your mother and grandmother want me to have a special gown for the wedding, Anton. It will take but two weeks to make…' Marietta saw the look in his eyes and smiled. 'Can you not wait that long to please them?'

'Will it please you to wait?'

'Yes, for it will give you a chance to recover your strength. I know that you have healed well, but you are not yet as strong as you were.'

'I know it,' he growled. 'But it is too long to wait, Marietta. I burn for you, my love. I want to make love to you.'

'You know I would not deny you,' she said, and smiled. 'Say the word and I will lock the door and join you in that bed.'

She leaned forward, kissing him lightly on the mouth. His hand held her locked to him, their tongues tangling in a sweet dance of delicious play. Marietta moved closer and he placed his lips to her throat, moving down to where the swell of her breasts was revealed by a dipping neckline. His tongue teased between them. He pushed the material lower, seeking the rose nipples that peaked beneath his tongue, sending tingles of pleasure running through her. Then he cursed and leaned back against the pillows, looking rueful as beads of sweat formed on his brow.

'Damn it, you are right. I am weak as a kitten.'

'Your strength will return soon. Tomorrow you can get up and come downstairs. I believe you will soon see an improvement once you are on your feet.' Marietta got to her own feet and his eyes narrowed.

'Where are you going?'

'To make a potion that will put iron in your limbs.'

'More of that foul-tasting stuff?'

Marietta made a wry face at him. 'Your grand-mother advised me to mix it with wine and sweeten it with honey—since you make so much fuss about taking it without.'

'Both of you should try drinking it,' Anton complained, and then laughed. 'You are a lot alike, you know. I have always admired my grandmother. Perhaps that is why I am so drawn to you.'

Marietta smiled. 'The sooner you regain your strength, the sooner we may be married...'

She laughed as he pulled a wry face, and went out. He was making huge strides in regaining his health, but he grew bored with lying in bed. She was certain now that his wound would not reopen or take harm. Once he left his bed he would soon feel more himself again.

Anton found his way to the nursery later that afternoon. The door was open, and he heard the sound of children laughing as he paused outside. That was Maddie, but he had not heard her laugh so freely before.

Pushing the door open, he paused. Marietta was down on the floor, lying amongst a pile of cushions. Both children were climbing over her, and she was tickling Maddie, making the little girl shriek with laughter.

His throat caught with emotion and his eyes stung. He could not recall Isabella playing with her daughter once, though she had loved her.

Something shifted in his mind, the shadows falling away. A part of him wanted to join the children playing with their mother...*their mother*. Yes, Marietta had already taken Isabella's place in Maddie's heart, for the child had hardly known her true mother.

He smiled, turning away so as not to disturb them. Marietta did not know she was watched. One day he would join them in their play, but not just yet. He had been told that Miguel had been seen in the woods but not yet apprehended. He must save his strength until he was truly well again.

'So, tomorrow we shall be wed,' Anton said, and reached out to touch Marietta's cheek. 'You were right to make me wait until your dress was finished, my love. I am feeling much better. I should not have wanted to come to your bed and find myself unable to consummate our marriage. I am almost back to my full strength, thanks to your disgusting potions.'

'I doubt there was much chance that you would fail to consummate our marriage,' Marietta teased. 'You would have performed your duty as a husband if it killed you.'

'Wretch! You have teased me back to health, Marietta. I do not know how I shall manage you once we are wed—am I to be petticoat-led?' His eyes challenged, and dared her to answer.

'I am not sure,' she responded in kind, knowing that he enjoyed this banter. He was just as she had seen him in her dreams, the shadows seeming to be banished from his eyes. She felt now as if the years apart had never been. 'I may demand more than you can give...'

'Witch,' Anton muttered, drawing her to him. He bent his head, kissing her lips with such hunger that she melted into him. 'My beautiful, lovely woman...'

'I love you so…' Marietta lifted her eyes to look at him, melting with desire. She felt the press of his aroused manhood as he held her crushed to him, her heart racing as hot liquid desire built in her. She wanted him, needed him more than words could express. He was her life, her love—her destined lover. 'I can hardly wait for tomorrow…'

'Nor I, my love—but we shall, now that I have waited so long…' He slipped the shoulder of her gown down, kissing her soft flesh. 'You are so beautiful—and you are mine.'

'For ever,' she murmured, moving her fingers into the hair at the nape of his neck. 'I thought when they condemned me as a witch and a murderess that my life was over, but now I have so much to look forward to.'

Anton caressed the sweet curve of her breast. 'I envy the babe that sucked at these sweet jewels, and I hope that your son will have a brother or sister one day.'

'I long to hold your babe in my arms.' Marietta pressed against him, her need to lie with him as great as his to take her. 'Are you sure that you wish to wait one more night?'

'Temptress!' Anton smacked her rump. 'Off with you now. This time I shall let you go, but watch how you tease me in future.'

Marietta laughed and ran from him. All the shadows of the past seemed to have faded away. There had been no sign of Miguel, at least as far as she knew. The Earl was of the opinion that he had taken himself off back to France to lick his wounds. Perhaps Miguel had decided that honour was satisfied and returned to Spain.

She could only hope that it was so…

* * *

'You make a beautiful bride, Marietta,' Lady Melford told her. She handed her a small silver casket. 'I brought this with me just in case. Anton was my first male grandchild, and I saved this for his wife.'

Marietta gasped as she opened the casket and saw the beautiful cross set with cabochon rubies and pearls.

'This is lovely! I have my own silver cross, but this is magnificent. How can I thank you for such a gift?'

'Be a good wife to Anton.' Melissa smiled. 'I know that you will—and I wish you both happiness.'

Marietta thanked her, then kissed her cheek. 'You are so good to me—' She broke off as the door opened and a young girl entered. Marietta had recently employed her to help Rosalind with nursing her son. 'Eleanor…is something wrong?'

'No, my lady. Lily is to take Mistress Madeline to church—and Rosalind told me to ask if you wished for your son to be present in the church when you are wed?'

Marietta hesitated. 'I am not sure. He may cry if his gums hurt, for his teeth are coming through…but I suppose you may take him home if he starts to fret.' She smiled. 'Yes, bring him to the church. He should be there.'

'Children often cry in church,' Lady Melford said as the door closed behind the girl. 'But I agree that your son should be there to see you wed.' She looked thoughtful. 'The girl is very young to have charge of the boy. Have you long employed her?'

'I took her on when Anton was ill. She is from the village. Her brother works for Sir Harry, and she asked Claire for work. Claire thought that I might like her to help with my son. She seems a pleasant, careful girl, and I have been satisfied with her work, but of course Rosalind is always there to keep an eye on things. And there is Lily too. She has had the care of Madeline, and must continue to look after her because it would upset the child to part from her nurse. I want us all to be happy together.' Marietta smiled. 'Anton is so good with the children. He says that I am a good mother but he is gentle and patient and they both love him.'

Anton turned his head to look as Marietta walked up the aisle towards him. He caught his breath as she halted at his side and turned to smile at him. She was so beautiful! Almost regal as she walked, her head held proudly. He could hardly believe that so much happiness was his. After Isabella's death he had felt that his heart was dead, but Marietta had wakened it, bringing him back from the dark place that had claimed him.

A ray of weak sunshine had managed to break through the clouds, piercing the stained glass window high above to shower the stone flags with a rainbow of colour. As she took her place at his side, Anton looked tenderly on his bride. For a while he had wondered if this day would ever come, fearing more mischief from Miguel, but nothing had been seen of him.

From somewhere in the church he heard the high, thin wail of a child, and then the sound of movement. Marietta turned her head for a moment to look. He raised his brows as she brought her gaze back to meet his, but she shook her head and smiled.

Anton reached out to take her hand as the priest

began the marriage ceremony. Marietta would be his wife, and tonight he would claim her for his own...

The bells were ringing joyfully as they came out of church. Marietta stood on the steps with her husband and smiled as the cheers of village people greeted them. Children came forward with tokens of friendship and small gifts for the bride, which she accepted gracefully.

'Are you happy, my love?' Anton's voice brought her thoughts back to him. She laughed as he drew her to him and kissed her, in full view of their friends and family. 'It is too late to change your mind now, for you are mine—my wife.'

For a moment she saw jealousy and possession in his eyes, and understood his mind. He could not quite rid himself of the fear that she might betray him, as Isabella had.

'It is all I have ever wanted to be,' she told him, her eyes meeting his. 'I love you, Anton. I shall never look at another man.'

'We should go, for they will be ready to begin the feasting.' He took her hand and they ran down the steps together, laughing as they were deluged with dried rose petals and rosemary. 'Come, for the sooner the feasting begins, the sooner it will be over.'

A giggle of delight bubbled inside her as she saw his hot eyes. She had made him wait for this day so much longer than he had wished, and she did not doubt that he would make her pay for it that night.

The Great Hall was filled with people. The Earl and Lady Claire had invited all their friends to this joyous occasion, and they were assembled to greet the bride and groom. Marietta was feted by the other ladies, and given so many gifts and good wishes that she felt she must be dreaming.

Were all these beautiful things for her? Anton's gifts had been lavish, and included a wonderful string of huge creamy pearls that wound twice round her throat and fell to her waist. She had not expected to receive so many gifts of silver, costly cloth, and precious glass which came all the way from Venice and was rare and expensive. His family had almost overwhelmed her with their generosity, and the Earl's neighbours had also brought gifts that were magnificent.

Anton came to her as the toasts were drunk and everyone began to find their places so that the feasting could begin. He led her to the place of honour, sitting at her right hand while the Earl sat at her left. Lady Claire sat to Anton's right, and his parents were a little further along the high board.

The entertainment began with minstrels singing love songs, and the first dish to be brought to table: carp swimming in a rich wine sauce with tiny onions. After this came the boar's head, capons, a huge side of beef, pork, venison, wood pigeons and sweetbreads, plums, tarts of quince, custards and almond comfits.

Marietta tasted each dish but ate only a morsel, though she could not resist the marchpane and ate two that were stuck with walnuts and dates. Quantities of wine accompanied the food, also mead and sweetened ale.

She drank a little of the wine but kept a clear head, noticing that Anton did the same. His eyes were constantly on her, throughout the feasting, and she knew that he was waiting for the moment when they could leave.

As the afternoon wore on the guests began to call for dancing. Anton stood up, offering his hand to Marietta. She took it and they walked behind their guests at the high board, descending down the steps at the end to the centre of the hall. As the music began she made her curtsey, and Anton led her through the steps of a stately pavane. For a while they danced alone, but then their guests began to join in, and soon the floor was filled with smiling, happy people.

'Are you enjoying yourself?'

'Of course. This is our wedding…' She gazed up at him, catching her breath as she saw the heat in his eyes. 'Anton…'

'I want to sweep you up and—' He broke off as Lily came up to them, looking distressed. 'Something troubles you?'

'Forgive me for disturbing you at your wedding feast, sir. Maddie seems to have taken a fever, and Lady Melford said that I should ask my lady to come…'

'Surely my grandmother can manage—?' Anton began, but Marietta smiled and put a finger to his lips.

'If the child is ill I shall tend her. We shall be together later, my love.'

'I shall come with you,' he said, looking anxious now. 'It is not like Maddie to take a fever.'

They hurried up to the nursery, where they found Lady Melford bending over the little girl's cot. She was stroking Maddie's forehead and looking anxious.

'What ails her?' Anton said. 'Is she truly ill?'

'I thought at first that it was simply a fever, but she does seem very hot and unwell,' Melissa said. 'I wanted to ask Marietta what she thought. It isn't a teething rash—have you seen anything like this before? I do not think it is the pox…'

'Let me see. I have treated the pox before…' Marietta bent over the child, stroking her damp hair back from her forehead. She examined her arms and her neck and face, and then straightened up. 'I do not believe it is the pox. Maddie was taken into the garden earlier this morning. I think she has touched something that has brought out this rash. She may have eaten something she ought not. I can make a mixture to help with the fever, and a lotion to spread on her arms and legs. Stay here with her and I shall go down to the still-room…' She smiled at Anton. 'Stay and comfort her, my love. Talk to her, for your presence may calm her…'

He nodded. 'Yes, I will stay. Though I think you are the one she needs. I believe she already thinks of you as her mother…'

Reaching the stillroom, Marietta set to work with a will. She took down various jars as she sought the herbs she needed. Maddie was not in danger but she was undoubtedly feeling ill, for she had a nasty rash and might have eaten berries that had made her unwell.

'I wonder if I should make her sick or simply ease her…'

Marietta did not realise that she had spoken out loud until she heard a sound behind her and turned. Her eyes widened in shock and fear as she saw the man watching her. Miguel was looking at her in such a way that her blood ran cold. She was not imagining it this time! He *did* hate her.

'What are you doing here?' she asked, her hand going to her throat as she sensed his evil intent. 'We thought you had returned to Spain. You tried to kill Anton…'

'May his soul rot in hell! You saved his life with your potions and your spells, witch—but I shall kill you, and then him.'

Marietta stared at him. 'Why do you hate me so? Why do you hate Anton? What have we done to you?'

'*You* took away his guilt and his pain. He was supposed to suffer for what he did to her…*my* Isabella. I saw her lying there, all the life gone from her. Her eyes looked at me…such accusing eyes…'

'Anton told me what happened. He merely asked her for the truth that day. She was his wife, and he was afraid that she had betrayed him with another…was it you…?' Marietta saw his face twist with agony. 'Yes— she was carrying your child. But you wanted more, didn't you? You wanted her to run away with you, and she would not, so…' A gasp broke from her. 'You were there when she died… What did you do, Miguel? What did you do to her?'

'I loved her. She was always mine. He stole her from me…' Miguel's eyes glittered as he moved closer to Marietta. 'I was her friend, and then her lover. She came to me when she was unhappy and told me she did not love him. We made love, and she conceived. She was terrified that he would know the child was not his because she had not slept with him, so she went to him and asked him to love her. I tried to make her understand that it was me she loved, to persuade her to flee with me…' His hand was shaking and she saw beads of sweat on his brow. 'It was his fault, not mine. He was her murderer, not I…'

'You?' Marietta saw the truth in his eyes. 'What did you do to her that day, Miguel? She ran from Anton because he was angry. But she didn't fall, and she didn't take her own life… *You* pushed her down those steps. It was you that killed her, not her husband.'

'I never meant to kill her,' Miguel said, and he was trembling. 'She told me that her life was over, that she must go into a convent to atone for her sin. She did not enjoy marriage and felt that she had failed as a woman. Even when she lay in my arms she was afraid of giving herself. That day she was weeping, and I tried to comfort her. I tried to take her in my arms but she pushed me away, and then…she just fell…'

'You grabbed her and she pulled away, losing her balance…and you watched her fall. You could not save her, and instead of blaming yourself you blamed Anton…'

'It was *his* fault! She was mine. He stole her from me…' Miguel cried, and then made a move to grab Marietta. 'He took my love from me and I shall take his from him. Before he dies he will learn what it is like to lose everything.'

Marietta backed away from him, her eyes on his face. 'You cannot bring her back. Vengeance is empty. You will still be guilty of her murder.'

'Be quiet, witch! I intend to have my way—but first I will taste you. You will have *my* kiss on your lips when you die, feel the humiliation of—'

He broke off as Marietta picked up the sharp knife she had been using to peel roots and strip bark from a branch of willow. She held it in her right hand.

'Come near me and you will feel this blade in your flesh,' she said, and made a threatening stabbing movement. 'The blade has been used to squash the berries of deadly nightshade. If it enters your flesh you will surely die…'

'Witch! They were right to name you murderess. You should burn in hell for what you have done…'

'I did not harm anyone. What little skill I have is used for good, not harm. *You* are the murderer. You killed Isabella by knocking her off balance so that she fell down the steps…'

'Damn you!' Miguel drew his sword, advancing on her menacingly. 'I shall not drink at your poisoned well. It is enough to see you dead…'

'Stay away from me!' Marietta screamed as he lunged at her with his sword, jumping back, retreating to the other side of the bench where she had been working. He was between her and the door. She could only draw him on and hope to get past him as he followed. 'Your soul is doomed to burn in hell. You cannot wash away your stain by taking my life…'

'If I burn in hell so be it—but you will be there first!'

Miguel lunged at her again. She screamed and jumped back once more. If she could just get past him and make a dash for the door…

He had seen her intention, and moved back to cut off her flight. He laughed, his eyes glittering with hate.

'You cannot escape. Your knife is of no use against my sword—'

'But my sword will match yours,' a voice rang out, and Miguel swirled round to face his new adversary. 'It seems that you are too much a coward to face me. You prey on defenceless women, and you make sure that I am not near. Are you a coward, or will you fight me?'

'He killed Isabella. He caused her fall, not you…' Marietta cried.

Anton gave no sign that he had heard her. His eyes were fixed on Miguel. Suddenly the Spaniard lunged at him with his sword. Anton sidestepped, drawing him on further into the room.

'Run, Marietta—rouse the house…'

Marietta ran towards the door. Opening it, she screamed for help, but she did not leave. Her eyes were glued to the men who were joined in battle. The chilling sound of steel on steel was echoing through the room. She could see at once that they were evenly matched, for Miguel was also a skilled swordsman, and they were of much the same weight, though Anton was a little taller.

Marietta's heart was in her mouth as the fight swayed one way and then the other. Anton drew the first blood, his sword-tip catching Miguel's left arm, but then Miguel struck back, his sword sliding across Anton's shoulder but failing to pierce his heavy leather jerkin. He swore and slashed wildly, catching Anton's arm with the tip, making the blood run. Marietta screamed again.

Anton parried, bringing his sword round with a movement that swept Miguel's blade from his hand. Miguel's eyes were wide with fear as he looked at Anton. For a moment Anton hesitated, then lowered the blade of his weapon.

'I shall not kill you, for it would be to take foul advantage,' he said. 'You will be taken into custody and tried for attempted murder—and may God take pity on your soul.'

Anton turned towards Marietta, his eyes seeking hers. 'Are you hurt, my love?'

As Anton turned his head, Miguel swiftly bent and retrieved his sword with his left hand. Even as he thrust it at Anton's back, Marietta threw the knife. It pierced Miguel's neck and he fell to the ground, a thick crimson tide bubbling as he tried to speak and failed.

Anton looked down at his fallen enemy and frowned.

'Have I killed him?' Marietta asked, and crossed herself. 'God forgive me! I have murdered him…'

'What nonsense is this?' Anton tipped her chin, gazing down into her tear-drenched eyes. 'Do not cry, my love. You have been brave and strong. You have done no wrong to any being—had you not thrown the knife, he would have murdered me.'

She swayed against him, her senses swimming as the terror of the ordeal came over her. Anton swept her up in his arms, the watching servants parting as he walked towards them, leaving the way clear for him to carry her upstairs to the chamber they were to share that night.

He lay her down on the bed and stood watching her as the colour slowly came back to her cheeks.

'You have done too much,' he said, in a harsh voice that hid his anxiety. 'You nursed me for weeks and then this…'

Marietta pushed herself up against the pillows as her head cleared. 'No, I have not exhausted myself,' she said, and smiled at him. 'It was just so…overwhelming. He wanted to kill me.'

'And would have done so had I not come in time.' Anton looked grim. 'It is little wonder that you felt dizzy just now…'

'It was just for a moment. I shall be better now.' She swung her legs over the bed. 'Your arm is bleeding, Anton. Let me bind it for you.'

'It is but a scratch. I can do it myself. I have had worse and survived it without nursing. Stay where you are, Marietta, and rest.'

'I do not need to rest, and Maddie needs me…' She bit her lip as he prepared to leave the room. 'Will you not stay with me?'

'My grandmother will care for the child. Rest for a few hours or you will make yourself ill,' Anton told her. 'I need to rest myself. I shall see you later…'

Marietta lay back against the pillows as he went out, then she shook her head, refusing to give way to tears. She was tired, and she would sleep later, but if Anton did not wish for her company she would go to the nursery and see if Maddie responded to the potions she had made.

'I came to take my leave of you,' Lady Catherine said the next afternoon. 'My husband hath business that will not keep. I hope that Anton will bring you to us soon.

I do not know where you plan to settle now that your enemy is dead.'

'Miguel *is* dead…?' Marietta swayed and gave a little moan, sinking down onto a padded stool. 'Anton would have spared him. Forgive me, I am feeling a little faint. Mayhap Anton is right and I am ill…'

Catherine looked at her for a moment, her eyes narrowed in thought. 'Is there any chance that you might be with child?'

'With child?' Marietta stared at her. 'It is possible…' She blushed as she remembered the night she had given herself to Anton as they travelled to London. 'I had not thought…one night…is it possible?' It had taken years of trying before she had been able to give her husband a son.

Catherine laughed. 'You were married to a man much older, perhaps an invalid?' Marietta nodded her head, looking bemused. 'Anton is young and strong. If you lay with him before your wedding then there is every possibility that you carry his child.'

'I believed that I might die in prison, or at the rope's end,' Marietta said, her cheeks hot. 'You will think me wanton…'

'I was young and hot-blooded once,' Catherine told her with a smile. 'I was forced to marry a man I was not sure loved me. If he had made love to me before we were wed I might not have suffered so much doubt or wept as many tears.'

'Oh…' Marietta laughed. 'I believe you are right concerning my condition, for now I think of it I have not seen my courses since before that time. I had not noticed, for there has been no time to think of myself.'

'I am no physician, but if you need confirmation ask my mother. She will know if you are with child.'

'I do not think I need to ask. I had not considered it, but now…' Marietta laughed. 'I am not sure what Anton will think of my news…'

'If I know anything of my son he will be delighted. He has a daughter he loves, but I am certain he longs for a son.'

'Thank you…' Marietta was suddenly glowing. She put her hands on her stomach. 'Our child… Yes, perhaps it will be a son…'

'You will come to us when you can?'

'Of course.' Marietta moved to kiss her cheek. 'I have no idea what Anton plans for the future. We have had little time to talk…'

'You must ask him when he comes to you—and tell him your news. I dare say the news that he is to become a father will sharpen his thoughts. It would please his father if he were to buy an estate that borders ours and has recently been offered for sale.'

'It would be pleasant to have you as neighbours, but Anton must decide…'

After Lady Catherine had gone, Marietta went to sit on the bed, piling the pillows up behind her. She was not tired, but she wanted to relax and think. She had already visited Maddie that day, and knew that the girl was recovering well. There was no need to be anxious for her. All Marietta needed to do now was think of the future.

She was carrying Anton's child! It was a blessing from God, and the shadows that had hung over her melted away as she realised how fortunate she was. She slipped back against the pillows and closed her eyes.

When Anton entered the bedchamber an hour later, he found Marietta sleeping. She looked so lovely! He stood watching her, resisting the temptation to touch her. If she woke he would want to make love to her, and it was obvious that she was still tired. When she had almost fainted in his arms he had been terrified that she was ill; the fear of losing her had made him harsh. He had spoken sharply and it would not do. He must learn to speak softly to his beautiful wife, because he did not wish to see shadows in her eyes.

He would leave her to sleep. They were due to leave the next morning. He had agreed to escort his grand-mother back to Melford, and stay with her and his grandfather for a while.

Anton had been told of two estates that might suit him. One was close to his father's house, the other a little closer to Melford but with more land. He wanted to see both manors for himself before he came to a decision.

Marietta might prefer to return to France. Anton frowned as he turned away. He could not blame her if she wanted to claim her son's inheritance. Unless a strong man was put in charge of the castle, it would fall into neglect and ruin.

Had Miguel not proved to be the traitor he undoubt-edly was, Anton might have trusted *him* to hold the castle. Without someone who could be trusted not to try

to steal the manor from the young Comte de Montcrief
it might be better to sell it—but would Marietta agree?

'Anton…' Marietta's sleepy voice stopped him as his
hand moved towards the door latch. 'Are you going?
Why did you not wake me?'

He turned and smiled, coming back to her as she
pushed herself up against the pillows. 'You looked so
peaceful. I did not want to disturb you, my love.'

Marietta yawned, and then swung her legs over the
side and stood up. She gazed up at him, her lips soft and
moist, slightly parted.

'I was dreaming of you. Are you angry with me,
Anton?'

'Why should I be angry?' He gave her a rueful smile.
'Yesterday I may have spoken harshly. You looked tired
and pale. I was anxious that you had made yourself ill
looking after others.'

'I am not ill, Anton…' She hesitated, her eyes searching his face. 'I think there may be a good reason for my
faintness—and the tiredness…'

'You have worked too hard—' he began, but she put
her fingers to his lips and smiled. 'Then what—?'

'You remember that night…when we travelled to
London?'

'Yes, but—' He broke off staring at her. 'What are
you telling me?'

'I am not yet certain, but I think it very likely that I
am carrying our child…' She saw his face darken. 'Oh,
no, please do not look at me so. Why are you angry? I
know it is too soon, but…'

'Too soon?' Anton looked into her face. 'Not too

soon, my love—but I wanted to have you to myself for a time…before you face the agony and danger that awaits you.'

'Childbirth is painful, and at times it can be dangerous,' Marietta admitted. 'However, I carried my son easily, though I lost others. My husband blamed himself, for he was not strong enough to give me more children, but *we* are both young. There is no reason to think we shall lose our babe.'

'It is not of the babe I think…though I should be loath to lose a child…but of you, Marietta…' He reached out to hold her close, his face buried in her hair. 'Isabella was always so sickly… If I lost you…'

She drew back, looking at him. 'I am not Isabella. I shall not draw back when you touch me, or run from you. We can only trust in God that I shall be safely delivered of a child, Anton—but I do not fear it.'

'You are so brave…' He touched her cheek. 'I love you more than life itself. I am a coward compared to you, my love.'

'You? A coward?' Marietta laughed mockingly. 'You won the silver arrow against all comers. You fought my enemy face to face and killed him—yet you would have spared Miguel. Why would you have spared him?'

'Because I felt pity for him. He loved Isabella and I took her from him. I wish that I had never seen her. Had I not asked for her, her father would have let her marry Miguel and both of them might still be alive.'

'Do not blame yourself for their deaths, Anton. Isabella's was an accident—for Miguel acted in haste, sending her to her death without understanding what he did—and he brought his own death on himself. I blamed myself at first, but I see now that I had no choice.'

'You speak truly. When he tried to murder me there was no other choice.'

'Miguel was mad with hate for you, Anton. He would have killed you if he could. We must neither of us feel guilt over his death.'

'I shall not, and nor must you, though we may pity him…' Anton looked down at her. 'I had thought to lie with you this night, but now…'

Marietta laughed softly. 'And so I should hope, my husband. We missed our wedding night. You have much to make up for…'

'Wicked wench!' he murmured. 'But should we not be careful?'

'We need not take care for a few months yet. I am hardly sure I carry the babe, but I have missed my courses and I feel it.' She reached up to kiss him on the lips. 'I see no reason why we should wait for the night, Anton. Secure the lock and come to bed with me.'

He hesitated, then, 'You are sure?'

'Yes, I am sure. I want to lie with you, my beloved. I want to seal my marriage vows. I am yours and I long to be in your arms…'

Anton smiled and moved to the door, turning the key in the lock. When he returned he saw that Marietta was trying to unlace her gown at the back.

'Come here and I shall do it for you,' he said, lifting her hair to kiss the back of her neck. She looked round and smiled at him. He kissed her lips and she moved against him. Anton wrenched the laces free and pulled the bodice over her head. Marietta swiftly untied the ribbon at her waist and let her overskirt fall to the ground. She stood before him in her thin undergown, holding out her hands. He took them, pulling her hard against him, suddenly fierce with need. 'I want you so much…'

'Your arm?'

'A mere scratch…' Anton said, bending his head to kiss her. 'Nothing that will keep me from your bed…' He reached out, gathering her up in his arms. 'I have waited so long for this…'

Marietta smiled and kissed him.

'You long for it no more than I,' she whispered. 'I have waited for you far longer than you know, my love…'

It was dark save for a chink of light from the small window when Marietta woke to find herself snuggled close to her husband. She could hear his even breathing and knew that he still slept. She stretched and moved away from him, getting up and going to the closet to relieve herself.

She could still taste his kisses on her lips, and feel the tingling between her thighs where he had loved her well. She had wondered if the excitement and pleasure she had known the first time in his arms could ever be repeated, but if anything this night had been better. Anton's tenderness, his care for her pleasure and her comfort, had carried her to new heights of ecstasy. All her dreams had been surpassed. She knew that she was the happiest, most fortunate of women.

A little cry came from the bed. Marietta went to see

what was wrong. Anton was having a dream—and a bad one, it seemed. He threw his arm out and kicked as if he were fighting.

'No! Do not leave me… I cannot bear it… You must not…' he muttered.

Marietta's smile dimmed. Did he still think of the woman he had lost? Even after the night they had just spent in each other's arms! He had sworn he loved her, but if he still called for Isabella…

'Stay with me…' Anton pleaded, tossing restlessly. 'Marietta…my love…'

He was dreaming of *her*! Marietta climbed on to the bed and bent over him, pressing her lips to his cheek and giving him a little shake.

'Wake up, Anton. Wake up, my love. I am here with you. I love you.'

Anton opened his eyes. He stared at her and then smiled. He reached out to touch her cheek, his hand moving in her scented hair.

'I was having a bad dream. I dreamed that you had the child, but then you—' He choked back the words. 'No! It was just a dream. A stupid, foolish dream. You are strong. I am a fool to burden you with my fears. Forgive me, my beloved wife.'

'Of course I forgive you,' she said, and kissed his mouth. 'I love you. I promise that I shall not leave you. I shall not die. When my time comes to have the child I shall be well cared for and nothing will happen. You must believe me.'

'Yes, I believe you,' he said. 'I shall forget this nonsense. Forgive me for waking you.'

'You did not wake me.' She held her hand out to him. 'Come, my love. Slip on your robe and come with me.'

Anton rose and put on the loose chamber gown that lay beside the bed. He looked at her oddly.

'Where are you taking me?'

'Just take my hand and wait…'

She led him along the passage to the nursery. Going in, they saw a candle still burned atop a chest some distance from the child's cot.

Marietta drew her husband close to the cot, gazing down at the boy as he lay sleeping, his arm curled about Maddie. He must have climbed in with her, mayhap to comfort her. His skin was soft, touched with pink, one fist curled under his head the other arm across her body. Maddie was sleeping peacefully, her face against her companion's curls. They looked so perfect together that it brought a lump to the throats of the man and woman who watched.

'Is that not beautiful?' Marietta whispered. 'Our children. Think of the other children I shall give you, Anton. Is it not worth a little risk for a son of your own?'

Anton looked down at the boy and smiled. 'He is beautiful, and I shall love him as a son. We are lucky to have these two…' He touched her face. 'I care not what our child is—a son or a daughter. I know that you will bear it without fear. You will not weep and curse me as she did.'

'Isabella blamed you for her discomfort?' He nodded, and Marietta smiled. 'All women complain and weep sometimes when they are with child, but it does not mean that they truly blame the father—it is just that they grow weary of feeling fat and ugly. Once it is over the pain and discomfort is forgotten.'

'You are so wise and lovely,' he said. 'Do you mean to absolve me of all blame, Marietta?'

'Isabella could not enjoy marriage as you might have wished, but that was not your fault. You must let the past go—as I have.' She led him from the nursery back to their chamber. 'Only then will you be free of the nightmares that haunt you.'

'Yes, I know.' He smiled and stroked his fingers down her cheek, placing a kiss at the little hollow at the base of her throat. 'Shall you be content to live in England? Or do you wish to return to the castle?'

'Could we have a house such as this?'

'I hope to find something as comfortable—is that what you would like?'

'Yes. I was never truly comfortable at the castle. It holds no fond memories—only those that I can create here with my son, Maddie and our children. I think I should be pleased if you could sell Montcrief and invest the money here in England for my son.'

'Then you have solved my problem.' He grinned as she raised her brows. 'My father wishes me to buy an estate next to his—and my grandfather sent word that there was an excellent manor near to Melford. I was not sure which to choose. If we bought both we should between us own a huge area of land—all of which is held by members of my family. It would make our family one of the most powerful in England.'

'Then purchase both and sell Montcrief,' Marietta said. 'If you need more gold I will sign so that you can use the money from the Comte's deposits with the gold-smiths at the French court.'

'I think the money would be better invested here,' Anton said. 'Your son will be raised as an English gentleman. Better that his land is here and well cared for than he inherit a neglected castle in France.'

They had reached their bedchamber. Marietta reached up to kiss him on the mouth, pressing herself against him.

'Do it with my blessing,' she said. 'Build for the future, for all our children—and now, my love, I want you to come back to bed with me...'

Anton gazed down at her. 'I almost passed by that day I saw the notice for the contest for the silver arrow. Had I never seen you, I might have refused when the King commanded me to take a message to the Comte de Montcrief. Had I not come, the rogues who tried to capture you might have killed you that day. I had decided that I would retire from court life, and would have liked to refuse the King, but it was the memory of your face as you gave me the arrow that drew me back to France, though I knew it not then. It has taken me a long time to let go and allow myself to love again, Marietta—but now that I have I shall love only you until I die.'

'It was fate, our destiny,' she said. 'You saved me from certain death beneath the hooves of that horse, and when the dog attacked me—and you have saved me many times since. Yes, I am certain it was fate that drew us together at the last, my brave and gallant husband...'

Afterword

'You must wait a little longer, my son.' Anton's father smiled as he motioned to him to sit down. 'Come, drink some wine and exercise patience. You are not wanted in Marietta's chamber for the moment. At times like these we must leave matters to the women. Your wife is strong and has already borne a living son. Your mother and grandmother are certain she carries a boy child, and they are usually right.'

'How am I supposed to just sit here while she is in such pain?' Anton demanded. He looked round as he heard another piercing scream. 'I cannot bear it a moment longer. If she dies…'

'There is little you do, Anton.' The Marquis of Malchester looked sympathetically at the Earl of Rundle. Both were strong fighting men, powerful and influential in their circles, and both felt helpless. 'Catherine will call us when you can go up to your wife.'

Hearing another scream, Anton started for the door.

He did not look round as his father called to him. 'I must go to her. Perhaps I can help...'

Anton pounded up the stairway to the little solar where the child was being birthed. His heart was racing wildly, for Marietta had been in labour some hours and he was terrified that she would die. Would to God that he could bear the child for her! She had become such a huge part of his life that he would not want to live if he lost her, even for the sake of the children.

As he reached the door of the chamber he hesitated, and in that moment he heard a thin, wailing cry. That was not Marietta! It must be the child. His throat tightened and he felt his eyes sting with unaccustomed tears. Suddenly his feet were rooted to the ground, and he felt as weak as a kitten, unable to take another step. He was not sure how long he stood there, but after what might have been minutes or hours the door opened and his mother came out. She was carrying something wrapped in a fine wool shawl and smiling.

'Your son is born, Anton.'

'My son?' He looked at her, almost stupid in his relief. 'My son... But Marietta? Is she...?' He was too fearful to ask the question.

'Marietta is tired, but well. She was very brave, and bore her ordeal as she ought.'

'Marietta is always brave,' Anton said, and glanced at the red face of his son. 'He is beautiful. Give him to me, Mother. I want to hold him when I see Marietta.'

Catherine handed over the babe. Anton took him carefully, then went into the birthing chamber.

Marietta was lying against a pile of pillows, her eyes closed. She opened them as he approached, and smiled.

'You have the son I promised you,' she said, and held out her hand to him.

Anton bent to kiss her on the mouth. He sat down on the edge of the bed, holding his son carefully and looking down at the babe. 'I think he looks like me. Charles looks like you, but that is as it should be. We have two sons and a daughter now, Marietta. Our family is complete.'

'Oh, I don't know. Maddie is such a darling. I might like to have another daughter.'

'I am not sure I could bear it,' Anton said. 'The birth of my son was almost too much for me…' He saw the mischief in her eyes and laughed. 'I know that you had to bear the pain, but it hurt me more than you will ever know.'

'My poor darling,' Marietta teased. 'Next time I will have you here with me, so that I can hold your hand.'

'Be careful, woman, you go too far,' he replied. 'Wait until you are well, and remember that I have the power to chastise you…'

Marietta was saved from replying by the arrival of her mother-in-law, who had brought Madeline and Charles to see their new brother. They were closely followed by the arrival of their grandfather, who was impatient to see the heir to his estates.

As Catherine took the babe and placed him carefully in his cot, Marietta felt her hand captured by Anton's. She smiled up at him, then closed her eyes, drifting into a peaceful sleep. Her happiness was complete, and the future would be all that she had ever dreamed of and more...

* * * * *

Harlequin offers a romance for every mood!
See below for a sneak peek
from our paranormal romance line,
Silhouette® Nocturne™.
Enjoy a preview of REUNION by USA TODAY
bestselling author Lindsay McKenna.

Aella closed her eyes and sensed a distinct shift, like movement from the world around her to the unseen world.

She opened her eyes. And had a slight shock at the man standing ten feet away. He wasn't just any man. Her heart leaped and pounded. He reminded her of a fierce warrior from an ancient civilization. Incan? She wasn't sure but she felt his deep power and masculinity.

I'm Aella. Are you the guardian of this sacred site? she asked, hoping her telepathy was strong.

Fox's entire body soared with joy. Fox struggled to put his personal pleasure aside.

Greetings, Aella. I'm the assistant guardian to this sacred area. You may call me Fox. How can I be of service to you, Aella? he asked.

I'm searching for a green sphere. A legend says that the Emperor Pachacuti had seven emerald spheres created for the Emerald Key necklace. He had seven of his priestesses and priests travel the world to hide these spheres from evil forces. It is said that when all seven spheres are found, restrung and worn, that Light will return to the Earth. The fourth sphere is here, at your sacred site. Are you aware of it? Aella held her breath.

She loved looking at him, especially his sensual mouth. The desire to kiss him came out of nowhere.

Fox was stunned by the request. *I know of the Emerald Key necklace because I served the emperor at the time it was created. However, I did not realize that one of the spheres is here.*

Aella felt sad. Why? Every time she looked at Fox, her heart felt as if it would tear out of her chest. *May I stay in touch with you as I work with this site?* she asked.

Of course. Fox wanted nothing more than to be here with her. To absorb her ephemeral beauty and hear her speak once more.

Aella's spirit lifted. What *was* this strange connection between them? Her curiosity was strong, but she had more pressing matters. In the next few days, Aella knew her life would change forever. How, she had no idea....

Look for REUNION
by USA TODAY *bestselling author*
Lindsay McKenna,
available April 2010,
only from Silhouette® Nocturne™.